D0355754

THE DANILOV FAMILY

Heirs to great wealth, pride, passion—and family secrets best forgotten—the Danilovs reserve their strongest loves and hates for each other . . .

MARGARET . . . The dying matriarch of the clan, she alone is privy to its darkest, most unimaginable secret.

BARRON . . . Chairman of Danilov Industries, he cares more for profit than for the family and its traditions.

SONYA . . . Neglected by her husband, Barron, she finds comfort in the luxuries of wealth—and the attentions of other men.

LYDIA . . . Barron's seductive sister, she shares Sonya's fondness for men—and sometimes Sonya's lovers. But she would sell her soul to possess the one man she cannot have.

and

ALEX DANILOV . . . The mysterious distant relative whose unexpected arrival ignites the family's darkest passions—and changes their lives forever.

*Don't miss THESE FALLEN ANGELS,
the enthralling sequel to THIS DARK PARADISE,
coming from Diamond Books . . .*

"*These Fallen Angels* is just as hauntingly poignant, chillingly original, and fast-paced as its predecessor. A beautiful love story . . . this vampire tale is destined to become a cult classic."
                                                    —*Affaire de Coeur*

THIS DARK PARADISE

Wendy Haley

DIAMOND BOOKS, NEW YORK

This book is a Diamond original edition,
and has never been previously published.

THIS DARK PARADISE

A Diamond Book / published by arrangement with
the author

PRINTING HISTORY
Diamond edition/April 1994

ISBN: 0-7865-0000-X

Diamond Books are published by The Berkley Publishing Group,
200 Madison Avenue, New York, NY 10016.
DIAMOND and the "D" design
are trademarks belonging to Charter Communications, Inc.

PRINTED IN THE UNITED STATES OF AMERICA

10 9 8 7 6 5 4 3 2 1

THIS
DARK
PARADISE

1

A hot breeze washed over Alex the moment he left the airport terminal. He breathed deeply, savoring it. Savannah in June—humid, slow-moving air carrying the scent of flowers, the heavy dusting of star gems across the night sky, live oaks with their ghostly bearding of Spanish Moss. Home.

The roar of an airplane's engines shattered his pleasant reverie. This, he reminded himself, was a new Savannah. Taxis, buses, honking horns, all the trappings of modern society. He must learn to accommodate himself to the changes. He shifted his suitcase to his left hand, feeling the heat radiating from the concrete sidewalk.

A limousine pulled up to the curb in front of him, its polished black length reflecting the lights of the terminal. One of the windows rolled down. A woman's throaty voice floated out from the shadowy interior.

"Hello, Alex. Welcome home."

He knew that voice, even after forty years: Margaret Danilov Crowe, matriarch of the wealthy Danilov clan. "Hello, Margaret. I didn't expect you to meet me."

She laughed. "Of course you did, or you wouldn't have sent that telegram telling me you were coming. Is that all the luggage you've brought?"

"Yes." He hefted the single suitcase. "It isn't much to show for all these years, is it?"

"Darling Alex, you've always carried all your baggage in that gorgeous head of yours."

"Now that, my dear, is the truest thing anyone has ever said about me."

He surrendered the suitcase to the chauffeur, then slid into the seat beside Margaret. "You look beautiful, as always," he said, leaning forward to kiss her wrinkled cheek.

"I look eighty, which is what I am." She pushed him to arm's length and studied his face. "You've changed, Alex."

He knew she meant that he looked much younger than when he'd left. The carefully cultivated gray hair, the stooped posture, the eyeglasses had all disappeared. He looked like a young man again.

Margaret, too, had changed. She was old now, her beauty ravaged by time. Only her eyes were the same, midnight blue and full of laughter. She had been a mischievous child, perhaps his favorite of all the Danilov brood.

As though she'd read his thoughts, she said, "I don't suppose I should call you Uncle Alex anymore."

"Just Alex will do for a distant cousin." Actually, he was her great-great-great—he'd forgotten exactly how many greats—grandfather. How many Danilovs had he held a similar conversation with? He sighed. Too many to remember, too many to forget.

Margaret opened her mouth to say something, then closed it again when the chauffeur slid behind the wheel. With a wink at Alex, she pressed a button on the door beside her. A glass partition slid smoothly into place, sealing them away from the driver.

"There," she said as the big car eased into motion. "Now tell me what you've been doing all this time."

"Wandering. Europe, Indochina, Australia."

"For forty-three years?"

"Yes." Forty-three years of waiting, of traveling through the world, a lonely expatriate, until he could come home again.

She cocked her head to one side like a wizened, sharp-eyed bird. "The sun is very hot in Australia, I hear."

He smiled. "I wouldn't know."

"I suppose you wouldn't." She was silent for a moment, studying him intently. Then she reached out to smooth his hair back from his forehead. "You know, I tried many times to have my hair dyed that same shade of dark gold, but they were never able to quite match it."

The unexpected touch of her warm, human hand stirred his Blood-Hunger. He repressed it sternly, hating it. It was not gone, however, just quiescent, waiting to grasp him in its razor claws the moment he relaxed.

Taking her hand away from his hair, he clasped it gently between his palms. Her bones were brittle with age, as fine and as fragile as a bird's. "Are you well?" he asked.

"I'm as well as you get at my age," she said.

"A gallant reply."

"A woman is gallant at forty, Alex. At eighty, it's called being crotchety."

"You haven't changed a bit," he murmured. "Even as a child you had a retort for everything."

"I *have* changed. I'm old now." She touched his face lightly as though to assure herself he really was there. "So many years. Why didn't you write?"

"Because Uncle Alex is dead."

"Is it always this way?" she asked.

"Always. I shed my past lives like a snake sheds its skin."
Shed them, yes, but I carry them on my back. So many, so

very many. He tried to smile, but felt his mouth twist into something else.

She looked away. "There were times during those years when I thought you were just a figment of my imagination."

"A dream?" he asked, genuinely amused this time. "Perhaps I am that."

"Will you stay?"

"Yes, Margaret, I'll stay." He knew what she was asking, and what he had just promised: to stay at the Arbor until she died.

"Thank you. I've outlived my husband, my brothers, and most of my friends. It will be a comfort to have someone from my past with me at the end."

He raised her hand to his lips. She couldn't understand how much that promise would cost him. He had seen her come into the world, had held her, a tiny, mewling baby, when she'd been baptized. And now he would hold her hand as she passed into God's embrace. It was his curse to watch the cyclic turns of birth and death and not be part of them. For him, it was eternal youth, eternal "life." Eternal hell.

The limousine entered the highway that led to the Isle of Palms, accelerating smoothly to enter the flow of traffic. A car sped past, horn blaring.

"People are in such a hurry these days," Margaret murmured.

Alex chuckled. "People have always been in a hurry. They just have faster ways of being in a hurry than ever before. Personally, I think the airplane is a marvelous invention."

"Dear Alex, always so adaptable."

"It's that, or walk out to greet the dawn."

Her mouth thinned. "Have you been tempted?"

"Not yet." If salvation waited at the end of *that* road, he would have taken it long ago. But there was no such thing for his kind, only damnation. Wishing to change the subject, he asked, "How is the family?"

"There is a whole new set of Danilovs," she said. "Jack and I never had children, you know, so the dynastic torch is being carried by my brother Everett's children: Barron and his wife Sonya, his son Justin and sister Lydia. You'll meet them tonight; they live at the Arbor. I moved them in ten years ago when I got tired of racketing around that huge house all by myself."

"Will I like them?" Alex asked.

"Of course you will. They're Danilovs."

He laughed, then sat forward as the limousine exited the highway. The lights and traffic noise faded as they left the busy road behind.

"Please open the windows, Margaret," he whispered.

She obeyed, and hot air swept into the car. Alex relaxed against the seat and closed his eyes. Fragrance surrounded him, the sweet, heavy perfume of camellias and roses, bee balm and honeysuckle. He drew it in deeply.

The sound of the limousine's tires changed. Alex caught the scent of the marsh, fecund and powerful, and knew they were passing over the bridge that led to the Isle of Palms. He opened his eyes. Mist was beginning to rise from the brackish water below, obscuring the thick supporting pillars of the bridge. A chain of tiny, tree-covered islands seemed to float upon the sea of spiky grass like a dark necklace upon the marsh's pale breast.

Wildwood Marsh—the perfect guardian for the Arbor, untamed, primeval, its paths known only to the alligators that abound here.

The car left the bridge and swung onto a palm-lined street. The night perfume returned, laden with roses and honeysuckle. There were no buildings here, no traffic lights; this was Danilov property. Here there was only the moonlight, gentling the rough edges of the landscape and making the shadows look like thick, dark velvet.

"The house is very much as you left it," Margaret said. "Oh, there are a few more bathrooms discreetly tucked away here and there, and the kitchen was renovated a few years ago, but that's all. I sent the maids into the west wing to clean today, and that's the first time a human being has stepped foot in those rooms since you left."

"Thank you, Margaret."

"You put your home and trust in my hands. I couldn't betray that." She smiled. "Besides, I seem to have inherited your love of old things. Look, here we are."

The limousine turned right, slowing as it reached the long gravel drive that led to the house. The crushed rock was pure white in the moonlight, a ribbon beacon leading Alex back. Excitement shot through him. *I'm coming home, Catherine. Can you feel me?*

"Brings back memories, doesn't it?" Margaret asked.

"Yes." Volumes were contained in that short word. Layers of memories all intertwined, regrets and happiness, good times and bad.

He could see the house now, its columns gleaming through the huge old trees surrounding it. Many, many years ago he'd built that house for his lovely young wife, and it was as beautiful now as it was then. The simplicity of its Greek Revival design gave it a grace that belied its enormous size. Live oaks spread their twisted, moss-shrouded limbs far out over the roof. A pair of towering magnolias framed the front portico, their huge white blossoms seeming to glow like cups of captured moonlight.

The limousine drew to a halt in front of the portico. Alex swung the car door open and stepped out onto the gravel. The voices of crickets and cicadas wrapped around him, singing their age-old song. Tilting his head back, he looked up the length of the columns. This was his home, his haven. Impatient now to be inside, he helped Margaret from the car and urged her toward the house.

Stepping through the door was stepping into his past. The marble-tiled foyer and the long, sweeping staircase with its carved balustrade seemed to enclose him, to welcome him. The breeze swirled in through the open doorway and set the crystals of the chandelier into movement. Whorls of rainbow light spun over the marble floor. Alex held his breath; he could almost hear the graceful lilt of a waltz, the whisper of Catherine's dancing slippers upon the stairs.

"The family should be in the parlor," Margaret said. "Come meet them."

He let his breath out in a long sigh. "I must have some time alone. Tell them I'll be down in an hour."

"Are you all right?" she asked, putting her hand on his arm.

"Yes. I am just . . . feeling the weight of my years just now." Gently disengaging himself, he turned and walked up the stairs.

The upstairs hallway was lined with portraits of many generations of Danilovs. He'd known them all. They were long gone, relegated to the churchyard, their memories remaining only in the portraits and his mind.

They seemed to stare at him as he passed through their midst. Whispering ghosts, brought to life by the presence of the man who had outlived them all. It pleased him. When he reached the end of the hallway, he turned and bowed to them, a graceful courtier's gesture he hadn't used in a hundred years.

Then he opened the door to the master suite that had been his since the house was built. Everything was in place, as though he'd left here yesterday. He ran his hand down one of the carved posts of the bed. Here, he and Catherine had slept, made love, laughed and cried and held one another. Here, she had borne nine children to carry on his line.

"Catherine," he murmured. "I'm back. Come to me, love."

The feel of her was strong in the room, so strong that he could almost smell her perfume. Lavender and musk, delicate but haunting. Wrapped in the memory of that scent, he went to the built-in bookcase on the far wall and pressed the hidden lever that would open it. The shelves slid forward with a small, protesting sound. He closed it behind him, bolting it so that no one could follow him.

Ahead, a narrow stairway plunged into a well of shadow. He didn't bother switching on the light; the night was his world. Even if he were blind, his feet would know these stairs. Every turn, every bump, even the delicate graining in the oak banister was as familiar to him as his own flesh.

There was another door at the bottom, this one made of steel, secure and strong. He unlocked it and stepped into the room beyond. This was his sanctuary, the brick-lined heart of the Arbor. Not even Margaret knew about this room. An old four-poster bed occupied the west wall, its heavy brocade draperies shrouding the mattress from view. There he would hide from the sun, secure in Mother Earth's hand.

Directly across from the bed was a full-length portrait of Catherine. Her dark hair was swept into a simple chignon, and she wore the sapphire gown that had been his favorite.

Dainty slippers peeked out from beneath the hem. Willow slim, willow graceful was his Catherine, with soft blue eyes and a mouth that never stopped smiling.

"I came back as soon as I could," he said. "I hope you didn't grow tired of waiting." The scent of lavender was strong. Closing his eyes, he gave himself up to it, opening his heart and mind in welcome.

"Ahh, Catherine, love, I missed you. If only you could come with me. Then my travels would be joy instead of banishment. But every moment I spend away from this house, from you, feels like a year, a year like a century." Then he chuckled. "I can almost hear you chide me for being maudlin. Feeling sorry for myself has always been my biggest fault."

Something passed over his face. It wasn't a touch or a breeze, but a gossamer sense of *presence*. Catherine. He held his arms wide as though to embrace her. But as always, they remained empty.

"I've kept my promise to you, Catherine. No lives have been lost to my Blood-Hunger. But it has been a torment, surrounded as I've been by warm, human bodies. I probably should not have come back here until after Margaret died, but it was growing more and more difficult to restrain the appetite that drives me. I need your strength, love."

The ethereal caress moved over his mouth, his closed eyes. It was almost, but not quite a touch. So close, so very, very close. And then it went away, leaving a yawning ache of loneliness in his heart. The scent of lavender faded.

Sighing, he dropped his arms to his sides. If he still possessed a soul, he'd gladly barter it to the devil to hold her in his arms one more time. But just the fact that a small part of Catherine dwelled in this house was miracle enough. It was what drew him back to the Arbor time and

again, when good sense dictated that he cut all ties with
the past. She had given him hope. Vampire and man, she
had loved him. And in loving him, she had freed him from
the demands of the hated Blood-Hunger. Her presence here,
however ethereal and fleeting, still gave him respite.

Because of her, this house was the only place on this earth
where he could find a measure of peace. Wanderer, drinker
of blood, revenant—peace was a precious commodity for
such as he.

"Thank you, Catherine," he said, turning toward the door.
"And now that I've touched my past, it's time to meet my
future."

2

Alex stood in the doorway of the parlor and watched Margaret and the rest of the family. They didn't see him; no one saw him if he didn't wish it. It was a simple spell, a mere tweaking of others' minds. Ordinarily, he wouldn't use it in his own home, but he wanted to observe the family when they didn't have their company manners on.

Margaret was playing solitaire at the desk nearby. The light from the Tiffany lamp over her head glinted off her silver hair, warming it to gold. As Alex watched she slipped a red four from the bottom of the deck and played it on the board. Amusement bubbled through him; Margaret *always* cheated at solitaire.

The man—Barron, evidently—was in his late thirties, tall and dark-haired, with aquiline features an eagle might have envied. His hands were restless, his eyes even more so.

The two younger women were both beautiful, but opposite in coloring and manner. One was blond and languid, the other a fiery redhead whose laugh was frequent and just a bit malicious.

The boy was dark like his father. Although he still had the soft face of a child, adult bones were beginning to show through the baby fat. He would be a big man one day, with a pugnacious chin and a heavy brow. He didn't want to be here; arms crossed, he stood in front of the window staring out into the night.

Alex smiled. Meeting each new generation was always the best part of coming home. This was his family. The Danilov dynasty, sprung, if not precisely from his loins, from Catherine's.

It was time to join the party. He waited until no one was looking directly at the doorway, and then allowed himself to be visible again.

Margaret was the first to notice him. "Ah, Cousin Alex," she said, rising from her seat. "I do hope you're feeling better."

"Much. Thank you for letting me rest. Eight hours on a plane wore me out, not to mention the time difference." He had flown from Paris in the early evening, heading west, and had almost doubled his hours of darkness tonight.

"Barron, this is Alex Danilov, from France," Margaret said.

"Welcome to the Arbor," Barron said, reaching to shake hands.

Alex felt the other man's curiosity and resentment come toward him like a gust of cold air. Then the red-haired woman took his hand and the room warmed considerably.

"I'm Lydia," she said. "Barron's sister."

She was lush and curved, and life was strong within her. There was bold sensuality in her gray-green eyes, petulance in the line of her generous mouth. She was wearing a green silk dress with a wrapped bodice that accentuated her heavy breasts. Alex's gaze focused on her throat, where the pulse beat beneath her skin. He felt his Blood-Hunger quicken. With an effort of will, he pushed it away.

"Enchanting," he murmured, raising her hand to his lips.

She smiled. "I can't tell you how happy I am that you're

going to be staying here with us."

"The pleasure is mine," he said. Just before he let go of her hand, her thumb moved to stroke the inside of his wrist. His internal temperature went up a few more degrees. Lydia stirred more than his Blood-Hunger; his body, too, bespoke its interest in her. A fascinating woman, he thought. Trouble, with a capital T.

The blonde came forward, her hand outstretched. She matched Alex's six-foot height, and had a greyhound's sleek, long-legged lines. Her slow-moving grace was an interesting contrast to Lydia's vitality.

"I'm Sonya, Barron's wife," she said.

Alex bent over her hand. She was as sensual a woman as Lydia, but her sensuality was a different sort. A slow burn, but no less consuming.

"And this is my grand-nephew Justin," Margaret said, going across the room to put her hand on the boy's shoulder and turn him around. Although Justin's expression was sullen, he slipped his arm around the old woman's waist. Alex's interest sharpened. He'd expected the boy to withdraw from Margaret's touch. The fact that Justin's reaction was unexpected pleased him. Very little surprised him any longer.

Sensing that the boy didn't want attention, Alex merely waved a greeting and turned back to Barron and the two women.

Lydia took his arm. "Would you like a drink, Alex?"

"Red wine would be nice."

"And make mine a martini, Barron," Lydia said, leading Alex toward the sofa.

Barron turned to the sideboard without comment, and Alex smiled. Lydia was a most interesting woman indeed. He allowed her to install him at one end of the sofa, and install herself beside him. Her long, gilded nails traced patterns on the few inches of fabric that separated them. Ivory damask on a Queen Anne sofa. The last time he'd sat here, the upholstery had been dark green. Catherine had chosen it, and now it was gone. He glanced around the room, looking for other changes. They were few and insignificant, but jarring nonetheless: the walls had been painted a pale peach and the landscape over the fireplace had been replaced by an abstract something-or-other in pastel green, orange, and aqua.

New faces, new furniture—thank God Catherine was constant.

"So," Lydia said, "why did you decide to come to America?"

He spread his hands. "Doesn't everyone want to come to America? No, actually it was loneliness that brought me. . . . Thank you, Barron," he said, pausing to accept the glass the other man offered. "You see, I'm alone in the world. My parents are dead, and I have no brothers and sisters. When I went through some old family papers, I found that Danilovs had emigrated to America in the early nineteenth century. I did some research, and voilà! I contacted your aunt hoping to begin a correspondence with the American branch of the family, and was surprised and pleased when she asked me to visit."

"And how long do you plan to stay?" Barron asked.

Alex spread his hands. "That depends on your aunt."

"True," Margaret said. "You see, I've asked Alex to help me research some of the more, ah, obscure branches of the family."

Alex smiled at her, pleased that she had given him an occupation that would account for his absence during the day.

"I didn't know you were into genealogy, Aunt Margaret," Sonya said.

Margaret accepted a tiny glass of sherry from Barron, then sat in the armchair opposite Alex. "As my future shrinks, I find myself growing more and more interested in the past." Her gaze was bird bright, mischievous.

"I prefer the present," Lydia said.

Alex raised his brows. "Enjoy today, because tomorrow may never come?"

"Exactly."

"But tomorrow *does* come," he said.

She shrugged. "But when it does, then it's *today*, isn't it?"

"I can't fault your logic," Alex murmured. But he doubted she was quite as unconcerned as she liked others to think; he sensed an urgency in her that went beyond her natural vitality. Lydia Danilov was not the sort of woman who would serenely accept the status quo.

Sensing another presence enter the room, Alex glanced at the doorway. A woman, a servant by her dress, was standing there holding a cloth-wrapped tray in both hands. He caught the delicious aroma of ham and roast chicken.

Margaret turned to look at the entrance, evidently cued by his expression. She was quickly falling into the old habits, Alex noted; when they had been uncle and niece, she had been very good at reading him.

"Ah, thank you, Eve," she said. "Would you set it on the sideboard, please?"

The woman obeyed, then turned back to Margaret. "Will there be anything else, ma'am?"

"No, go on to bed. I've kept you up much too long as it is."

When the servant was gone, Barron went to the sideboard

and lifted the cloth. "Mmm," he said, breathing deeply. "It looks delicious. But isn't it kind of late to be eating?"

As though to punctuate his words, the big grandfather clock in the hall began to chime.

Margaret laughed. "It's only midnight, Barron. I for one am not going to bed before getting much better acquainted with our newfound cousin."

"Here, here," Lydia murmured.

Raising her glass, Margaret said, "A toast, everyone. To Alex, and to research. I can't wait to see what marvelous skeletons he'll unearth in our family tree."

"To skeletons," Alex agreed, amused by the tart double meaning of her statement. Out of the corner of his eye, he saw Barron frown.

"Well, it's much too late for Justin to be up." Sonya set her glass on the sideboard. "Sweetheart, say good night to our guest."

"Good night." Justin's voice cracked a bit on the last word. He flushed painfully.

Ah, puberty! Alex thought. A terrible time. Setting his glass aside, he rose to his feet and clasped the boy's hand casually, as though he were a man. "Good night, Justin."

The boy flushed again, but Alex saw some of the tenseness go out of his shoulders. Good. He'd always had a soft spot for the young.

"Alex, dear, would you mind?" Margaret murmured, holding out her hands.

He helped her rise from the chair, then tucked her hand into the crook of his arm and led her to the sideboard.

Lydia took possession of his other arm. "Don't forget me," she said.

"An impossibility," he murmured, noting that she made sure her breast rubbed against his arm as they walked.

Margaret flicked the cover off the tray. Alex nearly sighed, seeing the small Limoges plates that were nestled amid the food. He'd bought that china during his second lifetime at the Arbor.

"This looks wonderful," Margaret said, piling thin-sliced chicken upon her plate. "By the way, Alex, our family has a tradition we share with all our guests on their first night at the Arbor—a sampling of our own scuppernong wine."

Alex's taste buds fairly quivered with anticipation. It had been many, many years since he'd tasted scuppernong wine. "I'd be delighted to try it."

"Do we have to?" Sonya asked.

"It's a tradition," Margaret said. "Barron, will you pour?"

Barron took a decanter of pale liquor out of a nearby cabinet and half filled four wineglasses. He handed the first to Alex. "You first. Tradition says that if the guest survives, then it's safe for the rest of us to drink."

Alex took a sip, then another. It was the same as he remembered, wild and musky. Not a good wine, as wines went, but it was a part of the past that he could actually feel and smell and taste.

"This is our own brew," Barron said. "Or rather, the gardener's. There are many scuppernong arbors on the property, which, of course, gave the house its name. I don't care for the taste myself."

"Barron has been after me to clear the arbors and plant something else," Margaret said. "A tennis court, I believe, was to be this year's crop."

Ah, Alex thought, Progress. The snake had invaded Eden.

Sonya took a sip of wine, grimaced, and set her glass aside. "The vines are old, and the grapes, well . . . they certainly don't seem to be of much use."

"But the birds like them," the old woman said.

"Well, *I* think a swimming pool would be better than a tennis court," Lydia said.

"Why do you want a pool, Lydia?" Margaret asked. "You never let the sun touch your skin lest you get a freckle or, God forbid, a *wrinkle*."

Lydia's eyelids dropped to half-mast. "True. But I do love to wear bathing suits."

"I'll drink to *that* picture," Alex said. But the tone of the conversation alerted him to undercurrents of emotions going on beneath the words. He'd played this scene thousands of times, and it was always the same: sarcasm, resentment, and old arguments thinly concealed behind the veil of repartee.

Lydia put her hand on his shoulder. Again the unexpected touch of a human hand triggered his Blood-Hunger, and again he suppressed it.

"What do you think, Alex?" she asked, glancing at her brother as if to gauge his reaction. "Should we have the tennis court or the swimming pool?"

"Or the birds," Margaret interjected.

"Ordinarily I wouldn't give an opinion in a private family matter, but since you lovely ladies insist, I'll do it. We're talking about change here, and there are times when change is a good thing. For example,"—he indicated the chandelier overhead—"electricity. Air-conditioning, the polio vaccine, telephones. But in this case . . ." Picking up his glass, he held it to the light, admiring the play of color in the wine. "I happen to be partial to birds."

"So there," Margaret said. "Justin wants the birds, too. It's three for, three against. A tie. You young people will just have to wait for me to die to break it."

While the others rushed to protest that statement Alex sat silently and studied the old woman. There was more to this than just the issue of the arbors. Things were going on in the Danilov family, things he ought to know more about.

Barron took a single sip of his scuppernong wine and put it aside. "I think I'll stick to my scotch and soda. Alex?"

"I'll finish this, thank you."

Lydia shuddered. "You're a brave man."

"Not brave." Again, he held the wine up to the light. "I just like to try new things."

"There will be plenty of time to redeem the sacrifice you're making tonight," Margaret said. "Our cellar is quite extensive; both my father and my . . . favorite uncle liked wines."

Alex inclined his head, silently acknowledging her reference to their past. "I look forward to it."

Her plate full, Margaret headed back to her chair. Lydia took a turn at the platter. "Alex, aren't you going to eat?"

"No, thank you. I'm not hungry just now."

"A pity." Her gaze dropped to his mouth. "Tell me, just how close a cousin are you?"

"Not very," he said. "Several times removed, I believe."

"I see." In a low voice only he could hear, she said, "I've never seen eyes quite that color. Pale, pale gray, like mist. Beautiful."

They used to be darker. One day they'll be entirely colorless, forcing me to wear contact lenses to look human. You wouldn't think them beautiful then. Aloud, however, he said, "I'm glad you like them."

He waited for her to ask if there was a Mrs. Danilov, but she didn't. Then he smiled, thinking that Lydia wouldn't care if there was.

"I'm ready," she said. Holding her plate in one hand, she took hold of his arm with the other. "I ought to be ashamed at taking so much, but"—she glanced up at him from under her lashes—"I have a very good appetite."

Alex couldn't help but laugh. She could have held her own in even the most notorious of the salons of Europe. He'd known uncounted numbers of women like her, and they were all compelling, delightful, and very alluring. And quite dangerous to the unwary male who was foolish enough to love them.

He took the plate from her when they reached the sofa. Lydia slid into her seat as though she were fitting herself to a man, then glanced up at him to make sure he got the message. He did.

If there weren't so many complications, he might have taken her up on her offer. Lydia appealed to all his basest instincts, both revenant and human. Sex and Blood-Hunger were inextricably bound, for pleasure was his gift to his partner for what he took. Lydia would be a poor choice for two very good reasons: one, she lived in his house, and two, she might like it too much.

He'd learned the risk of allowing himself to become entangled in a feeding-spawned relationship: *he* might like it too much. And then it would be easy to go too far, to take too much from his partner. He had renounced that aspect of being a revenant; for Catherine's sake and for his own, he would not kill.

Lydia sipped at her drink. "You know, Alex, there's something strange about you coming to the Arbor tonight."

"Why do you say that?" he asked.

"I knew something was going to happen tonight. Do you know how the air feels just before a thunderstorm . . . charged?"

His interest sharpened, focused. "Yes," he said. "I know how that feels."

"More of your crystal gazing, Lydia?" Barron asked.

Alex swung around to look at him. "Crystal gazing?" *My God, does she have the gift?*

"The newest fad of the bored, the eccentric, the frustrated flower children." Barron's smile twisted. "We've been through many of Lydia's fads. Let's see . . . there was the fire walking, the mail-order witchcraft courses, and now crystals."

Smiling, Lydia ran her fingertip around the rim of her glass. "Tease away, Barron. I know what I know."

"Give it a rest, Lydia," Barron said. "Now, Alex, may I compliment you on your excellent English? No accent at all. I don't remember when I've ever met a foreigner who could speak so perfectly."

Alex sat down beside Lydia and propped his wineglass on the arm of the sofa. "My Russian, too, is completely without accent. As are my Greek and German."

"Alex has been all over the world," Margaret said. "He's learned his languages from the natives."

Barron didn't take his gaze from Alex. "What do you do for a living?"

"Nothing," Alex said. "I'm a dilettante."

"I see." Barron's lips thinned. "And how do you support yourself?"

"I don't."

"Isn't being a dilettante expensive?"

Alex nodded. "Very, if one wants to do it right."

"Barron, why are you questioning him like this?" Margaret asked.

"I just want to be sure he is who he says he is, and that he isn't here to con us. As head of the family—"

"And I thought *I* was the head of the family," the old woman said. Her tone was light, but there was no humor in her eyes. "I seem to have been demoted."

Ah, there it is, Alex thought. The gauntlet has been thrown down. Would Barron take it up?

"Don't be silly, Aunt Margaret," Barron said. "I meant that as the *man* of the family, I feel it's my duty to look after everyone's welfare."

Challenge refused. Alex knew it wouldn't be forever, for the man's anger swept through the room like the tide, hot and powerful. Someday Barron would try for the brass ring.

"Perhaps I've come just in time," he muttered under his breath.

"Did you say something, Alex?" Lydia asked.

"Yes. I asked what perfume you're wearing."

"It's called Obsession. Do you like it?"

"Very much." Alex was hardly aware of her; his senses were filled with Barron's rage and frustration. To turn the man's attention away from Margaret, he said, "I'm sorry that my remark about being a dilettante misled you, Barron. Not because I admit to any legitimate profession, but because I don't have to work to support my dabbling."

"What do you mean?" Barron asked.

"I'm rather wealthy, you see."

"There's no need to sound so embarrassed about it," Lydia said.

Alex shrugged. "I didn't work for my money. When my parents died, I inherited everything. It isn't on the scale of Danilov Industries, I'm sure, but quite enough to support my modest little ventures."

"What scale are we talking about?" Lydia asked.

"Lydia!" Sonya cried, nearly dropping her plate.

Lydia laughed. "Come on, Sonya, we're all rich folks here. As long as Alex is discussing his financial standing, why not ask how much?"

"Ah, Lydia, you are refreshing!" Alex said. "Let's just say it's in the millions of francs and leave it at that." He raised his glass in a toast to Barron. "I'll be glad to furnish you with proof of my identity after supper. Will that do?"

Barron nodded curtly. The tone of his anger had cooled somewhat, however, and Alex was pleased that the diversion had worked. It was going to be an interesting time, he was sure. Games within games within games, with House Danilov as the prize.

Tomorrow he would be more than willing to play. Tonight, however, he was tired. Without the resources at the moment to deal with the currents of emotions in the room, he turned the conversation to other subjects.

Once the scuppernong wine was gone, he switched back to the red. Barron played the good host and refilled Alex's glass whenever the level dropped. Although Alex wasn't able to become drunk—another price of his condition—he managed to pass into a state of dreamy contentment that was very welcome. Somewhere between the fifth and sixth refill, he felt Lydia's hand close over his knee.

Ah, it was good to be home. Whatever else one might say about the Danilovs, they were never boring.

3

Bong! Bong! Bong! The mellow tones of the hall clock cut through the conversation.

"Heavens, three o'clock already!" Margaret set her coffee cup aside and stood up. "Alex, come for a walk with me. The garden is very beautiful at night."

"I'd be delighted." Alex extricated himself from Lydia and rose to help the old woman up from her chair.

He noticed a muscle twitching at the corner of Barron's jaw. Obviously, the scion of the Danilovs was not at all pleased by the attention the newcomer was receiving.

"Good night, everyone," Margaret said. "Come, Alex."

She led him to the back of the house, taking him through to the renovated kitchen. The room was a marvel of stainless steel and sleek black glass, the utilitarian hardness of which was tempered by the ocher tile of the counters and the buttery gleam of copper cookware. Alex was glad to see that the massive old oak table was still in use; he'd drunk many a cup of tea at that table.

"What do you think?" she asked. "Almost terrifyingly efficient, isn't it?"

He shrugged. "Who am I to say? I'm not one to make demands on the cook's services, as you very well know."

"It was Barron's idea. He likes to entertain business associates here. Dinner parties and such. We've become very fashionable."

"Thank you for warning me." He turned her toward the outer door. As they stepped out into the summer night he said, "Your nephew is growing tired of the reins, Margaret."

"I can handle Barron. He may be chairman of the board of Danilov Industries, but I hold fifty-one percent of the stock."

A gracefully curving gravel path led from the patio to the gazebo that nestled under the broad, feathery branches of a huge mimosa tree. Climbing roses, heavy with bloom, wound their way up the trellises that formed its sides. The white-painted building gleamed like marble in the moonlight, and Alex steered the old woman to it. "He'll fight you," he said, escorting her up the steps to the shadowy, rose-scented interior.

"Perhaps," she said, running her hand along one of the posts that supported the octagonal roof. "This structure is new. The old one was riddled with termites, but you see I had it reproduced faithfully."

"About Barron," he reminded her gently.

She let her breath out in an explosive sigh. "Barron's god is the almighty dollar. If I let him, he would sell the Arbor and put luxury condominiums in its place."

"And he assumes the Arbor will be his someday."

"Of course. What do you think he'd say if I told him the house and property are to go to the family vampire?"

Alex smiled. "There have been Danilovs who have been told exactly that."

"But they were carefully chosen. Picked by you, Alex. Would you choose Barron to hold your secret? Do you think he would take title to this place and agree to keep it unchanged until your return?"

"No."

She put her hand on his arm. "Then let me handle Barron in my own way. He won't like it, but he'll take it."

"All right, Margaret." He helped her into one of the big wicker chairs that squatted comfortably in the center of the gazebo, then took the seat beside hers.

They sat in companionable silence, listening to the wind play in the branches overhead. A mosquito's thin, hungry whine pierced the darkness. Alex knew that hunger. The insect flew closer, hovered just above his wrist for a moment, then moved toward Margaret. He reached out and gently brushed it away from her.

"Thank you for giving me such an interesting occupation while I'm here," he said. "Of all the things that ought to be my specialty, the genealogy of the Danilovs is surely at the top of the list."

She laughed. "I pulled it out of thin air. It's perfect, though; none of that lot—with the exception of Justin— would think of setting foot in a library."

"You like the boy, don't you?"

"Yes. He's a great kid apart from being the last male of the direct Danilov line. Smart, but in a different way than his father. Wants to be an engineer." Her brow settled into furrows. "It's a shame, really. I had envisioned spending my old age surrounded by shrieking Danilov offspring, but Sonya doesn't want any more children and Lydia was never interested in having children at all."

"And they look like such healthy brood mares," he said in mock disappointment.

Margaret laughed. "Alex, you're an idiot. But really, you'd think they might be able to have *one* more between them. Your wife had nine, for God's sake."

"And don't forget Edgar's wife, back at the turn of the

century. She had eleven, and four stillbirths."

"Good grief!" Suddenly the old woman's smile faded. "How old are you, Alex? You've never told me."

"I've never told anyone," he said. *Only Catherine. Only Catherine knew everything.*

"How old?" Margaret's voice was sharp, urgent.

He closed his eyes. Margaret had given him so much, how could he refuse her this? "I was born in the year of our Lord, one thousand and twelve."

"Ahhhh. So long ago? I never expected . . ." She drew in her breath with a hiss. "You've seen it all. The Crusades, the Renaissance, man walking on the moon. How wonderful."

"It hasn't all been wonderful. Don't forget the Black Death, the Inquisition, and all the innumerable wars mankind has waged in that time. And don't forget the boredom of being one's own company for nearly a thousand years."

The old woman cocked her head to one side. "I prayed for you to come home. Every day I prayed. You see, I hated getting older. At forty it was all right. But forty-five came, then sixty, then seventy. And it was no longer all right."

"Don't." He knew what was coming. Dread coiled his stomach into a knot.

She continued, inexorable. "You see, I knew there was an alternative. So I prayed for you to come home. Now would be a good time, I'd tell myself. I could stay like this forever. But you never came."

"And now it's too late," he said.

"No!" Her grip tightened. "It's not too late."

He disengaged himself gently, then stood up and began pacing the floor of the gazebo. "You don't know what you're asking."

"Yes, I do. Alex, I've lived a long life, and now that it's almost over, I find that I want more. I don't want to die.

You have the power to make me live forever."

"But I don't." He swung around to look at her, willing her to understand. "Only God has power over life. My power comes from death. This"—he tapped himself on the chest—"is only an extension of death. And there is no hope of salvation for me when it is over."

"I'll give that up gladly."

He shook his head. "Ah, Margaret, I said the same thing many years ago."

"It's my choice."

"No," he said softly. "It is *my* choice. And I love you too much to do such a thing to you."

Her hands gripped the chair arms like claws. "You'll let me die?"

"Either way you'll die. I'll just do you the kindness of allowing you to stay that way."

"Please, Alex."

"I can't."

"Please!"

He closed his eyes, tormented by the need in her voice. "I can't!"

"I can make it cost you," she hissed. "*I* own this house. I can leave it to Barron. You can sit and watch him build his damned condominiums!"

Alex sighed. Her voice trembled with many emotions, emotions that made his heart wince: fear, anger, betrayal, hope. *He* had caused this. In his weakness, his need to have one person in whom to confide, he had made Margaret want things no one should have. In his need to have one person love him, he had made his condition seem romantic—the age-old lure of immortality. She simply could not understand that for the vampire, immortality meant eternal death, not eternal life.

Even if he were not bound by his vow never to make revenants of his blood, he would refuse her. Whatever the cost.

He went down on one knee before her and took her hand in both of his. "The house is unimportant, compared to the value of your soul. Do as you wish; I will love you no matter what."

"You and your talk of souls!" She tore free and wrapped her arms around herself. "Do you really think there is such a thing as God or heaven?"

"Yes." *And Hell, for that is my world.*

"I would have been all right if you hadn't come back!" she whispered, the intensity of her words only enhanced by the quietness of her tone. "I had accepted the fact that my life was almost over. But then you showed up, and . . . and I thought it was for me!"

"It *was* for you, and for me as well. But not to turn you into what I am. Never that."

She began to cry. Slowly, her head fell forward upon his shoulder. He put his arms around her and held her, giving her the comfort of his embrace since he could give her nothing else.

After a time she quieted, her sobs becoming hiccups and finally fading into silence. He stroked her hair, just as he'd done so many times when she was a child. She let him, seeming to need the touch as much as he did. Then she pushed away, using his shoulders as support as she rose to her feet.

"I think I'll go in," she said. "No, don't get up. I need to be alone just now."

He watched her walk toward the house, her shoes crunching on the gravel path. Light flooded out onto the patio as the door opened, then abruptly disappeared when it closed.

The night seemed very lonely. Rising, he left the gaze-bo and went to sit on one of the stone benches that were scattered about the garden. Leaning back against the trunk of the tree behind him, he closed his eyes and let the busy insect sounds wash over him. Searching for peace. Even when he'd been alive, peace had eluded him.

With a sigh, he let himself slip back to that time so very long ago. Back nearly a thousand years ago, when he'd been young and foolish, the sap of life rising strongly within him. Son of a knight of Kiev, he had lived in a golden age. Gold glitters, and so did the court of Prince Vladimir, and later that of his son Iroslav. Kiev was the center of law, architecture, Christianity and art.

At sixteen Alexi Danilovich entered the prince's service. A strong, clever campaigner, the young knight helped extend Kiev's reign all the way to the Baltic Sea. He fought well and bravely, and rose high in the prince's favor during the next ten years. Life was good. More than that, it was simple, with well-defined truths. He dedicated his life to Kiev, to God, and to his prince, and expected to be rewarded for it in this world and the next.

But then Alexi fell in love with the prince's lovely young niece, Larisska, and life was no longer simple. Sweet Larisska, with her wide dark eyes and pouting lips. She was fifteen years old, but even then she knew how to drive a man to desperation. Alexi courted her, snatching brief, fevered moments of love in between campaigns.

But one summer day he returned from the front to hear that Larisska had been promised to a Norse warrior, one Olaf Borrson, in payment of a political debt. Alexi had done everything in his power to stop the marriage, even going to the prince himself. But Iroslav refused. Furious, Alexi challenged Borrson to a fight to the death. He found himself arrested and tossed in prison until the day Larisska sailed north to her husband's harsh homeland.

Alexi stood on a bluff overlooking the river and watched the ship disappear in the distance. His heart shriveled. Everything was gone. His wealth, his honors, the woman he loved, stripped away by the man he had loved like a father.

He turned to look at Kiev, that marvel of architecture dominated by Iroslav's elegant palace.

"Tyrant!" he shouted into the uncaring wind. "For ten years I served you with my heart and mind and strong right arm, and it meant nothing to you. Nothing!"

Something snapped in him. Prompted by an impulse that he neither understood nor resisted, he turned and hurled himself off the bluff into the rushing river below. The cold water snapped him back to rationality, and he began to fight for life. But the river had him now. He slammed into a rock with crushing force. Gripping it with frantic, bloodied hands, he tried to pull himself out. The current was too strong, however, and he was swept downstream.

As he sank beneath the surface for the last time, the setting sun dyed the river bloodred. Water filled his mouth, his nose, his lungs. Darkness closed around his eyes, but his mind saw a faint, beckoning light. He strained toward it. The light grew brighter and brighter until he was rushing through a blazing tunnel, yearning for the peace he knew was waiting at the end.

He felt, actually felt, the hand of God reaching to gather him in.

And then something pulled him back. He slid, protesting, along the path back to darkness. No! his mind shrieked. Let me stay! But he was drawn away from the light.

He opened his eyes. Above him was the night sky with

its dusting of star gems. Once he would have thought it glorious, but nothing would ever compare with the light that had been stolen from him. A face came into his field of view then, a cruelly beautiful woman's face and eyes as deep and black as death.

Darija Onskaya. Six years ago, he had been her lover for a brief time. A brilliant flame was Darija, violently possessive, her passion hot enough to sear a man's soul. He'd been eager to bask in her heat. Until she died.

"Am I in hell?" he croaked.

She smiled. "Perhaps, my handsome Alexi, perhaps."

"How . . . did I get here?"

"I brought you here. Death parted us once, but you don't think I would truly let you go, do you?" She stroked his wet hair back from his forehead. Her hand was cold. "I let you play with your royal lover. But I made sure that you would be mine in the end, Alexi Danilovich."

He shook his head in mingled bewilderment and dread. Her hand closed on his hair, holding him still.

"Ah, Alexi, of course you don't remember," she crooned. "But I visited you one night a year ago, and it was then that I made you mine forever. All I had to do was wait. Death tried to claim you, but my claim is stronger than his."

"Dear God—"

"Forget your God," she said. "He will not have you."

"What . . . are you?" he whispered, afraid to ask, but more afraid of not knowing.

"I am revenant," she said, smiling the cruel, sensuous smile he remembered so well. "And now, so are you."

Alex pressed the heels of his hands hard against his eyes, preferring pain to the memory of that beautiful, inhuman face with its mad, night-dark eyes. In the guise of love, Darija had condemned him. She had stolen his soul and left him only Blood-Hunger in return. Eternal "life." It had been a poor trade.

Then he met Catherine and found peace. For a time. So brief a time, compared with the rest of his life, but so precious.

As though the memory had summoned her, he became aware of the scent of lavender drifting upon the humid air. He welcomed her silently, content at the moment to sit in the comfort of her presence.

His nostrils flared as a stronger perfume overwhelmed the faint lavender scent. Obsession, and the blood heat of a live human body. He felt suddenly weary, as though every one of his many years had come to sit on his shoulders. Without opening his eyes, he said, "Hello, Lydia."

"Hello, Alex. How did you know it was me?"

"Your perfume."

"That's right," she said. "You liked it before."

He opened his eyes and looked at her. She had changed into a gossamer, clingy thing that may have been a dress or a nightgown; it was hard to tell these days. Whichever, she looked ready for bed.

Before she could sit beside him, he rose and stretched. "I'm afraid the journey has caught up with me," he said.

"You don't look tired," she murmured, moving so close that the pointed tips of her breasts grazed his shirtfront.

"But I am."

"All night I've been sitting beside you, trying to behave like a rational human being. And all the while I could feel you here"—she touched her heart—"and here"—her belly—"and in my soul. You came here to me. For me. You can't tell me you don't feel it."

Too much. "Lydia—"

"Come to my room," she said. "Or let me come to yours."

He looked down into her gray-green eyes and read the desire there. She had the gift. To be burdened with this now, when he was so weak . . . The pulse beat visibly in her neck, and the neckline of her garment gaped open, exposing enough of her breasts to make his hands itch to touch her. The drive of his Blood-Hunger was urgent, its sharp claws tearing at his insides. She was so rich with life, like a vessel filled to overflowing. He wanted to bury himself in it, in her, and take what she offered.

But Catherine waited for him downstairs. Knowing that, he had the strength to resist both Lydia and his Blood-Hunger.

Grasping her by the elbows, he lifted her up and away from him, then set her gently back on her feet. "I'm sorry, Lydia," he said, "but I'll have to pass."

"Alex—"

He turned on his heel and walked away. Saving her, saving himself.

4

Lydia turned the stereo up loud. The hot, urgent beat of Led Zeppelin felt like a physical touch on her naked body. She made a slow circuit of the room, lighting the candles clustered on every tabletop.

She leaned down to light a joint from one of the candles, drew deep, and held it in for as long as she could. When she let it out again, the familiar rush went through her like wine.

The lead singer's voice soared high, running fire along her nerves. "Stairway to Heaven." All about buying your way in.

Not she. Heaven wasn't her thing, and all the money in the world couldn't buy her what she wanted. She looked down at herself. Her breasts seemed a little slack these days. Cupping them in her palms, she lifted them. Yes, definitely. A few years ago, last year even, they'd been *here*.

"I don't want to get old," she said. Oh, God. Thirty-five years old, and it was already happening. Every faint line, every loss of tautness in her skin terrified her.

Alex was younger than she.

It didn't matter, not to her. No man had ever stirred her like he had, with his burnished hair and the strange,

35

mist-colored eyes that seemed to look straight through to
her soul.

There was something about him that drew her irresistibly,
a sense of power and danger that lurked beneath that smooth
imperturbability of his. She liked danger. She liked power.
Alex had been attracted to her, too. Desire raged in the
depths of his eyes when he looked at her, a hot and powerful
kind of desire she'd never sensed before. Consuming. She
ached to give herself up to it.

But last night, when she'd pressed herself against him
and invited him to come to her room, he had said, *"I'm
sorry, Lydia, but I'll have to pass."* And then he'd put her
aside gently but firmly, and she'd known he meant not just
then, but any other time.

And still the desire had flared in his eyes, hot and inviting.
How he had resisted it, she didn't know. *She* certainly hadn't
the strength; it was all she could do not to fall at his feet and
beg him to touch her.

Is it because he thinks I'm too old for him?

"No," she said, taking another hit on the joint before laying it aside. "I'm not too old. I'm not going to *be* too old."

Turning in a graceful pirouette, she went to the cabinet
at the far end of the room and opened it. Her crystals lay on
padded shelves inside. Clear quartz, amethyst, aquamarine,
citrine quartz, malachite—all old friends that had been tuned
to her.

She ignored them. Tonight she wasn't looking for healing
or inner balance, or even for the return of her youth. Tonight
she was going to try something new. Reaching into a drawer,
she withdrew a red velvet pouch. She carried it to the center
of the room, sinking to her knees before opening it.

Her breath went out in a long sigh. There it was. Pure power—a twenty-inch tabular quartz crystal, made even more

rare because of the cloudy image of a ghost crystal deep inside. Its flat sides caught the candlelight and cast it back out, glittering like a thousand leaping points of flame.

"Beautiful Tabby," she said, stroking it lightly. "Your talent is to balance energies between two people. But I'm going to try something a little different with you tonight."

Barron was an idiot. He thought she was an amateur, dabbling in the bizarre because she had nothing else to do. Well, he was wrong. She *had* fire-walked. She *had* channeled. But the first time she'd held a generator crystal in her hand, she knew she'd come home. She'd read all the books about crystal lore, studied them, then gone beyond. Tonight, she felt stronger than ever before.

"It's you, Alex," she said. "You're the source."

She curled herself into the lotus position, then took the crystal between both hands. Emptying her mind of everything but her awareness of the stone, she began tuning it. She'd never worked with a crystal this big. Its power was immense, dwarfing anything else she'd ever worked with. The vibration set her body thrumming, her nerves singing in counterpoint. Suddenly it all meshed, blending crystal, Lydia, stone, and soul. And all around was the driving beat of the music, primal, urgent.

Heat settled deep in her belly, warming her like a man's hands. Sexual energy, a woman's power. She sank into it, letting the crystal absorb it, magnify it, send it outward.

Alex. She imagined his hands on her, stroking. What would it take, she wondered, to shake him out of that cool control? And what would it be like to make love to him if she succeeded? An ache spread through her groin at the thought.

Alex. His lean, sharp-planed face stared back at her, that marvelous lion-tawny hair falling forward on his forehead.

Passion narrowed his crystalline eyes, parted his lips. She could feel him in her veins, bringing her arousal to a fever pitch. Shivers ran up and down her spine, raising the fine hairs upon her back.

Her breath came in quick pants. Alex. Alex, Alex, Alex.

"Stairway to Heaven" was reaching its crescendo. Up and up, carrying her with it, helpless now despite the sudden clamor of fear. The voice and guitars blended, became both, then neither. The sound seemed to be *inside* her head now. Like thunder, like the beating of great wings.

It was too much. "Stop!" she screamed. "Stop it!" She fell backward, dropping the crystal.

The roar faded. She rolled onto her side and began to take deep, shuddering breaths. After a while she calmed enough to push herself to a sitting position.

What had that been? Imagination? Nightmare? The big crystal looked clear and unharmed. And totally unthreatening. She heaved a sigh of relief.

"Thank God you're all right, Tabby."

As she picked it up, however, she noticed something different about it. It *was* clear. Completely. The ghost crystal was gone. Stunned, she turned the stone over and over in her hands.

Suddenly she spotted a glint in the carpeting in front of her. She leaned forward and picked it up. It was a small tabular crystal, pointed on both ends, and exactly the size of the ghost crystal.

Her hands trembled. If this *was* the ghost crystal, the implications were astounding, incredible. Could she have somehow pulled it into reality, given it substance?

The tiny crystal felt warm against her skin, almost as though it were alive. She felt the edges of its power in her mind. High-pitched, higher than anything she'd ever felt.

Hold me, it seemed to say. *Keep me with you.*

With a gasp, she dropped it.

It glittered at her, beckoning. She wanted it, wanted its power, its strangeness. But she shrank from the memory of the roaring darkness that had filled her mind. The small crystal had been born of that darkness. If she took up the crystal, she would take up its birthright as well.

Did she dare face that again? But then the picture of Alex's face coalesced in her mind.

Take me up, the crystal sang. *I am power. You have only tasted a fraction of what I am.*

Lydia closed her eyes. Power. She liked the sound of that. Power and Alex, the perfect combination.

She reached for the ghost crystal again.

Alex opened his eyes. Although it was always dark here in his underground haven, he knew night had come. His time to walk the world of men.

Suddenly he was surrounded by the smell of lavender. His love had come to greet him, just as she'd greeted him every night of their lives together. Ahhh, heaven! To wake from oblivion to Catherine's arms!

"Come to wake me?" he murmured.

The presence slid over him and through him, rousing him as her hands had done so many years ago. Sweet, sweet desire, free from the taint of Blood-Hunger.

His love for Catherine was his link to his conscience, his reminder that he had once been a man. Without that, human beings would become nothing more than prey, food for his bottomless Blood-Hunger. He had traveled that road before, and it was a bitter one.

Something hovered at the edge of his vision, almost seen yet elusive. He sat up, hope running through his body in a rushing tide. This had never happened before. Had Catherine finally found a way to bridge the gap between the spirit world and this one? Dear God, if he could look into her face once more . . .

"Catherine, let me see you," he said.

Again the sense of presence, again the almost-seen phantom fluttering just out of sight. There was an urgency about that will-o'-the-wisp movement, as though she knew her time was short.

Catherine. Come to me, love. With every bit of power he possessed, he strained to bring her closer. *Catherine!* He flung his love toward her like a rope, hoping it would be strong enough to pierce the barrier between their worlds.

Almost, he heard a whisper. Almost. And suddenly it was all gone—scent, presence, everything.

His breath went out in a low groan. It had been so close! The hope had been great, the disappointment equally cruel. He'd lost her. If he'd been a little stronger, he might have brought her through.

"I'm sorry, love," he said, resting his elbows on his knees. He had been so close, so tantalizingly close. Orpheus at the threshold of joy, only to lose his beloved to death once again.

Worse, the Blood-Hunger had come back. It was even stronger tonight. Appetite, the revenant's need for blood was like white-hot needles driven into his flesh.

He pulled the bed's draperies aside and got to his feet. With his Blood-Hunger riding hard upon him, the cool air felt like sandpaper upon his naked skin. He glimpsed Catherine's portrait out of the corner of his eye. Although she was still smiling, it seemed a very sad smile tonight. She knew where he had to go.

"I'm sorry, love," he said. "I no longer have a choice."

He went upstairs and opened his closet. It was just like Margaret to have preserved the clothes he'd worn forty-three years ago. Then he smiled, thinking of the gold pen she'd given him for Christmas one year. He still had it, after all this time.

His revenant's senses alerted him to someone approaching the room. He strode to the door and opened it. Margaret stood outside, her fist raised to knock.

"I'd forgotten you could do that," she said, lowering her hand. She surveyed him from head to foot. "You look very dangerous tonight, Alex."

"I am . . . dangerous." He could hear the beat of her heart, feel the blood moving through her veins. "I'm going out."

"To Savannah?"

He nodded.

She looked away, her face betraying her knowledge of what he was going to do. Then she met his gaze again. "I'll send for the limo."

"I don't think that would be a good idea."

"Then I'll drive you," she said. "I want to talk to you anyway."

"This isn't a good time, Margaret. Tomorrow night I'll be all yours." He started to brush past her.

"I have an appointment with my lawyers tomorrow," she said, her words stopping him in midstep.

He took both her hands and raised them to his lips one by one. "If it's about your will, there's nothing to discuss. As I told you last night, I will accept any decision you make."

"Is your . . . life so bad that you'll give up the Arbor to keep it from me?"

"Look at me, Margaret." Bending so that she could look directly into his eyes, he let her see it all: the despair, the terrible weight of too many years and too many sins, and most important of all, the deadly, bestial need that was driving him out of the house.

Then he began to speak in a voice that burned his throat in its intensity. "I can walk through a roomful of people unseen and unheard. I can lift a car from the ground or break a man like a twig. I am, for most practical purposes, immortal. But I can't walk out on a beautiful spring day and feel the sun on my face. My sustenance is the fresh, warm blood of human beings. I can't even dream, for my rest is that of oblivion, not sleep."

He grasped her by the shoulders, as though his touch would make her understand his words. "I'm trapped, Margaret. Like a hamster running in one of those little exercise wheels. 'Round and 'round and 'round: new places, new identities, new lovers, new prey. Blood and guilt. Blood and desperation. Blood and fear—fear that I might forget myself and kill someone."

He suddenly became aware that Margaret was sagging between his hands. The old woman's eyes were closed, her head thrown back. For one awful moment he thought he'd done something to her. Dear God, had his blood lust gotten so bad that he wasn't aware of his own actions?

"Margaret!" he said sharply, his stomach clenching in horror as he checked her for wounds.

Her eyes opened. They were filmed with tears, her lashes spiked with moisture. "I never knew . . . you felt that way about yourself. Oh, Alex, do you hate yourself that much?"

Relief shot through him, making his hands shake. With an effort of will, he forced them to steadiness again. "I hate what I must do. I hate not having control of this . . . demon that drives me." Somehow, for her sake, he managed a smile. "As for Alex, well, sometimes he's not such a bad fellow. Has a bad habit of pitying himself, however."

She straightened. As soon as he was sure she was solidly on her feet, he let her go and stepped back.

"There's a car in the garage," she said. "A gray Celica I bought for Sonya to run errands in. The spare keys are in the lacquer box on the table in the foyer."

"Thank you."

"Alex." She raised her hand to her throat. "Are you going to . . ."

"Yes," he said, deliberately, brutally blunt. "Tonight I'll drive to Savannah in search of food. Tomorrow a prostitute will wake up feeling a bit tired and wondering where she acquired several hundred dollars."

"She won't remember you?"

"No." He turned away. "None of them remember."

5

Alex looked down at the prostitute. She was sleeping soundly, her chest rising and falling with her breathing. A small, red wound marked the skin between her breasts, and he reached out to smooth it with his fingertips. So young, he thought, so very sad. Pleasure had been a surprise for her, who was so skilled in giving it to others.

"Prey to everyone and everything," he murmured. "And now to me."

Only her death would have satisfied his Blood-Hunger. But the worst of the agony had been blunted, and for that he was grateful. He brushed the woman's hair back from her forehead, then dropped five one-hundred-dollar bills on the pillow beside her. After a moment he added two more.

"Thank you," he said.

It was nearly midnight when he got back to the Arbor. The house was dark, but the porch light had been left on to welcome him home. Margaret's kindness, he knew. Some things never changed.

A noise at the side of the house attracted his attention. Silently, he drifted across the lawn. No spell was required to make him unseen; the night's own shadows were quite enough. He turned the corner in time to see one of the

second-story windows sliding open with stealthy slowness.
Justin's room. A moment later the boy's thin, blue-jean-clad
legs slid out the window, his feet groping for purchase on
the tree limb beyond.

Amused, Alex crossed his arms over his chest and watched
as the boy climbed down, dusted himself off, and started
toward the back of the house.

"Ahem," Alex said.

Justin froze in midstep, then wheeled around. "I . . . I . . .
was just . . . Oh, all right. I was sneaking out."

"Yes?" Alex prompted.

"I've got some friends out in Delano. We're building a
ham radio. But these guys aren't from our so-called social
circle, and Mom and Dad don't want me out 'slumming,' "
he said, mingled wariness and defiance on his face. "I ride
my bike. It's only three miles."

"You like this ham-radio thing, then?"

"Oh, yeah." Excitement crept into the boy's voice. "We've
talked to people all over Europe and South America, and
now we're saving to buy a bigger antenna so we can talk
to Australia and Japan. We're into computers, too, and
I'm going to ask for a Mac for my birth—" He broke
off, obviously dismayed that he'd said so much about it.
Obviously thinking that Alex was going to tell his father.

"Please, go on," Alex said. "It's very interesting."

"No, I gotta get going."

Alex sighed. He'd lost him for now. "Good night, then."

Surprise erased the wary defiance on the boy's face.
"You're not going to tell?"

"Tell what?"

"About . . . about me sneaking out."

"I don't see that it's any of my business," Alex said. "Tell
me, though—why don't you just use the door?"

"Dead bolts. They lock up at night, and you need a key to get in or out."

"Ah, I see." Alex delved into his pocket and took out the keys Margaret had given him. "You mean one like this?" he asked, holding it up.

"Yeah."

"I'll be stuck in the library during the day, but I'll be around in the evenings," Alex said, pocketing the keys. "If you get a chance, come on up to my room sometime and tell me more about your project."

Without waiting for a reply, he walked away. He could feel the boy staring after him until he passed around the corner. As he went into the house he heard the sound of a bike's wheels on gravel. He grinned, cheered by the knowledge that the boy seemed to have inherited a full measure of Danilov drive and independence.

Upstairs, he found a note taped to his bedroom door. *We're having a party tomorrow night, Alex darling*, it said in Margaret's horrible scrawl. *Do come; I won't have any fun without you. Oh, and we're going to be formal, I'm afraid.*

He pulled the note free and folded it, his senses registering the life around him. Sleeping human beings inside, outside the nightlife of the marsh edge: alligators, raccoons, opossums, a mated pair of owls gliding on silent wings. And bats, of course. It always amused him to see movie vampires turning into bats. If he were to choose to live out the rest of his existence as an animal, it would be as one of those beautiful owls.

Wry amusement speared through him. Why hadn't he picked something innocuous, like a field mouse? Always the predator, never the prey.

His smile faded as his senses focused on Lydia. She burned like a flame, that one. Her gift was strong and raw, rooted in the sensuality of her nature. It called to him. He could almost feel her, taste her. His Blood-Hunger quickened.

"Help me, Catherine," he whispered.

The scent of lavender surrounded him. He closed his eyes and gave himself up to it, letting it draw him to his underground haven, to safety. Catherine. She knew his weakness.

"I shouldn't have come back," he said. "I should never have promised Margaret I'd stay."

The perfume wrapped him close as he lay upon the bed. *She* knew. He needed the Danilovs. The human connection anchored him to the world, gave him the strength to resist his own nature. When he was here, he was dressed in the skin of Alex Danilov—III, IV, or whatever. Without that, he was . . . what? Revenant. Monster.

A gossamer touch brushed over his eyelids. Tender. Accepting. "Yes, I know," he murmured. "Good night."

Alex sensed Margaret outside his room, but gave her the courtesy of letting her knock before opening the door.

"Breathtaking," he said, surveying her beaded gown.

"It's new. That's why I arranged this formal party." She put her hand on her hips. "Your tie is a disgrace."

"It would be easier with a mirror," he said, bending so that she could fix his tie.

"After a thousand years, I'd think you could learn to knot a bow tie without looking."

"The tie is a relatively new innovation, Margaret. And may I add, not one of the most notable things man has come up with?"

"Idiot," she said. "There. I don't know why I bothered; you always look elegant no matter what you're wearing."

He held out his arm to her. "Shall we go?"

The house was ablaze with light and laughter. Music drifted out from the ballroom. Delight rippled along Alex's veins; had Margaret arranged an old-fashioned ball just for him? He paused at the top of the stairs to enjoy the view of the foyer below. Huge vases of white roses flanked the door, and a basket of gladioli and carnations graced the drop-leaf table.

"This doesn't seem to be the usual sort of cocktail party people do nowadays," he said.

"I thought you might enjoy something different." Margaret pulled him to a halt at the top of the stairs. "Alex, about my visit with the lawyer—"

"Shh," he said. "Whatever you decided will be fine."

"But I want you to know—"

"Margaret." Gently, he smoothed a stray hair back from her face. "I love you. I always will. That's the only thing that matters to me."

Lydia walked out of the parlor and went to stand at the foot of the stairs. She was dressed all in white, but it didn't lend her innocence. A single emerald blazed green fire between her breasts. "Hello, Alex," she said. "I've been waiting for you."

"Dear Lydia," Margaret murmured. "I wish she'd devote her time to more . . . serious occupation."

He smiled. "I think she's very serious."

"God forbid." The annoyance in Margaret's eyes suddenly turned to amusement. "Watch where you allow yourself to be lured; there are mirrors all over her room."

"Thank you for the warning," he murmured.

As he walked down the stairs he felt as though he were walking into an oven.

Lydia claimed his other arm. "You look marvelous in a tux."

"You should see me in a courtier's uniform. The cape drives women crazy." He felt Margaret's nails sink into his forearm, and smiled.

A rush of memory overwhelmed him as he entered the ballroom. Courtesy of his imagination, the waltzing couples of the present were accompanied by generation upon generation of past Danilov guests. Ghosts in bustles, Empire gowns, corsets and crinolines, cravats and tailed evening coats; ghosts of his own lives. He banished them ruthlessly.

"Let's dance, Alex," Lydia said.

Gently but firmly, he pulled his arm from her grasp. "I'm sorry, but I promised this dance to Margaret."

"Coward," the old woman whispered as he led her onto the dance floor.

"Definitely," he said. "One thing I've learned in my long, long existence is the value of cowardice when dealing with certain women."

"Lydia has proven too much for three husbands so far. Perhaps you are just what she needs."

"Please!" he said in mock horror. "*Three* husbands?"

"Three. Let's see. She married one for money, one for love, and the third for . . . I'm not sure. The first ran out of money, the second ran out of love, and the third just ran out. He was the smartest of the three, in my opinion. And . . . damn it, here comes Faye Delacourt, ready to cut in. If you think Lydia's dangerous . . ."

Alex glanced over his shoulder to see a woman threading her way purposefully through the dancers. Blond, lovely, elegantly turned out, her eyes as hard and predatory as a hawk's.

"This is a tight-knit group of people," Margaret said. "All much too rich to schmooze with anyone else. So we're stuck with one another. And since few of us are at all interesting, we've become extremely bored with one another's company. You, however, are fresh blood."

He raised his eyebrows. "Really, Margaret, your metaphor—"

"May I cut in?" the blonde asked.

"No, Faye, you may not," Margaret said. "He's mine."

Alex swept her away, leaving the astonished woman to stare after them. "You're terrible, Margaret."

"I know. Always have been, haven't I?" Her indigo eyes were full of laughter. "Remember the time I was eleven and sneaked into my parents' Christmas ball?"

"I remember." He closed his eyes, maneuvering through the dancers by instinct. Almost, he could smell lavender. Almost.

"Daddy ordered me upstairs. But you just laughed and swept me out onto the dance floor. It was a waltz. You had me stand on top of your feet, and then we danced and danced and danced."

"I let you taste champagne—when your mother wasn't looking."

"Mother knew. She took my dessert away for a whole week."

He opened his eyes. "You never told me that."

"I didn't want you to feel bad."

"And now you do?"

"Don't be an idiot, Alex. Old people just like to reminisce." She reached up, smoothing his hair. "I'm glad you came back."

"So am I." A small lie. He'd told many lies in his many lives, and this was one of the kindest.

Eventually, Margaret gave him up to another. He danced with a series of women, hardly noticing their faces or their names even as he conversed with them. None appealed to

him, either as a man or as a revenant. It was a relief, even
as he steeled himself for the time that Lydia would slip into
his arms.

Finally, the press of warm human flesh around him
became claustrophobic, and he slipped out into the garden.
Mosquitoes whined shrilly on the hot, heavy breeze. The
grass was dew wet beneath his feet, the stars cold and hard
and beautiful overhead. He passed a few couples out to enjoy
the garden, but nodded without speaking. For a moment he
wanted solitude.

Then he felt something in the air, a hushed sense of
secrecy, coupled with urgency and sharp, malicious delight.
He passed into the heavy shadow beneath the mimosa tree,
knowing that no one would see him emerge on the other
side. Then, shielded by his revenant power, he followed that
piquant scent.

He found the source in a copse at the far end of the
garden, and it surprised him considerably. There, he saw
Sonya Danilov in the arms of a man. Not Barron. The
couple was tightly entwined, their heat an almost palpable
thing. Then the man lifted her gown, and her legs flashed
palely in the moonlight as she wrapped them around his
waist. Hushed sounds of coupling drifted on the night air.

Alex stepped backward, away from the wave of hot sensuality that threatened to engulf him. He wasn't shocked,
nor did he want to sit in judgment. But he was becoming
more and more entwined in the complexities of these people's lives, and he didn't want to be.

Then you shouldn't have come back. It was the cynical
revenant's part of him speaking, the part he'd spent nearly
a millennium fighting. This time, however, he agreed with
it. He had to gain a measure of objectivity if he were going
to deal with this situation.

The scent of Obsession drifted on the breeze, but the real perfume was the bright, burning life force of the woman who wore it. He turned to face her as she stepped off the path and walked across the grass toward him. Time for objectivity. Definitely.

"Hello, Lydia."

"Alex." She moved closer, her hair catching the moonlight and casting it back in a glory of ruddy sparks. "Are you enjoying the Garden of Earthly Delights?"

"I beg your pardon?"

She laughed. "I saw you come from the far end of the garden, looking like you'd gotten an eyeful. Sonya detailed me to make sure Barron doesn't follow her while she had her fun."

"Then you should be on duty."

"Barron doesn't even know she's gone. I must admit, I can't blame Sonya for finding a little fun elsewhere. Barron's a cold fish, always has been. The only thing that excites him is money and/or power. But then, they're pretty much the same, aren't they?"

"Not necessarily."

"No?" She looked terribly young, the fine lines around her eyes and mouth veiled by the diaphanous moonlight.

It was on just such a night he'd met Catherine. She *had* been young, only twenty. Innocent. And yet she'd had the maturity of soul to recognize his pain, the courage to take it into herself, and the strength to mold it into love. She had taught him humanity.

"Are you in there, Alex?" Lydia asked.

He blinked, refocused on the present. The woman before him was lovely, sensual, as bright as a flame. But her eyes, no matter how beautiful, were greedy, and reflected the hard green glitter of the emerald she wore.

"Of course I'm here," he said. "Who could be distracted around such a beautiful, charming woman?"

"If you really mean that . . ." She slid one hand around his neck. Her palm lay hot against his skin, demanding, tempting. "Why are we just talking?"

He took her hand and clasped it between both of his. "We weren't talking. We were gossiping about Sonya's infidelities, which is far more interesting than mere conversation."

"Are you trying to distract me?"

"Yes."

"Why?"

"You terrify me," he said. It was no lie; she touched things in him he'd rather not acknowledge. Things that could kill her.

"I don't see terror in your eyes."

"Shall I scream?"

"Only if that pleases you."

He smiled. "That's a lovely emerald, Lydia."

She shrugged, setting her breasts into graceful movement. "This is a very special stone, Alex. You see, most women wear emeralds because of the color, or the value. I don't. I searched through hundreds of them to find one that was right for me. Here," she said, taking a step forward. "Touch the stone. If you're sensitive enough, you can feel its vibration." She did not, however, lift the stone from its nest between her breasts.

Alex could feel the stone and the woman from here, and both raced through his veins like wine. But not his heart. *That* belonged to him. Recklessly, he reached out, sliding his fingers beneath the stone. Testing himself. Taunting the Blood-Hunger, proving that he was its master. Her skin was hot, pulsing with life. She looked up at him with slitted eyes, and he knew she was aware of the battle he was fighting—albeit not the cause—and thought he was going to lose.

Not tonight. He held the stone in his palm for a moment, then let it drop back against her chest. Disappointment and uncertainty flashed in her eyes.

"Come, Lydia," he said. "It's much too hot out here. Let me get you a glass of punch."

It wasn't until he put his hand on her back to urge her toward the house that he realized her gown was all but backless, plunging almost to her derrière. He resisted the urge to stroke his hand down the curve of her spine. Truly, he thought, this would be much easier if he'd been able to give up his baser human instincts along with his humanity.

"I'm driving up to Hilton Head tomorrow," Lydia said. "Would you like to come with me?"

"Sorry. I'm afraid I'm going to be tied up at the library all day, and—" He stopped, every nerve in his body screaming alarm.

Then a wave of fear and pain washed over him, so powerful that his mind shuddered beneath the onslaught. And it had a name.

Margaret!

Her pain tore at him as he ran toward the house. Pain. Tremendous, crushing weight on her chest. His chest. Everything began to grow hazy, and he knew she was slipping away.

Stay with me! It was both a plea and an order, and went out with all the power at his command.

The French doors burst inward as he approached them. He didn't know if he'd done it with his hands or his mind, didn't care.

Margaret lay on the floor beside the buffet table, her hair spread out around her in a white aureole. Barron knelt beside her. Alex stalked toward them, vaguely registering the crowd that melted from his path, bleating like a flock of sheep, only to re-form again in his wake. Far off, he heard the wail of an ambulance.

Barron rose, extending his arm as though to bar the way. Alex brushed him aside, then dropped to his knees beside the old woman. He could see death in her eyes, feel it in her mind. From the moment she'd been born, he'd known he would lose her. But not now, tonight. He wasn't ready. For the first time in many, many years, he was afraid.

Feeling Barron pressing close, Alex turned his head to look at the other man. Barron took a step backward, then another.

Alex turned back to Margaret. He couldn't control his trembling as he took her hand in his, then stroked her gnarled knuckles along his cheek. So many times he'd done this, her fat baby fingers feeling like tiny, silken pillows against his skin. He created a subtle spell, privacy for these last moments together. That, at least, he would have.

"I'm here, Margaret," he murmured.

"Unc . . . Alex." Her voice was the merest breath of sound. "Can we talk?"

Even now she protected him. "Yes," he said.

"I'm afraid, Alex."

"There's nothing to be afraid of."

"Is there something . . . after?"

"Yes," he said. "Oh, yes."

"Why . . . do I listen to you? Of course you . . . You're a damned . . . Byzantine Christian."

He brought her hand to his mouth and kissed her palm. "That's the best kind. Real belief, my darling. Trust me on this."

"I trust you," she said. "I always . . . have."

He sighed. "Thank you."

Her eyes drifted closed. Alex pressed her hand against his cheekbone, willing her to stay. Her pain centered in his chest, solidified into a solid mass. He fought it, breathing for himself and for her. In. Out. *Stay with me, just a few more moments.*

She opened her eyes, looked deep. "Alex . . . let me go."

"Margaret—"

"Let me go." A whisper, a plea. Too powerful to resist. Drawing in a deep, shuddering breath, he obeyed.

"Oh, Alex. I . . . It's so beautiful." Her gaze shifted, focusing on something beyond him. "I never knew anything could be so . . . beautiful. No wonder you wish . . . wish . . ."

"Wish I could go with you?" he finished for her.

"Yes." The light went out of her eyes. Her fingers relaxed against his cheek.

He felt something rise up from her body. Her soul— young and carefree, the Margaret that had never grown old, never stopped laughing, never stopped loving.

She moved forward to him. Eagerly, joyfully, like Margaret the child always had. Then she touched him. *Entered* him, passing through flesh and blood and mind. Then she left him, and he caught the barest taste of the bright and shining place that awaited her.

Take me with you! It was a scream in his mind.

But he was revenant, and bound. With a sigh, he laid her hand gently upon her chest. "Fare thee well, Margaret Danilov," he murmured. "Pray for me."

"She's not breathing!" someone shouted. "Does anyone know CPR?"

"The ambulance is just pulling in!" someone else shouted.

Alex allowed himself to be elbowed aside as people crowded around the old woman's motionless form. He knew they would fail; Margaret was gone. And with the joy awaiting her, nothing could bring her back to this.

He strode out into the garden, aware of nothing but the loss inside him. Not for Margaret; who could begrudge the joy that had welcomed her? His pain was for Alexi Danilovich, that soulless hulk of flesh too stained for redemption. Sins upon sins, centuries upon centuries of damnation.

"Alex!" Lydia called.

He registered her voice, dismissed it. She came running out of the darkness, flame woman in a dress as pale as moonlight. He kept walking.

"Alex, stop," she panted, trotting beside him. "Where are you going? Alex!"

He increased his pace. She floundered on her high heels, steadily falling behind. He passed from manicured lawn to the tougher grass of the borderland between the property and the marsh.

The odor of the marsh reached out and surrounded him. Wildwood. He walked straight out into the reeds, letting the water soak his pants and the mud fill his shoes.

"Ahhhhhhh, God!" he screamed.

The marsh took his cry and made it part of itself, blending it with the challenging bellow of a bull alligator. As the clamor died away Alex stood with bowed head, thinking that Wildwood had no prejudice at all. Man, beast, bird, revenant—all were accepted into its fecund vastness.

"Very well," he said. "Take me."

He spread his arms wide. They became elongated, grew wider, stronger. Feathers shimmered into existence, eclipsing flesh and skin and cloth.

A moment later a white owl glided off into the mist on silent wings.

6

Four nights later Alex walked out of the marsh. Four nights of prowling Wildwood's damp breezes, trying to be an owl, trying to think owl thoughts, do owl things. He had failed. No matter how much he looked like an owl, he was still revenant.

The beasts knew. And they had shunned him. Expatriate still, he had spent his nights alone as always, his days burrowed in the damp ground. Wildwood accepted him, uncaring of him as it was of all the myriad creatures that lived out their lives in its fecund depths.

The Arbor sat in the moonlight, unchanged by the tides of human life that came and went inside it. It was a part of him, perhaps the most important part. Leaving it would be hard.

Then he stiffened, his nostrils flaring as he caught the air of anticipation that permeated the house. He noticed a strange car parked in the driveway, and knew it belonged to a guest who was much more than casual.

Hidden in a cloak of revenant power, he walked in. If need be, he'd walk out again and never come back. It was the lack of sound that drew him into the study; silence was the last thing he'd expected.

He surveyed the room from the doorway. Lydia and Sonya sat at either end of the sofa, both looking very bored. Barron sat at Margaret's desk with an air of possessiveness that gave Alex a jolt.

The queen is dead, long live the king! And off with the arbors, on with the tennis courts. *You made your choice.* Alex reached deep inside for balance, and managed to find it.

His gaze moved to the stranger, who stood at the window, his back to the room. The family's attention was centered on him, although they tried to hide it. Judging from the thick tension in the room, the Danilovs weren't getting what they wanted from him.

Interesting. This merited some investigation. Alex took a step backward, out of the doorway. With a flick of his mind, he erased the reek of the marsh from his clothes and body.

Lydia turned around the moment he stepped back into the doorway, her head coming around as though pulled by a string. Almost as though she'd *felt* him.

"Alex!" she gasped.

She ran to him, and he grasped her outstretched hands to stop her from embracing him. Just now he felt like flawed glass, ready to shatter at the slightest touch. He put her to one side, retaining his grip on her wrist to make sure she stayed there. Her gift was surging high tonight, and ran up through his arm like heat lightning.

"Where have you been?" she demanded. "We've been so worried about you!"

"Margaret's death hit me hard. I just needed to be alone for a few days."

"Rather an extreme reaction, isn't it?" Barron asked. "Considering that you barely knew her."

The man's resentment rolled over Alex. He breasted it, met it with his own. "Margaret was a very special lady. Time had nothing to do with the place she took in my heart." *Special, yes. I was more her father than the man who sired her.*

The stranger came forward, his hand extended. "Mr. Danilov, I'm Charles McGinnis, Margaret's lawyer and executor of her estate."

Alex didn't miss the subtle distinction the man had drawn: not "the family's lawyer," but "Margaret's." A distinction with vast implications.

"Pleased to meet you, Mr. McGinnis." Alex shook hands, studying the man closely. He was perhaps fifty years old, a square, solid fellow with sandy hair and shrewd blue eyes. Good poker face—an asset in his business.

"Mr. McGinnis has been coming here every night in the hope of catching you," Barron said.

"Indeed. Why?"

"The will, Mr. Danilov," McGinnis said. "Margaret's instructions were that it be read at night, with the entire family present. That includes you."

"The funeral, too, was at night, also per her instructions," Barron said. "Too bad you missed it."

"I said my good-byes," Alex said.

"Ah, yes, you spoke to her just before she died," Barron said. "What exactly *did* you say to my aunt?"

Alex smiled. "Good-bye."

"Gentlemen," McGinnis interposed smoothly, "I'd like to get started, if you don't mind."

Barron relinquished the desk and went to sit beside his wife. Alex crossed his arms over his chest and watched the lawyer extract a thick folder from a briefcase and set it upon the desk.

"This is a very long document," McGinnis began. He donned a pair of half glasses and peered at the papers before him. "There are bequests to a number of individuals and charities—"

"Just summarize the pertinent details, Mr. McGinnis," Barron said.

"Yeah, get to Barron's money," Lydia offered, sotto voce.

McGinnis adjusted his glasses. "As far as Danilov Industries itself, Mr. Barron Danilov is to continue in his duties as chairman of the board. Margaret's fifty-one percent of the stock . . ."

The lawyer paused for breath. Alex glanced at Barron, saw triumph on his face.

"Is to go to Mr. Alex Danilov—"

"WHAT?" Barron leaped to his feet.

"The house and contents, as well as all properties connected with the estate known as the Arbor, is now the property of Alex Danilov. However, Margaret requested that he continue to share his home with the family—"

"This is an outrage," Barron hissed. "She only knew the man a short time! He conned her, got her to change the will in his favor—"

McGinnis laid the papers aside. "Mr. Danilov, your aunt changed only the portion relating to Danilov Industries. As far as the house and contents go, that bequest to Alex Danilov has been in her will the entire twenty years I represented her."

"Twenty years . . . ?" Barron swung around to Alex. "How long have you known about this?"

"It's as much a surprise to me as it is to you," Alex said. That much was true. Only the house was to have gone to him; until now the company had always been the property of the current generation.

"I don't understand," Sonya said. "How did she know about him? And why didn't she say anything until now?"

"Your aunt had very far-ranging interests, both business and personal," McGinnis said. "Apparently she learned about the foreign branch of the family and followed Alex's career for many years."

"He's not a citizen." Barron's hands were clenched so tightly the knuckles were white. "The legality of this—"

"Sorry, Barron," Alex said. "My mother was American, and my parents happened to be vacationing in the U.S. when I was born. I hold dual citizenship."

Barron whirled away from the sofa and began pacing. "I can't believe Aunt Margaret would do this to me. I'll contest this will. I'll tie you up in court for a hundred years. A confused old woman—"

"I strongly advise you not to do that," McGinnis said.

Barron stalked to the desk and thrust his face into the lawyer's. "Danilov Industries is *mine!* This house is *mine!* And I'll be goddamned if some slick operator is going to cheat me out of it!"

"I was hoping I wouldn't have to do this," McGinnis said. Reaching into his briefcase, he took out a single piece of paper. "Your aunt was a very astute woman, Mr. Danilov. Much more astute than you give her credit for, I'm afraid. Let me read you this letter she left for me."

He took a deep breath. "It reads, 'Dear Charles: Tell Barron for me that if he challenges my will, I want you to send to the IRS those documents showing the million and a half dollars he has siphoned off from Danilov Industries in the past year. Not a lot of money, in Danilov terms, but added to what he's taken during the fifteen years he's headed the company, it runs into a tidy sum. Also, tell him that if he's going to steal money, to be smarter about it. I discovered it the first time he did it.' "

The color drained out of Barron's face. Without a word, he turned and walked out.

Sonya rose with languid grace and followed her husband. She was smiling.

"Wow," Lydia breathed.

"Wow, indeed," Alex said.

The lawyer cleared his throat. "Mr. Danilov, there are a few things I'd like to go over with you. Privately."

"No one ever said I couldn't take a hint," Lydia said, brushing past Alex with elaborate casualness. As she went by she whispered, "Better lock your door. Barron may come sneaking in to stick a knife in your back."

"I always lock my door," he said.

"A pity." She winked at him as she walked out.

McGinnis rose and closed the door, then took his brief-case over to the sofa.

"Would you like a drink, Mr. McGinnis?" Alex asked, moving toward the sideboard.

"Bourbon on the rocks, thank you."

"So, Mr. McGinnis, I gather Margaret trusted you with all her business dealings?"

"I handled everything for her. After twenty years, we were as much friends as lawyer and client. Thanks," he added, accepting the glass Alex held out to him. "I've been trying to get Margaret to do something about Barron for years, but she just said, 'Wait and see, Charles. I'll fix him. I've got an ace in the hole.' I gather that was you."

"Apparently," Alex said. "I must admit, I wasn't expect-ing it. And I don't quite know what to do about it; my circumstances do not allow me the time to deal with the day-to-day running of a large business."

"You don't have to. That's what they have presidents and

vice-presidents for. All you need to do is call meetings often enough to keep the fear of the Lord in them. And you need a good watchdog."

"Is that what you did for Margaret?"

"That, among other things."

Alex read only truth in the man, textured by a spark of wry amusement. If Margaret had trusted him for twenty years, he must be a very capable watchdog, indeed. But it was that spark of amusement that decided Alex. Capable lawyers were easy to find; the real jewel was one with a sense of humor.

"Are you interested in working for me?" Alex asked.

"Yes, Mr. Danilov."

"Call me Alex. And consider yourself retained."

McGinnis inclined his head. "Margaret hoped you would do so. Oh, she said to remind you that although Barron is a mediocre thief, he's still a Danilov. As she said, 'Judgment is not upon all occasions required, but discretion is.' "

"She didn't say it," Alex said. "She stole that little gem from Lord Chesterfield. I'll counter with Ecclesiastes—'He that observeth the wind shall not sow; and he that regardeth the clouds shall not reap.' "

"So you want him out."

"I want him controlled."

"It would be easier to get him out," the lawyer said. "A smart dog can slip the tightest leash."

Alex spread his hands. "Margaret wanted him in."

"Yes, she did. All right, Alex, if you want him, you've got him. I strongly suggest, however, that you do some housecleaning; the best way to pull his claws is to get rid of the people who've been helping him with his little swindle."

"Cleanliness," Alex murmured, "is next to godliness."

"I think I know which heads need to roll, but I want to be sure I get all of them."

"Sounds good to me," Alex said. "But how do we coordinate all this? I'm very hard to reach during the day."

"Got a fax machine?"

Alex shook his head. "I'm a rather old-fashioned fellow."

"I'll see that you get one. We can fax documents back and forth almost instantly. If you need to tell me something, you fax it to my private machine. If I can't tag up with you, I can act on your instructions, then fax you the results."

"I see." The image of a thousand-year-old vampire running his business via fax machine was a very funny one, and Alex struggled not to laugh outright. "Just like magic."

Lydia held the small ghost crystal in her palm. It glittered back at her knowingly, its high-pitched vibration shivering through her mind.

She could feel Alex, actually feel the strange, far-reaching power that had first drawn her to him. Like a tiger, trained to the whip yet not tame, it was beautiful and frightening at the same time. *If you turn your back, you might find yourself gobbled up.*

"What an interesting thought," she murmured.

The crystal whined shrilly. She closed her fingers around it. For once, she needed neither drugs nor music to draw her into the stone; it was like falling into an abyss, almost hitting ground, then soaring upward on vast wings.

Power. Lifting her up, drawing her forward. Ahead, a dark mist. It reached out to pull her in, wrapping wine-red tendrils around her. A face hung high above her, blazing power like the sun. Alex's face, his smile inhumanly beautiful, his pale eyes glittering with hunger. She flew toward him, wanting the beauty, wanting to feed the hunger.

And then her wings failed her. Like Icarus, she soared too high and was singed. Screaming in ecstasy and terror, she spun down a dizzying vortex. She fell into an endless well of purple-black clouds. Incandescent lightning crawled along the madly spinning walls, a spider-leg webbing of power.

The face swooped after her, but it was no longer Alex's. The gray eyes had become black and monstrous, whole galaxies trapped in their depths. And the mouth . . . No longer smiling, it gaped after her in a beast's roar, surrounding her with the stench of carrion.

And then came the touch of the vast, shadowy presence she had touched last time. No longer threatening, it enveloped her in velvet arms. Soothing, protecting, and yet possessing utterly. It was like being held by a god.

The presence filled her, overfilled her. Its knowledge was immense, its cruelty total. She was drawn to the knowledge, repelled by the cruelty; either way, she was helpless in its grasp. Raw power vibrated around her, through her, making her nerves sing like violin strings.

Power, it whispered to her. *Taste it. Is it good?*

Yes.

Take it, then. If you dare.

Power. More than she had ever hoped to find. Youth. Beauty. Alex. Everything she'd ever wanted. All she had to do was reach out and grasp it. But did she dare? *I'm afraid.*

Fear will not give you what you want. Only I can do that.

Will it hurt?

Amusement washed over her, vast and inhuman. *Pain is irrelevant. Power is the beginning and the end and everything between. Either take it, or stop wanting it.*

She reached out, touched the swirling wall of the vortex. A finger of lightning crawled along the clouds toward her, touched her, ran in rivulets along her skin, in her flesh.

Her body arched. God! She felt bigger, stronger, younger. With a wild laugh, she plunged both hands deep into the vortex. It carried her with it, spinning, spinning, as more tendrils of lightning humped their way along the clouds toward her.

She hung there, a pulsing heart of power sustained by the veining of bolts that ran up through the vortex. Exquisite pleasure, exquisite terror.

Until pleasure became pain.

She convulsed, screaming. Her arms and legs thrashed as she tried to escape the agony. But she was trapped, pinned like a butterfly on a collector's board.

Let me go! I'll do anything you want, just let me go!

The agony stopped. Everything stopped.

She found herself lying prone on the floor of her room. The carpeting felt like a thousand needles digging into her skin. Slowly, she pushed herself up onto her hands and knees.

"Ohhh," she gasped, shuddering.

The crystal hummed in her hand. Shuddering, she hurled it from her. Then she caught sight of herself in the mirrored closet doors. Crouched, her hair whipped into a tangle, her eyes haunted and wild—she looked as though she'd been to hell and back.

But there was something else. She rose to her feet and padded to the mirror, peered closely. Her breath went out in a long gasp.

The fine lines at the corners of her eyes were gone. The triple crease in the center of her throat, gone. The faint droop of her breasts, gone. She'd always been beautiful, but now there was a different quality to it, as though a light were shining just beneath her skin.

"Oh, God," she breathed, reaching out to touch her reflection. "I thought . . . I thought it was a dream. But it was
real!"

She whirled away from the mirror, searching the side
of the room where she'd thrown the crystal. It called her.
Following its vibration, she found it wedged in the crack
between the mattress and headboard.

Power thrummed in her mind, ran along her veins like
fire. But the pitch was different than it had been before, both
higher and more insistent. And the color had changed. The
stone had darkened, as though it had absorbed some of that
wine-dark mist that had claimed her. Rather than reflecting
the light, the crystal seemed to absorb it, pulling it deep
inside to power some strange incandescence of its own.

Lydia reached for it, then drew her hand back. Fearing
its power, fearing her own desire to possess it.

"What are you?" she whispered.

It glinted at her, cold and inviting. Its misted depths roiled,
as though a wind had stirred them. She could almost feel that
breeze. No, she *could* feel it. It tickled along her skin, still
cold, still inviting.

I am Power. Even Death bows before me. The beautiful,
inhuman voice spilled through her mind, wrapped her up
like a smooth, dark blanket. *Pick me up. Hold me.*

"No," she whispered, still afraid.

Its need thrummed in her ears, down along each nerve
and tendon, settled deep in her body. Or was it hers? Her
need, traveling through the crystal, magnified, and then sent
back to her again?

Yes. Yours, his, mine, ours.

"His? You mean Alex?"

Don't you?

"Yes," she said. Of its own volition, her hand crept up

to touch the now smooth expanse of her neck.

Youth is only a small part of what I can give you.

She closed her eyes. Wanting. Youth, beauty, Alex—those were only a small part of what she wanted. "You hurt me before," she said.

Your own weakness hurt you. I merely forged the vessel anew so that you can hold the power you need. Let me show you how to take it. How to use it. Take me up.

Lydia reached out and grasped the stone. It lay in her palm like crystallized blood, pulling her down, pulling her in.

She found herself floating in the vortex again. The spinning walls of dark, lightning-shot clouds stretched above and below her, seemingly without end. Even as she watched, the bolts began to move toward her, scuttling along the cloud surface like incandescent spiderlings.

Fear clawed at her. Then the presence closed around her, possessive, all-encompassing, its beauty and cruelty equally matched. She hung unresisting in its embrace. It would give her youth, beauty, wealth, anything she wanted. It would give her Alex.

No. You will do all those things, Lydia. Do you see the power all around you?

Yes.

I cannot touch this power. Only you can. Reach out your hand. Call to it. Draw it into you, and I will show you how to control it.

Despite her fear, Lydia stretched out both arms to the lightning. Bolts leaped to each of her splayed fingers, crawled in spirals up her arms.

Now, Lydia, open yourself to the power.

Terror was a hot blade in her guts. *How?*

Pretend it's Alex.

That vast, almost malicious amusement lay cold in her mind. But the lightning played across her body, through it, banishing that chill touch. She lay cradled in the searing light, burning yet unburned. Power. It felt like Alex, smelled and sounded and tasted like him.

"Alex," she whispered.

That's it. Call him. Bring him in to you.

"Alex."

Heat coursed through her. Breasts/nipples/groin—an endless loop of arousal. She arched, giving herself up to it. Her skin was aflame, her nerves quivering, her mind awash in sensation.

"Oh, God," she moaned.

God has nothing to do with this. Call the one you really want.

More lightning stabbed toward her. She spun, arms and legs splayed, while power played across her skin like a man's hands.

Call him!

"Alex."

Again.

"Alex."

The sensations were overwhelming now, her body straining as she slid up the slope of a giant wave of pleasure.

Call him! The voice flowed over her, through her. Erotic. Alluring. Promising fulfillment.

"Alex!"

Louder!

"ALEX!"

She screamed as a climax ripped through her. Shuddering, her back arched at an impossible angle, she hung impaled in the center of a web of light that pulsed and flared in time with the contractions of her orgasm.

Very good, Lydia. You're part of the power now, and it is part of you. You may go now.

Again, she found herself lying on the floor, her body throbbing, satiated. More than satiated. But her mind . . . her mind wanted to experience it again and again and again.

She felt somehow larger than life, as though the old Lydia had come bursting out of her cocoon. A whole new being—strong, desirable. The crystal lay on the floor beside her. It looked darker than before. No, not darker, but deeper, as though it no longer encompassed the few square centimeters of stone that was the ghost crystal, but had become a window. A window into . . . something else.

A few minutes ago she might have been afraid. But not now. She gazed deep, deep, wanting to see the other side. A thrill of fear ran up her spine, almost as if someone had touched her. Warning her. "Don't look," the touch seemed to say. "Don't look."

A faint trace of perfume surrounded her. She couldn't place it at first, registering only the awareness that it was terribly old-fashioned. Then she placed it: lavender.

She felt her lips stretch in a smile. "Begone," she said in a voice that didn't sound like hers at all.

The perfume faded.

7

Alex walked along the path to the gazebo. The breeze was sluggish and heavy, seeming to add more heat and moisture to the air rather than cooling it. He was surrounded with flowers, but all their myriad scents were lost in the simple, sweet essence of lavender. None had ever been planted on the property; that scent was Catherine's alone.

"Well, my love," he murmured. "I'm up to my ears in Danilov infighting again. This brood of ours continues to be unruly, difficult, and ambitious."

Almost, he could feel her walking beside him. Her amusement was obvious, washing over him like a cool breeze.

He chuckled. "Yes, I know. I wouldn't have them any other way. How boring it would be to be surrounded by nice, polite, undifficult people."

Sensing another presence nearby, he stepped into a wedge of shadow, pulled it around himself like a cloak. Then he located the other person. Justin. The boy sat on the ground beneath the mimosa tree, his face resting on his upraised knees, so silent and still that even the revenant's fine-tuned senses hadn't caught him until now.

Alex walked toward him, deliberately making some noise to alert the boy to his presence. Justin's body tensed, but he didn't look up.

72

"Hello," Alex said.

"Hi." Sullen, but polite.

"What are you doing out here alone?"

"Nothing."

Alex sank to a sitting position. Folding his legs Indian style, he leaned his back against the trunk and regarded the boy. "Do you want to talk about it?"

"Uh-uh."

"Is it Margaret?"

There was no answer, but Justin's grief was an almost palpable force. Surrounded with Catherine's perfume, Alex was able to manage his own pain enough to deal with the boy's. "I miss her, too."

"You hardly knew her."

Not true! "That doesn't mean I didn't love her."

"Dad says you conned her."

"Do you think Margaret could be conned by me or anyone?"

Justin's head bobbed, an indefinite answer. Suddenly he looked up, his cheeks wet with tears, his eyes red from crying. "I don't care about the stupid house or the stupid company! I never wanted them anyway!"

"I miss her, too," Alex said softly, wishing he could take the boy in his arms and comfort him. He would have, if the boy were a few years younger.

"I knew she was old. I knew she'd die someday. But I thought I'd have more time—" Justin's voice broke.

"Me, too."

The boy's head went back down. "That was a great talk. I don't feel any better for it."

"Neither do I."

Silence fell. Alex closed his eyes and leaned his head back against the tree. He could wait. After all, he had nothing but time. How ironic that he had so much of it and couldn't lend a bit to Margaret, whom he loved so much.

He could have. He could have given her Time itself. She had begged him to, and he had refused. The scent of lavender grew stronger, and a gossamer touch brushed over his eyelids. *Yes, love, it was the only decision I could make. But sometimes I wonder if I know right from wrong anymore. Perhaps it's only Alex's way, what Alex thinks at any given moment. That power, I never expected to have.*

She touched him again, reassuring.

"Dad wanted to put up condominiums," Justin said. "Tear down the house to make room for tennis courts and a golf course. It made Aunt Margaret nuts."

"I can understand why."

"Oh, Dad planned to go first class all the way. A quarter of a million per unit."

"Definitely first class."

"Dad says you're going to throw us out," Justin said.

Alex opened his eyes. "I wasn't planning to."

"What are you going to do with the place?"

"I think it's rather nice the way it is."

The boy ducked his head. "That's why she gave it to you, you know."

"I expect it is."

"Look," Justin said. "I don't even know what to call you. Mr. Danilov sounds stupid, and—"

"Why not Alex?"

"Okay."

There was another long interval of silence, but the tension had gone out of it. Finally, Justin spoke.

"My dad and I had a fight tonight. He caught me sneaking out."

"And?"

"He nailed my window shut." His voice was full of anger, desperation. "Will you let me use your key?"

Alex sighed. "I deserve that, for teasing you with it earlier. But it wouldn't be right for me to go against your father—"

"But—"

"Please, hear me out," Alex said, raising his hand. "In good conscience, I can't help you disobey your father. But what's wrong with having your friends come here?"

"*Here?* My low-life friends running through the house, messing up all the nice antique furniture . . . Dad would croak."

Alex smiled. "They'll be *my* guests, then. There's plenty of room in the west wing."

"Huh?"

"I don't want anyone in my bedroom, but other than that, you kids can have the run of the place. I'm rarely there in the evenings, anyway."

"It's really going to piss Dad off."

Smiling, Alex spread his hands. "So, what do I have to lose?"

"Yeah, that's true."

Ah, the refreshing candor of the young, Alex thought. An adult would have babbled some social lie.

But Justin just accepted the fact of his father's hate, then went on to other things. "What about the antenna?" he asked. "We've got to have an antenna."

"The Arbor is a grand old lady, Justin. I expect she'll weather that indignity as well as she's handled all the rest. I'll arrange to have an antenna installed." He looked up, hearing a door open and close at the rear of the house.

Sonya came into view a moment later. The breeze lifted her hair and swirled her skirt around her legs.

Combined with her smooth, languid movements, it made her look almost as though she were floating toward him.

"Justin," she called. "Are you out here?"

The boy rose to his feet, dusting his backside off with both hands. "Yeah, Mom."

"I've been looking for you all over. It's time for . . . Oh, hello, Alex. I didn't know you were with him."

"We were just talking about Margaret," he said, rising. "I'll let you and Justin—"

"Actually, I'd like to talk to *you* for a moment. Justin," she said, without taking her gaze from Alex, "go inside and get ready for bed."

The boy hesitated uncertainly, then swung around and headed for the house. Alex crossed his arms over his chest and regarded the woman, aware of her heavy-lidded sensuality, but more aware of the lavender perfume surrounding him.

"What can I do for you, Sonya?" he asked.

"I was just wondering what our status was. Should we start packing our bags?"

"Not at all. I hope things can go on as before," he said.

There was an edge to her smile. "You mean we continue living in someone else's house?"

"If you wish to phrase it that way, yes. But like Margaret, I find the Arbor far too large to occupy alone."

"My husband swears that he'll break you."

It was his turn to smile. "Do you think he will?"

"Maybe. But then again, maybe not; you look like you might be able to take care of yourself." She moved closer, put her hand on his chest. "I despise Barron."

"Why do you stay married to him, then?"

"Because I like living here. I like being a Danilov."

"Is that why you dally in the garden with other men?" he asked.

"Dally?" she echoed. "How funny! Tell me, Alex, what century are you from, anyway?"

"The tenth." He took her hand, which was moving up toward his neck, and put it from him. "And terribly old-fashioned."

"Scruples?" she breathed, apparently not at all upset by his rejection. "You'll lose those soon enough, or Barron *will* break you. He's got a lot of experience breaking people."

"Apparently he failed with you."

"Now there's where you're wrong," she said. "Barron made me what I am." Her eyes had turned hard and cold. Years ago, perhaps, there might have been tears in them. Alex realized she'd cried all her tears long ago.

"I'm sorry," he said.

She turned away sharply. Then she paused, hand on hip, and swiveled to face him. The coldness was gone. Her languid sensuality drifted like a drug on the hot night air. Alex could almost taste it.

"You can have us both," Sonya said.

Alex stiffened. Had she read his mind? "Who?"

"Me and Lydia. We've shared men before. Special men, men who like the . . . contrast between us."

Flame woman and moon goddess, Alex thought. Yes, a very intriguing contrast. His Blood-Hunger flared, raking along the edges of his mind with razor claws. *Take her. Take them both. They will love you. Pleasure addicts that they are, they will worship you.*

He shuddered. No. Better that he walk out to greet the dawn. "Good night, Sonya," he said.

"You didn't say no."

"All right then. No."

She turned on her heel and walked toward the house. Alex sighed. Satan himself couldn't have devised a more exquisite temptation for him.

"Ah, Catherine," he murmured. "Always you spoil me. Before you, I would have played with them both. The wife of the man who swore to break me, his sister as well, and all living under the same roof . . . I would have plunged in, enjoying the danger, the sheer, malicious drama of it." He sat down again in the hot, private shadow beneath the tree. "Using others' emotions to try to make myself feel alive— now *that* is true vampirism."

The scent of lavender was stronger now. He could almost feel her hand upon his cheek, but when he reached up to touch it, he felt only his own skin.

"Please, Catherine. Without you, I am only a shadow of a shadow. Come to me."

The night seemed alive, almost seen sparks that danced in the edges of his sight but disappeared when he tried to focus on them, almost heard music that lilted just beyond his hearing. The hair at his nape lifted with some unnamable force. He stood poised on a threshold. Here, was Savannah. There . . . just there, where he couldn't quite see, couldn't quite hear, was another world.

A magical world. A world, perhaps, where he could be with Catherine.

Mist crept along the grass, swirled around his ankles. It glowed with a radiance of its own, softer than moonlight, and it smelled of lavender.

"Come to me," he commanded, heart and mind and soul.

Wandering tendrils coalesced, drew together, rose into a pale, glowing column. Faintly, deep in the radiance, he could see Catherine's face. She was smiling.

"Oh, God," he rasped, scrambling to his feet. "Step forward, love. Let me pull you through."

Her hand, wreathed with mist, reached toward him. He tried to grasp it, but his own hand passed right through. His whole being focused on the slim, pale hand that seemed to beg him. He *would* hold her again. If he had to fight God and Satan together, he would hold her.

He tried again. The awareness of soft, warm skin passed across his hand. Almost. Almost.

And then the mist turned dark. Blood dark. Dimly, he could see Catherine's mouth open and close as though she were calling a warning. Then she was sucked away from him.

He sprang after her, only to be blown backward by a tremendous bolt of lightning that stabbed out of the retreating mist. Wind tore at him.

"Catherine!" he shouted. "Catherine! Noooooo!"

The wind snatched the cry from his mouth, flung it away. Then it stopped abruptly. The lightning-shot fog contracted, folding in and over upon itself. It dwindled rapidly; now the size of his head, now his fist, now a pin . . . and then it was gone.

Catherine was gone.

He lay on his back, too stunned to do anything but stare up at the sky. He'd almost won. A moment more, and he would have been able to hold her hand.

The shock faded slowly. There was only the garden. Serene, fragrant, normal. Just now, it was a mockery. Anger rose in him, and with it, the Blood-Hunger. Icy shards of need in his brain, in his guts, razor claws of desire raking across the fabric of his being.

Fists clenched, he fought it. In fear and loathing, he fought the bestiality of it. Pure appetite—if he let it rule him, he would be no better than a beast. Stalking the night, feeding off those who had once been his kind.

"No," he said. "I will not."

Like a lion tamer with his whip and chair, he beat his Blood-Hunger into abeyance. But there was a waiting sort of quality about it, as though it knew he wouldn't be able to hold it forever. As though it knew it would win.

For now, however, he retained his humanity. He stood, fists clenched, chest heaving, his face lifted to the sky.

"Was it you who took her from me?" he asked. "Did I trespass on your precious domain of life and death? If so, damn you! My very existence is a trespass, and yet you allow it. Why not Catherine? Why not the good along with the bad?"

There was no answer. He knew there would never be an answer.

Suldris stood at the far end of the bridge that led to the Arbor. This was as far as he could go without giving himself away to his enemy. This was the vampire's home ground; the air, the land, even the water of the marsh were tainted with the aura of the being who owned them.

"Alexi Danilovich," Suldris whispered. "We meet again, my old enemy."

After years of searching, he'd run his quarry to ground. The woman had brought him here, the one with hair like flame and the remarkable ability to tap the power of her crystals. He had touched her almost by accident. Touched her, claimed her, and now directed her. Under his tutelage, she had tapped straight into Alex's Blood-Hunger, using his own power to banish the ghost he held so dear.

"I've taken that," Suldris said. "And soon the rest. When you come to the final battle, Alexi, you will be stripped of everything."

But first the game. It was his favorite; playing the strings, making the puppets dance. He'd waited four hundred years for this. Centuries of pain, of hate, of wandering the continents in search of revenge.

He glanced over his shoulder at the woman he'd taken from a street corner in Savannah. Once, she might have been pretty. Now, however, she was merely sluttish, her once gamine face made haggard by the life she lived. He'd paid well for her company. Amusement bubbled through him. She was too stupid to realize what he'd paid for. But she would, in time. And then even stupidity couldn't save her.

"What is your name again?" he asked.

"Lisa."

"Ah, yes. Lisa, come stand here with me." When she obeyed, he put one arm around her shoulders and turned her so that she could see the lights of the Arbor. "Do you know what that is?"

She shook her head.

"That is the house of my enemy. I've been searching for him for many years now. Can you guess how many years, Lisa?"

Another negative.

"Four hundred years," he said. "Yes, Lisa, four hundred years. You see, Alexi is a vampire."

"You're kidding, right?"

"A living, breathing vampire, my dear." Then he chuckled. "Although that is rather a contradiction in terms. Now," he said, shifting his hand to her neck so as to savor the blood pulsing within, "let me tell you why he is my enemy. You see, he stole everything from me. My realm, my people, my life, all sacrificed to his god of morality. Greed I could accept, but morality?"

He knew she didn't understand. But she was afraid, and

that pleased him. Fear added savor. He'd fan it higher and higher, and when she reached the peak of terror, he'd take her. He needed a great amount of psychic energy to replenish what he'd used in binding the red-haired woman.

"And since we're talking about gods, Lisa, did I ever tell you that a long time ago I was almost one myself?" Suldris asked. "My people belonged to me, body and soul. There were those who covered their eyes rather than look at me, so afraid were they. But they refused me nothing. Dared not look at me, lest they attract my notice. Life and death, Lisa, held in the palm of my hand, and they knew it. Do you want to know what they called me?"

She shook her head. He tightened his hand on her neck, a gentle warning, and she changed it to a nod.

"They called me Suldris the Bad. The Demon. Seventh son of a seventh son, blood brother to Satan himself." He pointed to the glow that marked the house. "And then the vampire came. Old, powerful even then. He spoke out against me. He dared *judge*. 'You have no right,' he told me. Me!"

Suddenly realizing that the woman had gone limp in his hands, he loosened his hold. She slid bonelessly to the road, and he knew she was dead. The satiation of drinking her life force was lost to him. Now she would provide only blood. Wine as compared with ambrosia.

"Ah, well, another tally to add to what I already owe you, Alexi," he said. "For distracting me."

He took what he wanted from the woman. Then he tossed her over the side of the bridge. A sinuous tail whipped the water as an alligator followed the line of bubbles left by the sinking corpse.

He turned away. It was time to go back to Savannah; he needed *real* sustenance.

8

Alex woke alone. The underground chamber, which had been such a haven yesterday, seemed a dank and sullen tomb today. Now he realized how completely Catherine was gone.

"Perhaps it's best, love," he said, rising to stand before her portrait. But it, too, had lost something. It was merely oil paint and canvas now, a picture of a pretty woman. "I held you long past your time, long past what was fair."

The day's oblivion had not eased his Blood-Hunger. It snapped at the dry husk that had once been his soul, tearing at him like a ravenous dog. Worse than it had been yesterday, worse than it had been since his mad, early days as a revenant.

He needed conversation, lights and music, and the comfort of the night breeze, however hot, however empty. As soon as he reached his room upstairs, he got one part of his wish: music. A primal rock beat poured over him in a tidal flood, vibrantly, aggressively alive.

"Ah, yes," he murmured. "Justin and his friends."

A music lover always, he made a point of keeping up. Blues, jazz, rock, country-western—he liked them all. Perhaps not quite as loud as Justin and his friends did, but then the young were always louder, faster, and more alive than their elders.

He stepped out into the hallway, where the air fairly vibrated with sound, and made his way downstairs, only to meet more noise. It came from the dining room, where the family was embroiled in a seething argument. Or rather, Barron and Sonya were arguing, while Lydia injected caustic comments from time to time. He didn't have to hear the words to know they were arguing about him.

At another time he might have avoided it. But tonight any diversion was welcome. He preferred facing acrimony to hunting the streets of Savannah. The voices grew louder, the words clearer as he neared the dining room.

"I don't give a damn about your ego," Sonya shouted. "You've taken millions out of that company. I didn't know anything about that, did I, Barron? And *I* haven't seen any of it, that's for sure. All these years, you've held the purse strings so tight I had to ask your permission to buy a toothbrush."

"Tight! What about the five-figure credit-card bills I paid every month? Ten women couldn't use all the clothes you have. And you, Lydia. Don't try that innocent look on *me*. I'm the guy who bailed you out of your last marriage. I'm the guy who keeps you in clothes and jewelry and those ridiculous stones—"

"They are not ridiculous!"

"Thirty-two hundred dollars for a fucking piece of quartz, for God's sake!"

"Well, brother dear," she said. "You're not going to be able to be so *terribly* kind to us now that you can no longer embezzle from the family's company. And now that we're living on Alex's generosity, you're going to have to learn to be a whore, just like me and Sonya."

Acrimonious indeed, Alex thought. He walked through an almost palpable wave of anger as he entered the room.

The table was strewn with the remains of a meal, and coffee sat cooling in cups that apparently hadn't been touched.

"Hello, everyone," he said.

Barron swung around. Anger had drained the color from his face, pulled his lips tight. Beside him, Sonya lounged in her chair with her usual indolent grace, but her eyes were ugly with hatred. And Lydia . . . Lydia blazed like the sun, the fiery bronze of her hair eclipsed by the woman herself.

"Hello, Alex," she said. Her smile seemed to settle deep in his belly. "We were talking about whores. Would you like to join in?"

"How can I refuse such a fascinating subject of conversation? Just let me get a glass of wine."

He settled in the chair at the foot of the table, leaving an expanse of polished tabletop between him and the others. Setting his glass down, he leaned back in his chair and clasped his hands over his stomach. "Now, where were we?"

"We were talking about whores," Lydia said.

"We were not," Barron growled. "And we *are* not. Alex, I have a bone to pick with you about Justin."

"Yes?"

"I caught him sneaking out his window. Apparently he's been doing that regularly, riding his bike to Delano to hang out with his friends. Tonight these same boys show up at the front door, insisting that *you've* invited them."

"That's true."

"You have no right to interfere with my discipline of my son."

Alex raised his eyebrows. "As I recall, Justin's punishment was to stay here at the house. Nothing was said about him not having visitors."

"Technicality," Barron said.

"True." With a smile, Alex added, "But then the world is run on technicalities."

"We wanted to separate him from those friends," Sonya said. "They're not, ah . . ."

"Socially correct?" Alex supplied.

Lydia laughed, a lovely, malicious sound. "They're poor, Alex. Poor as dirt. Sonya and Barron are afraid it might rub off."

"I'm too rich to get dirty," Alex said. "And I don't mind the boys building their radio in a room I'll never use. God knows there are worse things for them to do."

"They're not our kind," Barron said.

"No," Alex agreed. "They'll probably do something useful for a living."

"Oooo, now you're getting nasty," Lydia said.

Alex leaned forward and picked up his wine. "But far be it from me to interfere with a father's discipline. Barron, if you want those boys out, feel free to go upstairs and ask them to leave."

"Then I can be the heavy again, right? Then you can slip right in and endear yourself to my son. But then, maybe not; he doesn't have any real cash value, does he?"

Alex met his gaze levelly. "He's a fine young man. You should appreciate him more."

"I don't need your advice," Barron snarled. "Oh, hell! Let them play their little games. They'll get tired of it and move on to other things."

Conciliatory words. But his eyes weren't conciliatory at all. "Watch your back," Lydia had said. Now, gazing deep into Barron's hate-filled eyes, Alex realized just how right she'd been.

"Mr. Danilov?" the maid called from the doorway.

"What is it, Eve?" Barron asked.

She flushed. "I . . . meant the *other* Mr. Danilov."

"We'd better do something about that," Alex said. "Since you're used to calling my cousin Mr. Danilov, I suppose you'll just have to call me Alex."

"Yes, sir. A package came for you today. From Mr. McGinnis."

"That must be my fax machine." Alex set his glass aside and pushed away from the table. "Excuse me, Barron, ladies. As much as I've been enjoying this conversation, I must give myself up to learning this particular facet of modern life."

"How nice to be able to sit at home and run everyone's lives," Barron said.

Alex smiled. "Yes, it is."

"Almost done," Justin said.

Alex nodded, admiring the boy's expertise with machines. In just a few minutes, he'd gotten the fax installed. The machine sat on the nightstand, its sleek modernity a sharp contrast to the nineteenth-century elegance of his bedroom.

"Look, Alex," the boy said. "You don't have to dial the number every time, okay? You can program a whole bunch of numbers into the memory, so all you have to do is push one button. The machine will dial it for you."

"Astonishing."

Justin glanced over his shoulder. "You know about this stuff already."

"I *did* read the instructions before begging humbly for your help," Alex said. "I may be almost over the hill, but I'm not exactly from the Middle Ages, you know."

"Yeah, yeah. Want me to program the numbers in for you?"

Alex found McGinnis' card and held it up. "Let's see . . . McGinnis—5-5-5-4-8-3-1."

"Okay, got it. What's next?"

"That's the only one."

"The only one?"

Alex shrugged. "I don't know anyone else."

He expected the boy to laugh. But there was no amusement on Justin's face, only understanding. Evidently he was familiar with loneliness.

"Aunt Margaret knew *everybody*," Justin said. "Too bad she . . ." He gulped the last of the sentence, his face flushing scarlet.

"Too bad she died before she could introduce me around?" Alex asked.

Justin nodded. "She was on the phone all day long, talking to everybody. 'As long as Γ keep the network going,' she used to say, 'I'll never get senile.' And you know what? She hated most of my parents' friends. Called them a bunch of spoiled slugs that had never done a full day's work."

Alex laughed. "That's rich! Margaret calling someone else spoiled."

A sudden, powerful memory gripped him, pulling him back to a day, many years ago, when six-year-old Margaret cajoled her usually dignified father into giving her a horsey-back ride. Alex caught them at it. In the midst of a shrieking gambol, Margaret looked up at him, her midnight-blue eyes dancing with delight—and the triumphant awareness of her own power. And from then on, her father had been helpless against her. Alex, who had been helpless from the moment he first held her in his arms, was glad to know there was someone else riding in his boat.

It wasn't until he saw the answering grin on Justin's face that he realized that he was smiling. "She was something else, wasn't she?"

"She was cool," Justin said. "A cool old lady."

They grinned at each other a moment more, foolishly. Then Justin sighed and set the now empty box aside.

"I guess I'd better get going," he said. "It's after midnight. Good night, Alex."

"Good night. Thanks for the help."

"No problem."

Alex carried an armchair over to the nightstand and settled into it. Foolish as it was to be faxing someone at this hour, he couldn't wait to try out this new toy. When he pressed the button that dialed McGinnis's number, the screen flashed *Insert Document* at him. He took a piece of paper and wrote *Dear Charles. Please arrange for a radio antenna to be installed at the west wing of the house. Thanks, Alex.* Then he fed it to the machine. It was devoured, processed, spat slowly out the nether end. The screen flashed *Message Received.*

"Fascinating," Alex murmured.

He lifted his head as the Blood-Hunger surged sickeningly high. Heat, cold, slices of pain as though shards of broken glass were being thrust through his guts, scrabbling mouse feet clawing through his brain. Then his being tightened, focused.

Lydia stood in the hall.

He could almost taste her. All he had to do was open the door and reach out . . . *I will not!*

"Alex," she called.

Her voice slid over him like a summer breeze, hot, sultry, inviting. He could hear her blood moving through her veins, hear her heart pumping. He could feel her desire, taste the wine-rich essence of her life. If he took it, he would feel alive again. It had been so long, so very long. His vision clouded as the Blood-Hunger thrust white-hot needles into his spine. *Take her.*

"No," he rasped. "No."

"Alex, open the door."

"Go away, Lydia."

Her laugh was low and throaty, and fanned the fires that threatened to consume him. "You don't want me to leave. I can feel you, Alex."

He gripped the arms of the chair, resisting. Wood splintered in his hands. "You don't know what you're doing."

"Yes," she said. "I do. Open the door."

His body obeyed her, even if his mind did not. She stood in the dark hallway, her white nightgown almost seeming to glow with a light of its own. He registered curves, smooth, creamy skin revealed by tantalizing wedges of lace. Her feet were bare. His hand shook as he reached up to stroke her bright hair. Then he gently clasped her neck, feeling the beat of her pulse against his palm. He craved her.

"If you were wise," he said, "you would run away now."

She smiled. "But I've never been wise."

That smile, so sensual and knowing, was the finish for his restraint. He drew her into the room and closed the door. When he kissed her, he sank into a mist of heat and Obsession. Desire, sharp and visceral, ran like a flame through his mind. For now, it would be enough.

He lifted his head to look at her. Slowly, she opened her eyes. Shock rippled through him when he saw a hunger in them almost equal to his.

"I knew it would be this way," she whispered. "From the moment I first saw you, I knew."

She slid the straps of her nightgown over her shoulders and down her arms. The garment slithered to the floor, pooling at her feet like liquid moonlight. She rose out of it like a flame, Aphrodite born of the sun instead of the sea.

Like a man in a dream, Alex closed the distance between them. He ran his hands lightly down her neck to her shoulders and down to her breasts, cupping the ripe, firm flesh, circling her nipples with his thumbs.

Her gasp of pleasure sank deep in him. Drawing her closer still, he spread his hands out over her curving hips. She lifted one knee against his thigh, inviting him further. He felt as though he were falling into a bottomless well. And all around him was Lydia, her need and his drawing him deeper and yet deeper.

Her head fell back, exposing the long, lovely line of her throat. He saw the pulse beating just beneath her skin, felt her life pumping through her veins. He groaned, in pleasure and in torment.

Sweeping her into his arms, he carried her to his bed and laid her down. She lay upon the coverlet, beautiful and sumptuous, the personification of every man's most sensual dream. Her hair spread out over his pillow like a river of molten copper. Fascinated, he combed his fingers through it. Everything about her was flame bright, flame hot. An enticing sort of flame, one that beckoned a man to come and be burned.

"I want you," she said.

He took her hand, which was roaming the front of his body, and brought it to his lips. "Slowly, Lydia. It's always better for the wait."

"I've been waiting too long already."

"Shhh." He kissed her wrist, her palm, drew her fingertips one by one into his mouth and sucked gently.

She gasped. Her eyes narrowed, the irises darkening to bottle green. "Kiss me," she said.

He fitted his mouth to hers. She tasted of honey and woman and desire, and he sank deeper and deeper into the burgeoning sensations. The Blood-Hunger was no longer painful; it fanned the pleasure higher, sharpening every kiss, every caress, every gasp and sigh and murmur.

Alex gave himself up to the delight of the woman, sight and feel and taste of her. There were times when he felt as though he were drowning. Like a whirlwind, she drew him in, spun him in a dizzy loop of sensuality. Her heartbeat thundered in his ears, his chest, setting up an answering resonance in his body.

Then she arched beneath him. Her hands sank into his hair as she cried out. Lost in blood lust and rocketing pleasure, Alex took her up again and again. And again. She screamed that time, and he felt her nails raking across his shoulders. Then she went limp in his arms.

Reason swept in, cutting through the fever in his brain. And with it, terror. Terror that he had gone too far. Frantically, he felt for a pulse.

"Thank God," he whispered, finding it. "Thank God!"

Her eyes were closed, her chest rising and falling in slow, shallow breaths. Alex bowed his head in shame. He'd almost taken her over the threshold. What had happened to him? Had the strength to govern himself vanished with Catherine?

"God help me if it did," he said.

He laid his hand over the small wound above her heart, as though to hide the evidence of his lack of control. "I'm sorry, Lydia. It won't happen again."

I should leave. The Arbor is no haven for me with Catherine gone.

And yet he couldn't just run off to Europe for forty years again. If he did, Barron would destroy the Danilovs. Margaret had seen the danger, and had trusted her beloved uncle Alex to take care of it. Also, he'd backed Justin's defiance of his father; how could he walk away now, leaving the boy to carry a load that was too heavy for him?

He looked down at the woman beside him. Beautiful, spoiled, her sensuality burning within her like a white-hot coal. The sight of her brought his Blood-Hunger surging high, a tide of pain and need and clawing appetite. Appetite.

I am not a dog to drool over a juicy bone, and she is not a herd beast raised to the slaughter. Get thee behind me, Satan!

Still, the hunger burned. He ignored it as he gently dressed the sleeping woman, then picked her up and carried her through the silent house to her room.

Crystal song filled the chamber, high, pure voices only a special few could hear. So many voices, so many stones. Knowing Lydia, with her immaturity and self-indulgence, it was astonishing that she could order her gift so well.

Then he caught a dissonance in the lovely chorus. Slight but, once noted, impossible to ignore. It grated along his nerves like the beginnings of Blood-Hunger. Perhaps Lydia didn't have things quite as ordered as it seemed.

She stirred as he laid her down on the bed. "Alex?" she murmured.

"Shhh. Go back to sleep."

"Tired . . . so tired."

"Yes, I know," he whispered. "You'll feel better in the morning."

She turned over on her side. He pulled the covers up around her, thinking that she looked very young and innocent asleep. So lovely, so dangerous. He wished he had the power to erase what had happened from his own mind as well as hers.

His instincts screamed for him to leave. Safety lay in running, burying himself in another life, another identity.

In a way, it might be a relief to lay Alex Danilov to rest.

But he couldn't. Wouldn't; he and Catherine had begun this dynasty, and by God, he was going to see that it endured.

It was all he had.

9

"Hello, Alex," Lydia said.

Startled, Alex whirled to see Lydia standing in the doorway of the gazebo. He hadn't sensed her coming. Strange. She wore a green sundress that echoed the color of her eyes and made her skin look as though it was lit from within. A reddish stone, perhaps a garnet or ruby, hung upon a simple chain around her neck. It nestled in the valley between her breasts. Beneath it, he could see the tiny wound he'd left upon her skin.

"Aren't you going to say hello?" she asked.

"Hello, Lydia."

"Six days, Alex. Six days you've managed to avoid me. Quite a feat when we're living in the same house."

"It's a big house."

"True. But I tried hard. I lay in wait for you in the dining room, the family room, the hallway outside your room. Somehow I never seemed to be able to catch up with you. I'm beginning to think you can walk through walls."

"I assure you, walking through walls is not one of my talents."

"Avoiding me is, however."

She came into the gazebo, passing over the lacy shadows cast upon the floor by the mimosa tree. Her hair caught the starlight and cast it back again in a thousand fiery glints. Alex could feel her frustration, her anger, and the life force fountaining high within her. Blood-Hunger flared. It grew stronger with every step she took toward him, and he clenched his hands as he struggled for control.

"I want to make love to you again," she said.

He stared at her in astonishment. She wasn't supposed to remember. Rarely, oh, so rarely, did he encounter a woman whose memory he couldn't tamper with. "It should never have happened," he said.

She drew in her breath sharply. "You regret *that*? Why? Is there something wrong with me?"

"No. *I'm* the problem. You're very beautiful, Lydia, very desirable, and you caught me at a time when I was lonely and vulnerable."

"And now you're not?"

He sighed. "I never intended to become involved with someone living in my house, particularly the sister of the man who has sworn to break me. It's a dangerous relationship. Believe me, if I let it begin, it will end badly."

"But it's already begun. What do you think happened six nights ago?"

"A mistake. One for which I must beg your forgiveness."

"It was beautiful, Alex," she whispered, moving closer. "Was it good for you, too?"

His hands itched with the desire to touch her; his being thirsted for her, to consume her even as he himself was consumed. Her eyes were twin, smoky-green flames, drawing him in, demanding things he was afraid to give.

He maintained his outward composure with difficulty while inside he shook and rattled like the Tin Man. She stopped in front of him, her breasts an inch from his shirtfront. Heat radiated from her.

She put her hands flat on his chest, then ran them upward to clasp them behind his neck.

"I love you," she whispered.

Alex closed his eyes for a moment, rocked by her declaration. She was almost right for him. If he'd been younger, less aware of the pitfalls of loving such a woman, he might have fallen for her. But Catherine had taught him the difference between love and lovemaking. *He* knew it, whether Lydia did or not.

With a sigh, he reached up to caress her cheek with his fingertips. "I wish I could love you, Lydia."

"Then just make love to me," she said. "You can learn the rest as we go."

He wanted to, so badly that it frightened him. "I'm sorry, but no."

"I don't believe you mean that."

She wound her hands in his hair, rising up on her tiptoes to kiss him. He found himself awash in sensation, helpless to do anything but pull her closer and return the kiss. Her skin was hot beneath his hands, her life force surging high. Beckoning him to take it.

Monster! The image hung in his mind, etched in fire by what was left of his conscience. It pulled him out of the drugged fog of his Blood-Hunger and gave him the strength to gently disengage the clinging woman.

"I'm sorry," he rasped. "I can't."

"You mean you won't."

"That's right. I won't."

She merely smiled, the secret, knowing smile of a woman who hasn't given up the battle. "All right, Alex. We'll talk about it later. When you're in a better mood. Later tonight."

God help her. God help me. For centuries he'd fought the lure of the Blood-Hunger. He'd only taken the bare minimum to keep himself "alive," always treading the edge of pain, sometimes, it seemed, of sanity. But he'd won. No lives had been lost to his hunger, no souls to his appetite.

But if he touched this woman again, that might end.

He left her there in the gazebo, turning once in the doorway to look back at her. She'd moved into the shadow, and all he could see was her shape and a glint of red from the stone she wore.

Blood-Hunger beat through him, an obscene imitation of life. It hammered at the back of his brain. *Go back! Take her, she'll give it willingly, and never know the price.*

But he would.

He avoided the house, turning instead toward the garage that had been built on the site of the old carriage house. Some rakehell scion of the Danilovs—Alex couldn't remember the boy's name, only his face—had accidentally burned the old building down in the early 1900s. Margaret's father, the first Danilov to own an automobile, built the garage for his brand-new Model T.

The garage held four cars: Barron's silver Jaguar, Sonya's Celica, Lydia's red Corvette, and Margaret's sedate black Lincoln. "Jack always told me to buy American," she would say. "It keeps the country strong."

Alex took Margaret's key ring out of his pocket and searched through it until he found an ignition key. "Ah, Margaret," he murmured. "You knew that I avoid flashy cars."

The Lincoln's interior smelled of leather and Margaret's perfume. Noticing a crumpled piece of white fabric on the floor in front of the passenger seat, he leaned over and retrieved it.

He smoothed it on his knee, and the scent of perfume grew stronger. It was an old-fashioned ladies' handkerchief, edged in lace and monogrammed in one corner with an *M*.

"Why, thank you," he murmured, tucking it away in his breast pocket.

A few moments later he pulled out of the garage and headed down the drive. *Running away?* the cynical revenant voice asked.

Yes, indeed.

Alex walked along Savannah's riverfront. For three nights now, he'd spent his waking hours in the city. Trying to lose himself, trying to escape the Blood-Hunger that tore at his guts whenever Lydia was near.

"Why her, of all the women in the world? She stirs neither my heart nor my mind," he muttered, staring up at the windows above him as though they might be able to answer.

They couldn't, of course. They merely stared down at him with blind glass eyes, as they had for many, many years. No thoughts, no feelings, just wood and brick and mortar—he envied them.

The old Cotton Exchange stretched above him, an impressive five stories high on the river side of Yamacraw Bluff, two stories on the street above. The sight of it triggered a tidal wave of memory. In the days when King Cotton ruled his world, fortunes were won or lost in that building, a man's future hanging on the caprices of the weather and the prevailing price of his crop. And all run on the blood and sweat of slaves. He'd hated slavery; it had haunted man throughout his history, and was ever an abomination. How had he, a plantation owner, gotten away with not owning slaves?

His mouth quirked upward in an involuntary smile. Money. He'd been rich enough to get away with it. Very rich men are considered eccentric, never subversive.

He'd had Catherine then, for nearly forty years. Then came the time when a stoop and whitened hair were no longer enough to maintain the fiction of age. In 1841, his "character" was sixty-three years old. Catherine was fifty-seven. Her hair was almost completely silver, but she was still slim, still graceful. Although she was quick to shed tears over a beautiful sunset or a poignant sonnet, she didn't cry when she told him it was time for him to leave.

They had both known this time would come. But Alex wasn't ready. It was Catherine who had the strength to insist, to make him see that he was endangering not only himself, but his children and grandchildren as well. After he left, she continued to run the estate and family as well as she ever had. She pulled the Danilovs through the War Between the States, and later, Reconstruction. On the eve of her eighty-eighth birthday, she went to sleep and never woke up again.

He'd never visited her tomb. When he had next returned to the Arbor, Catherine's ghost had come to him with her gentle touch and her perfume, and that had been enough.

Raucous laughter brought him abruptly to the present. He looked up as two women strolled toward him, their profession advertised by their clothes and makeup. One was blond, one a redhead of a shade too close to Lydia's for comfort.

"Hello, gorgeous," the blonde said.

"Out for a stroll, ladies?" he asked.

"Yeah." She took his right arm, the redhead his left.

Alex noted that the redhead had managed to shift her knit top down so that her right nipple was exposed. She was young and lush, and his Blood-Hunger soared. Then he sensed the taint of AIDS within her. That, even his Blood-Hunger wouldn't touch.

"You look lonely," she said.

"I came here to be lonely," he said, disengaging himself from both women.

He left the waterfront, his feet automatically taking him down Bay Street, then on to Bull Street and toward Johnson Square. He and Catherine had walked this way many times, arm in arm in the moonlight.

So much was still the same in Savannah. Take away the cars, the electric lights, and the tourists, one might almost be able to recreate the past. He stepped off the curb, intending to cross the street, and was honked back up by an impatient motorist.

"Watch where you're going, will ya?" the driver shouted.

Sometimes, he thought, the present was just too hard to ignore. Like Lydia. Why did she affect his Blood-Hunger so powerfully? God knows it wasn't sex. After a thousand years, all women feel the same. Except the one he'd loved.

The measured clip-clop of hoofbeats caught his attention. A moment later a horse-drawn carriage turned the corner and moved toward him. Alex felt his mouth drop open in astonishment. Not because of the vehicle; carriages were common here in the historic district. But the two female passengers were wearing hoop skirts and crinolines, the two men, Confederate uniforms. For a moment Alex thought they were ghosts. The Confederate uniforms, however, disproved that theory; the Civil War was not part of his personal history.

"So, perhaps I've merely gone insane at last," he murmured. "It was bound to happen sooner or later."

A fellow pedestrian, apparently overhearing that remark, edged away.

" 'The lunatic, the lover, and the poet are of imagination all compact,' " Alex quoted. "Shakespeare, you know."

Apparently the man didn't, for he turned hastily and walked away. Alex smiled.

The traffic light turned red, stopping the carriage almost directly in front of him. One of the men lit a pipe, and the sweetly pungent aroma of tobacco drifted on the breeze. Alex's nostrils flared as he savored it. His senses narrowed, discarding the automobiles, lights, signs of shops and restaurants, focusing instead on the two parasols, one pink and one green, that bobbed above the carriage. Slowly, with great concentration, he wrapped the past around him like a cloak.

The passengers chattered away, oblivious to the profound effect they had on him. When the light turned, the carriage moved on, spilling a drift of laughter in its wake.

Unable to do otherwise, Alex followed it.

It led him finally to Jones Street, which was paved in hard red brick. Alex's feet automatically adapted to the change in texture; it was welcome and familiar, like shaking an old friend's hand.

He stopped a few feet behind the vehicle as it discharged its passengers at the steps of a modest brick Federal-style house. Alex didn't remember the structure. A "new" home, built perhaps in the 1850s. It was square and stolid, but the lights blazing in every window gave it an air of gaiety. The front door opened, admitting the newcomers and letting music flood out into the street.

A woman stood framed in the doorway, the breeze stirring the fine drapery of her Empire gown. Her hair was brown/blond tawny, limned with light from the room behind her. It was caught in a simple knot at the top of her head, a few fine tendrils escaping to frame her face. She was somewhere around thirty, slim and tall, an inch or two shorter than he—perhaps five-nine.

The carriage pulled away, leaving Alex standing exposed on the sidewalk. The woman gave a start of surprise.

"Oh, hello. I didn't see you there at first." Her voice was low and sweet.

"Hello," he replied.

"You were supposed to wear period costume, you know."

She thinks I'm a guest! Well, why not? "I . . . missed that particular detail."

"Or Mother forgot to put it on your invitation," she said, a hint of a laugh in her tone. "It doesn't matter. Please, come in before the mosquitoes eat you alive."

Moving like a man in a dream, he walked up the steps toward her. She wasn't beautiful. Some, seeing the overlong chin and strong features, wouldn't even call her pretty. But Alex saw only her eyes. They were pure, dark amber, with depths he'd never seen in a woman's eyes before. There was pain in those depths; she was a woman who had lived, loved, and lost, experienced disappointment and betrayal.

And yet there was an innocence of spirit about her that transcended all life's blows. She had endured, and somehow had found serenity. It flowed through him like a cool sea breeze, washing away the clinging taint of Blood-Hunger. Surcease. He stared at her, stunned. Even in an existence as long as his, he hadn't expected to find this again.

"I . . ." A flush reddened her pale cheeks. "I'm sorry; I was staring."

"I don't mind," he said.

"Please come in."

"Thank you." An empty politeness; had she tried to bar him from the house, Alex would have torn the door off its hinges. And why? Only to spend a few minutes with her.

He extended his arm to escort her. Instead of tucking her hand in the crook of his arm as a modern woman would do, she placed her hand atop his forearm. An old-fashioned gesture.

"Are you an old friend or a new?" she asked.

"Don't you know?"

"I've only been here a few months. I came to stay with my parents for a while after . . ." Her voice checked oddly. "Well, since you didn't know I moved here from Virginia, that makes you a new friend. Are you a member of the faculty?"

He smiled. "No. I'm a businessman by trade, a haunter of libraries by preference."

"Business?"

"Container shipping, warehousing, this and that."

She cocked her head to one side. "Libraries?"

"Genealogy," he said. "I'm researching the Danilov family tree."

"You, then, are a Danilov?" She didn't seem to know the name.

He smiled. "Alex to you."

"Liz Garry." Apparently just realizing that her hand was still on his arm, she dropped it to her side. "Mom and Dad are holding court in the parlor. Come on; I know they'll want to see you."

Alex had absolutely no idea what he was going to say when he met his host and hostess. An insane notion; after centuries of dissembling, he ought to be able to think of some clever lie. But his mind was full of this unusual woman beside him, and the lie escaped him.

As she led him through the entry hall and toward the parlor, he saw that the house, although comfortably furnished, was hardly luxurious. It was the home of a man who worked for a living, and judging from the number and quality of the books, the home of a scholar.

The parlor was a tiny, stuffy room, furnished with a monstrosity of a horsehair sofa and a pair of Queen Anne wing chairs. Costumed gentlemen and ladies filled the room almost to overflowing. The costumes ranged the course of human history, from togaed Romans to twenties flapper. Most guests, however, seemed to have chosen the Civil War era. Conversation swirled amid the rustle of crinolines and the clatter of hoop skirts fighting for space.

The sofa was occupied by an older couple in medieval dress. Although the man wore his velvet and lace with perfect aplomb, his thin, ascetic features would have been better graced by a monk's robe. The woman had Liz's face—thirty years from now. She had the same air of serenity, but it had deepened and matured.

"We're never going to get through that crush," Liz said. "Just smile and wave, and I'll take you to the kitchen to get something to drink."

Salvation! Alex smiled and waved, then let Liz lead him toward the back of the house. The kitchen was as cluttered as the parlor, but infinitely welcoming with its warm-oak cabinets and polished copper pots. No servants' kitchen, this, but the workplace of a woman who liked to cook.

Liz deposited him at the table and went to open the refrigerator. Another wisp of hair had escaped her bun. It curled against the back of her neck, and he had to resist the urge to tuck it back into place. It was too soon for that. With merely human vision, she could only see the surface of him. To her, he was a stranger.

"What would you like?" she asked, peering into the depths of the refrigerator. "We have Coke, Sprite, lemonade, some kind of white wine—"

"Lemonade, please," Alex said, recoiling from the prospect of "some kind of white wine."

She poured two glasses, one for him and one for her, and Alex was pleased to find it was real lemonade. "Do you want to try the parlor again?"

"Do you think there'll be more room now?"

"I doubt it."

"Why don't we just stay here, then?" he asked.

"Mom and Dad—"

"I'd rather talk to you."

A blunt admission. He saw her take it in, consider it, accept it. A straightforward woman, was Elizabeth Garry.

She sat in the chair opposite him, placing her hands, palm down, on either side of her glass. "All right, talk," she said.

"When you were telling me earlier about moving here from Virginia, you looked sad. Why?"

Her breath went out in a rush. "I thought we were going to have light party conversation."

"If you'd wanted that, you would have gone back to the parlor," he said.

"You don't pull any punches, do you?" she asked. "All right, I'll tell you my sordid little story. It's not a blight on my life, just a little . . . bruising. I came to live here after my divorce. To lick my wounds, so to speak."

"Did you?"

"Lick my wounds?" She shrugged. "Yes. My pride took a bit longer to heal; he left me for another woman. A friend of mine, actually. She was prettier, blonder, and a lot more, ah . . ." She cupped her hands, making a sweeping curve several inches out from her chest.

"I get the picture," Alex murmured.

"Apparently they'd had an affair going for some time. It just took me a while to figure it out."

Alex shook his head, as always surprised by the blindness of men. To be married to such a woman, and not be able to *see* what she was . . . Truly, it was astonishing. "He was a fool."

"No," she said. "*I* was the fool. Both for not seeing it earlier and for not doing something about it sooner." She took a sip of lemonade. "I've known you ten minutes, and already you've pried my darkest secret from me. Will you reciprocate?"

"You wouldn't believe my darkest secret."

"Try me."

"Will you settle for next darkest?"

"For now. I warn you, though, I'm not one to settle for less than a hundred percent."

"Neither am I." Alex smiled. "And now for my secret, and I hope it doesn't burn me. You see, I don't know your parents, and I never had an invitation to your party."

She drew in her breath sharply. "Then why—"

"Because you asked me to come in. I wanted to get to know you, and I took the opportunity to do so. I've learned not to let opportunity pass me by."

Her expression flickered from annoyance to amusement to exasperation, finally settling on amusement. "A bit of a pirate, aren't you?" she asked.

"Among other things. Are you going to throw me out?"

"Should I? Are you dangerous?"

"Very," he said, with utmost seriousness.

She smiled, propping her elbow on the table and her chin in her hand. "Tell me you're not a salesman. My ex-husband was a salesman."

"I'm not a salesman."

"What are you, then, Alex Danilov?"

"A man"—*Not quite, but tonight I feel like one for the first time in so long*—"who appreciates less-than-blond hair and less-than-overblown curves."

"Is that a compliment?"

"Assuredly."

She laughed. "My father will love you; besides him, you're the only person I've ever met who has the nerve to say *assuredly* in conversation and the air to carry it off."

"Later you can introduce us," he said. "It will be a pleasure to meet a fellow atavist."

"You're not from here, are you?" she asked, startling him with the sudden shift in direction.

"How can you tell?"

"When you relax, a definite European inflexion comes into your sentences. Not that your English isn't perfect; it's just that you fall out of idiom when you're not watching for it. Don't look so startled, Alex. I'm a writer by trade. Textbooks."

Her perception was both astonishing and welcome. Astonishing because he *should* have expected it of her, and welcome because it had been far too long since someone had seen something of him he hadn't intended to show.

"You're right," he said. "I'm French. Or rather, a Frenchman of Russian extraction. I came to this country only a few weeks ago to visit some distant relatives."

"So you'll be leaving soon."

"Not necessarily." He caught her gaze, held it.

A man and a woman came into the kitchen, shattering the moment. "What are you two doing in here?" the man asked. "Are you hoarding the canapes?"

Alex rose to his feet as Liz made the introductions. Dr. and Mrs. Greg Barringer were an ill-matched couple; he was large and square, with a florid face and intolerant eyes. She was thin and pallid, her handshake as limp as wet tissue.

"Danilov, as in Danilov Industries?" Barringer asked.

"Yes," Alex said.

"Are you the French cousin who ended up with the whole caboodle?"

"Greg!" Liz cried.

Alex went very still. "I beg your pardon?"

"In many ways, Savannah's a small town, Mr. Danilov," Greg said. "People talk. And the Danilovs are rather high profile."

"Ah, I knew there must be a reason why you felt you could pry into my private business." Alex's tone was curt and cold. In another century, it was one he would have used on a servant who had overstepped the bounds.

An awkward silence reigned. Smiling, Alex let it continue. Finally Barringer left, taking his limp wife with him.

"I'm sorry," Liz said. "Greg likes to be outrageous. You'd be surprised at how many people find it entertaining."

"Yes, I would."

"Oh, sit down, Alex. You've got the look of a Victorian matron who's just been told her petticoat is showing."

Again, she astonished him. He sat. "You really know how to puncture a man's self-image, Miss Garry."

"And you didn't tell me you were a rich society snob."

"Ouch. Did I sound like one?"

"Terribly."

Her eyes were warm, dancing with humor. He slid right into those amber depths, effortlessly, painlessly. Slid in, and was accepted. But he knew she didn't yet realize what was happening between them. No, what already *had* happened. If she did, she'd be frightened.

So was he. He was frightened of walking away from her, yet even more frightened of what would happen if he did not. He knew the price Catherine had paid for loving him. For all her wit, her sharp-edged intelligence, Liz was both gentler and more vulnerable than Catherine.

He'd ruined Catherine's life; he had no right to destroy another. His love demanded too high a price. Catherine's voice echoed through his memory, saying the last words he'd heard from her in this world. "I never regretted it for a moment, Alex. No woman has ever been loved quite like this. I've had nearly forty years of heaven, and I thank God for it."

He closed his eyes. Why that memory? Why now, when he needed strength to resist?

"Alex?" Liz asked. "Are you all right?"

When he looked at her, he saw concern in her eyes, and an unconscious invitation he had no right to take. "I should go," he said, rising to his feet.

"Go?" Her hurt and bewilderment were obvious. "Is something wrong?"

Dear God in heaven, give me strength! "I have another engagement," he said. The lie felt like bile in his mouth.

"At midnight?" she asked. Then her eyes narrowed. Rising to meet him, she put both hands flat on his chest. "What are you afraid of?"

He felt exposed, more vulnerable than he'd ever felt before. She'd stripped away the facade and seen the true, raw emotion in him. He grasped her wrists. It took all his will to force his arms to move her away instead of pulling her closer. He should lie to her again; for her sake, for his. But he couldn't. "I've got to go," he said. "You don't understand. But if you did, you'd *beg* me to go."

Still, he couldn't keep himself from raising her hand to his lips. Her fingers were cool, and cupped around his mouth in a way that invited much more. His own hands shook as he put her from him.

"Good-bye, Elizabeth Garry," he said.

"*Au revoir*," she whispered.

Until we meet again. She had chosen that farewell carefully. Alex left by the kitchen door, striding across the garden and out the gate as though the Furies themselves were chasing him.

10

Lydia twisted and turned, tangling the bedding around her legs. Alex walked through her dreams, no longer reluctant, no longer holding back. He was hers. Finally, irrevocably. Sweet, searing pleasure, the feel of his hands, his mouth . . .

"*Lydia.*"

She tried to push the voice away. Alex was what she wanted now. Only Alex.

"*Lydia.*"

Alex's face exploded into tiny, bright shards. They hung before her for a moment, then winked out of existence. She opened her eyes to darkness.

Not quite darkness; a faint glow, almost like moonlight, came from the mirrored closet doors. She swung her legs over the edge of the bed and got up. Her body felt heavy, drugged with the arousal of the dream. The air was cold on her too sensitive skin, and she pulled her robe on before going to the closet.

The glow intensified as she got nearer. The reflection of the room behind her faded, and it looked as though she were walking through a sea of bright fog. Wonderingly, she put her hand out to touch the mirror.

And reached *through* the glass.

With a cry, she snatched her hand back, turned it over and over, inspecting her skin for wounds. Then, hesitantly, she reached out again. Her hand went through again.

She stared at the spot where her wrist touched the glass. There was no pain, no sensation of touch, only a coldness against her skin. She pushed farther, and her arm was engulfed to the elbow.

"Come, Lydia. Don't be afraid."

She should be afraid. But she felt numb, as though the coldness in her arm had crept throughout her body. Stepping toward the mirror was weird, coming face-to-face with herself, passing into and through herself. The coldness was all around her now. The bright mist enveloped her feet, crept upward along her knees, pulling her. She let it, for she didn't know the way.

Voices swirled around her. Sly voices, sometimes whispering half-heard secrets in her ear, sometimes singing songs that were almost known. They were frightening and alluring at once, offering things she wanted deep in her soul, things she knew no one should have.

"Lydia."

The summons was powerful. It banished the voices and pulled her unresistingly along. The mist swirled and thinned, and she felt a breath of fresh air against her face.

A moment later, she stepped out into a room. A forest of candles lined the opposite wall, their flames guttering wildly as though a wind had swept through the chamber. With a shock, she realized she was in the old True Faith Church outside Delano. It had been abandoned for nearly forty years; the walls were dank with moisture and mildew, the few remaining pews ravaged by rot. Empty bolts marked the place where the cross had once hung.

A shadow came between her and the candles, and for a

moment the flames burned red. Then the shadow coalesced into a man. She shook her head, denying that image. It had always been a man; in her confusion, she had let her imagination run away with her perceptions.

"We meet at last, Lydia," he said, coming forward.

She drew back. He stopped, his mouth curving into a smile. "You're not afraid of me, are you?" he asked.

"A . . . a little."

"You shouldn't be. We know each other very well now; we've shared dreams, after all. Don't you remember?"

He reached out to her. Without thinking, she placed her hand in his and let him draw her forward.

"See?" he asked. "There's nothing to be afraid of. I'm your friend, Lydia."

"You . . ." She shook her head, trying to grasp what was happening to her. "You're the crystal?"

"The crystal is the conduit between us; because of your ability to touch the power of the stone, I was able to use it to speak to you. Come, sit down with me for a moment."

Without willing her body to move, Lydia obeyed. The pew creaked beneath her, and the sound skittered off into the far reaches of the building.

The man sat beside her. He was handsome as a sword is handsome, sharp-edged and harsh, the angularity of his features intensified by straight, reddish-blond hair that hung to his shoulders. His eyes were midnight dark. The candle flames were reflected in those depths, spinning like tiny galaxies in the velvet blackness of space.

"Who are you?" she whispered.

"I call myself John Smith," he said.

"But that isn't your name."

He spread his hands. "John Smith suffices for this time and place."

She knew she ought to be frightened. But the cold from the mirror had settled somewhere in the center of her chest, taking away her capacity to feel. Even when he cupped her chin in his hand and tilted her face upward, she felt no alarm.

"Do you know how rare a talent you are, Lydia? In this age of computers and television, a gift such as yours is astonishing and very welcome. Many, many years I've searched for someone like you. Someone with whom I can share *my* talents."

"You . . . you're like me?"

"Of course. How else could we speak through the crystal?"

"How did you bring me here?"

He smiled, reaching out to touch the ghost crystal. Heat blossomed in it, spread out to warm her skin. "I just opened a different sort of door than what you're accustomed to. An easy spell, once learned."

"Spell?" she echoed.

"Magic, Lydia. And not the sort done on the stage for entertainment. What did you think was happening here?"

"I . . . I . . ." Astonishment warred with the gut-wrenching realization that she'd known this all along.

He smiled. "Once, magic was a very real part of humankind's existence. It was forgotten, however, in the foolish pursuit of more mundane things. Technology is for the masses; it gives them a sense of control over their world. But magic . . . Ah, that is reserved for the few. It cannot be turned on and off with a switch or a button. But mankind always takes the easy path, and so left magic behind."

Lydia studied him, her gaze finally focusing on his night-dark eyes. "You rediscovered it?"

"No," he said. "I never forgot."

"Who are you?" she whispered.

"If I told you, you would simply not believe. But let me show you." He took her hand in his. Holding it so that her palm lay against his, he passed his other hand across her fingers.

Her skin smoothed, the network of tiny lines at knuckles and wrist disappearing. Lydia brought her hands up and examined them, laughter bubbling up in her chest.

"They're younger," she said. "My face, too?"

"Yes. Just now, you look like a girl of twenty. Do you feel twenty, Lydia?"

She did, she actually did! Her body felt slimmer, more limber, her life flowing faster, harder, higher. She jumped to her feet and twirled, her robe swirling high around her legs.

"Charming," he murmured.

Lydia held her hands out again. But they'd changed. Gone back. No, they'd gone further. Horror rose in her as she realized the wrinkles were just a little deeper now.

"Oh, God!" she gasped, reaching up to feel her face, her neck.

Everything was back: the beginning crow's-feet at the corners of her eyes, the fine brackets around her mouth, the triple creases in her throat. Were they deeper now, like the wrinkles in her hands?

"What's happening to me?" she wailed.

"There is a price for power, my dear. The spell that creates the illusion of youth merely borrows time. Like any other debt, it must be repaid."

Lydia shuddered. "I'd rather *die* than get old!"

"Most people fear the dying," he said.

"Not me. My mother got old. And then Daddy dumped her for a woman twenty years younger. She drank herself to death, and Father screwed himself into a heart attack a year later. That's not going to happen to me."

"No," he murmured. "You're going to be young forever, and hold on to your Alex forever."

"Yes. This 'spell' or whatever it is. Can you teach me?"

"Teach you?" He smiled, the candle flames flickering madly in his eyes. "Of course. Are you willing to pay the price?"

Something about that smile chilled her, but she pushed her reservations aside. If she kept renewing the spell, the debt might never have to be paid.

"Yes," she said. "I'll pay the price."

"There are dangers involved for us both. I must have your loyalty, and obedience."

"Sure," she agreed, without any sincerity at all.

"You must swear."

Good God, where is this guy from? She raised her right hand. "I swear. Girl Scout honor."

"Ah, Lydia, your soul is as dishonest as you are beautiful. But I accept your fealty." Taking her raised hand, he held it cupped between his.

A stab of pain lanced across her palm, and a moment later she saw bright blood welling up. "Hey, what . . ."

"Silence!"

His shout stopped the words in her throat. She tried to pull away from him, but although his grip didn't tighten, she was powerless to move. Blood continued to rise in her cupped hand. Frozen in place, she could only watch in horror as he bent and drank the crimson liquid.

He raised his head and looked full into her eyes, his pupils swimming with star-shot specks. His lips were red. "Now I believe you."

"Please," she whispered. "Let me go."

"I never held you," he said. "Your oath did."

She snatched her hand back and examined the palm. There was no wound upon her skin, not the slightest trace of blood. Her breath went out in a rush. "I thought—"

"I wouldn't hurt you," he said. "I want only to help you."

She studied him, wanting to believe. Wanting what his help could do for her. "You do?"

"Of course. We're friends, bound in magic and purpose. What you want, I want."

Closing her hand into a fist, she made herself believe.

The Blood-Hunger returned almost as soon as Alex left Liz Garry. He walked Savannah's quiet late-night streets, feeling it rise in him like a foul tide. It clawed at his brain, sank searing needles into his spine, his guts. After the respite he'd had in Elizabeth's presence only a few minutes before, it felt like failure.

He was tempted to go back. With her, he could forget what he was. "Is that so bad?" he asked the solitude.

Yes. Because you put the burden of your salvation on her.

Catherine had built a world around him, one in which he was protected. One in which he could feel like a man again. He'd let her because he'd needed that so very badly.

And he'd been wrong. He'd let her shoulder the burden of what he was. *His* burden. Either he bore it himself, or he should walk out to meet the dawn.

The scent of flowers grew stronger as he neared Oglethorpe Square. The Lincoln sat where he'd left it, in the shadows beneath a lush maple tree. The street was empty but for an elderly woman in a bathrobe who was being pulled along by an impatient Pomeranian. The dog's claws scrabbled on the concrete as it strained at the leash.

"Slow down, Georgie," the woman panted. "Wait for Mama."

Alex saw her eyes widen as she spotted him, saw her register male, stranger, it's-late-and-there's-nobody-around-to-help-me. Her slippers slapped the pavement as she hastened to cross to the other side of the street.

If she only knew.

His footsteps slowed the closer he got to the car. He didn't want to leave; only Blood-Hunger waited for him at the Arbor, and Lydia. Here there was Liz Garry, and surcease. He could feel her heart calling to his. Urging him to go back. Siren song, as piquant as the woman herself.

No. If there was to be any chance for him and Elizabeth, he had to shake loose of the Blood-Hunger and the woman who triggered it so powerfully. He wouldn't go to Liz as he'd gone to Catherine—ridden with guilt and demons, needing her touch in order to live with himself. He lengthened his stride, precisely because he wanted to go back so badly.

A half block farther on, his revenant senses registered three men moving toward him from three different directions. He stopped. His nostrils flared as he caught the heavy scent of menace on the air.

They came out of the shadows, blocking his path to the car. One was a skinny young man with a pockmarked face and a baseball cap pulled low over his eyes, one a huge brute of a man with a bristling red beard and dull animal eyes, the third a short, slender Mexican teenager who moved with feral grace.

"Hey, mister," Pockmark said as his friends came up to flank him. "Whatcha doin'?"

Alex crossed his arms over his chest. Footpads, brigands,

muggers—whatever they were called, from Elizabethan London to the timeless, overcrowded fastness of Hong Kong, these men were all the same. Like him, they inhabited the night. Like him, they dwelled on the fringes of civilized society. Predators.

He smiled.

They hesitated for a moment, apparently taken aback by the smile. But then Pockmark started forward. The others fanned out on either side of him. A knife appeared in the Mexican boy's hand, catching the light in a deadly silver glitter.

Hands at his sides, Alex waited for them. Odd that they didn't demand his wallet. Not that he would have given it to them; he could see by their eyes that it was the fight they wanted. Tonight, he was more than willing to oblige.

"I give you fair warning, gentlemen," he said, knowing the warning would only spur them on. "Go home. You're out of your league."

"Fuck you." Pockmark pulled a handgun from the waistband of his pants and aimed it at Alex's chest.

Alex lunged forward, reacting with the warrior reflexes trained into him nearly a thousand years before. He reached Pockmark just as the man's finger tightened on the trigger. With a single, smooth motion, Alex broke the gun and the hand holding it. Pockmark staggered backward, then fell to his knees at the side of the road.

"He broke my fuckin' hand!" he wailed.

Redbeard's burly arm snaked around Alex's neck with a force that would have crushed a man's windpipe. Alex broke the hold, whirled, and clamped his hand on his assailant's neck. Although Redbeard was several inches taller and fifty pounds heavier, Alex lifted him clear of the ground and let him dangle.

Catching the glitter of metal from the corner of his eye, Alex swung his free arm in an open-handed slap that sent the Mexican boy in one direction, the knife in the other.

Redbeard kicked and gurgled. When his face gained the proper shade of purple, Alex let him fall. He sprawled on the asphalt, sucking air with great, gulping sobs.

"Kill him, Ramon," Pockmark growled.

Alex turned to see the boy rise to his feet, knife in hand. Rage burned in those black Latin eyes, but also fear.

"Yes, Ramon," Alex said, spreading his arms wide. "Come kill me."

"*Hijo de puta!*" the boy spat.

"*Hijo de puta y la puta que te pario!*" Alex replied, almost good-naturedly. Spanish was a most expressive language.

Ramon's face darkened. He shifted the knife from hand to hand, and for a moment Alex thought machismo would prevail over self-preservation. Then the boy turned and disappeared into the shadows of the square.

The street was silent but for Redbeard's labored breathing. Alex fought his Blood-Hunger, which had been roused to white heat by the violence. These men weren't victims, it whispered to him, but vanquished foes. *Easy. The issue isn't their value, but yours. A life is a life is a life, even such as this.* But he'd been raised for war, taught to wield battle rage like a weapon, and a thousand years hadn't dulled that lesson.

A scrape of shoes on asphalt brought Alex around to face Pockmark, who was scuttling backward on his rear end.

"Going somewhere?" Alex asked.

The man froze.

"It seems Ramon has declined to kill me. How about you? Would you like to try?"

Pockmark glanced at his companion, then at the gun,

which lay like a crushed insect upon the asphalt. His terror pooled around him, sickening and powerful, as he leaned over to vomit onto the street.

This isn't battle, Alex thought as the sour smell of vomit rose. There was no sense of victory in this, none of the clean triumph of defeating a worthy foe. Perhaps that, too, was a past he'd lost forever. And perhaps guiltless killing belonged only to men.

Whimpering, Pockmark tried to crawl away. Alex bent and caught him by the collar with one hand.

"Please," the man sobbed. "Please, don't kill me!"

"I'm not going to kill you. But in the future, I suggest you be more careful. You never know who you're going to meet on a dark street these days."

"What are you?"

Alex crouched so that he could look directly into the man's eyes. "My name is Death. I spared your life tonight; maybe you should think about finding something more constructive to do with it than knocking people over the head for a few dollars. Now get out of here before I change my mind."

He stood up, brushing dirt from his clothes. Behind him, he heard Pockmark scuttling away. Vermin. The sour reek of their terror hung in the air. Alex grimaced. He'd seen too much fear in his long existence upon this earth. Too much blood.

A hell of a thing for a vampire.

11

When Alex got back to the house, he noticed that a light was still burning in Margaret's study. A shadow crossed the curtain, a tall, wide-shouldered shadow.

"Barron," he muttered.

There was no reason why Barron shouldn't be in that room. But Alex's sense of violation wasn't born from logic. It was sheer, visceral dislike of anyone touching her things but him.

He tried the front door, found it unlocked. "Waiting for someone, are you?" he asked softly. "Interesting."

Silently, he made his way through the quiet house, stopping just outside the closed study door. Anticipation permeated the air. Barron was waiting for something, something he wanted badly. And there was a taint of furtiveness to the air to indicate that it was something he shouldn't have.

Alex pushed the door open with the flat of his hand. Barron stood with his back to the door, rocking back and forth on the balls of his feet. An impatient man, Alex thought.

"Hello, Barron," he said.

Barron whirled, his face blank with shock. "Wh—*Alex!*"

"In the flesh." Alex watched with interest as the man struggled for control. This went far beyond mere surprise; it was almost as though Barron had never expected to see Alex Danilov again. A fascinating revelation to a man who'd been attacked by three thugs only a short time before. "Were you expecting someone else?" he asked.

"What makes you say that?"

"The front door was unlocked."

"I . . . must have forgotten to lock it."

"I had an interesting evening," Alex said. "Three men tried to mug me tonight."

Barron's face congealed. "Oh?"

"Actually, it was a rather strange encounter; they didn't once ask for money."

"That *is* strange. Three men, you say?" Barron's facade was locked tight now. Smooth. Urbane. Brittle. "I'm amazed you were able to get away without getting hurt. Did the police pick them up?"

"No."

"Too bad." A slight relaxation of Barron's shoulders betrayed his relief.

Alex tipped his head back to study the taller man, delving deep to expose the shadow of rage at the back of his eyes. This was a new brand of Danilov. Oh, the others had had an equal capacity for ruthlessness; Catherine's progeny were an ambitious, high-tempered, stubborn lot. But it was the sort of ruthlessness that came at a man straightforwardly and damn the consequences, not this furtive stab-your-enemy-in-the-back approach. Or have someone else do it.

Without taking his gaze from Barron, Alex pulled a folded piece of paper out of his pocket. "I received a fax from Charles McGinnis today," he said.

"So?"

"This is a list of men who have been using their positions to benefit themselves at the expense of Danilov Industries."

Barron held out his hand. "Let me see."

"I'll read it to you. Let me see . . . Thomas Scanlon, vice-president of accounting. Richard Adarinson and Emmett Silvestre, eastern district managers, and Neville Moreley, payroll." Alex looked up. "Friends of yours?"

"Employees."

"Good. Then there won't be any social consequences to their dismissal."

"You're going to fire them?"

"No," Alex said. "You are."

"I am not!"

Alex smiled. "These men have been helping you steal, and they've been helping you cover it up. If you fire them, I'll see it as a gesture of future good faith."

"And if I don't?"

"I'll assume I can't trust you to behave yourself."

"And I'll be out."

"You'll be out," Alex said.

Barron's expression wavered between outrage and self-interest, settling finally on the latter. "All right," he spat. "I'll do it."

With a sigh, Alex folded the paper and slipped it back into his pocket. The Danilovs he'd known would have died rather than accept such terms. Disappointment rode him hard as he turned to go.

"Alex."

Alex turned, alerted by the hard, flat tone of the man's voice.

"I've seen the way my wife looks at you."

"How is that?"

"The way she looks at every other man who competes with me. It's not you she wants. It's the attention she hopes to get from me through you."

Alex smiled. "How Freudian. Are you warning me off?"

"Will you take my company away if I do?"

"A good point. You've nothing to lose, then."

He waited for Barron to rise to the challenge. And waited. But the man only stared, his hawk face impassive while storms of rage churned in his eyes.

Finally, Alex turned on his heel and walked away. A wave of malice followed him out into the hall and up the stairs.

He unlocked his door and swung it open. Without Catherine's perfume to welcome him, the room seemed empty. The three hours of night remaining yawned ahead, as empty as the chamber, as empty as his life.

Elizabeth Garry can fill that void.

"And what," he murmured to the treacherous part of him that had whispered that thought, "will I do for her?"

Then he sensed another presence nearby. Justin—perhaps the only person he'd be glad to see just now. He turned away from the room, relieved to be shed of his own company for a while.

Alex found Justin in what the boys called the Radio Room. He was asleep, his head resting on the table in front of him, his body slumped in a position that looked terribly uncomfortable. He'd probably fallen asleep in midconversation.

"Justin." Alex bent and touched his shoulder.

The boy awoke with a start. "What time is it?"

"Nearly three A.M. Time for you to get to bed."

"I was waiting for you. We've got to talk." He stretched, then scrubbed his face with his hands. "I heard Dad talking on the phone to some lawyer. He's hiring somebody in France to check you out. He's hoping to find something shady in your past so he can regain control of the company.

I sure hope you're who you say you are, or the stuff's gonna hit the fan."

Alex laid his hand on the boy's shoulder. "Thanks for the warning. But my past is as well documented as it is boring. I'm afraid your father is going to spend a lot of time and money for nothing."

"Are you sure? I mean, I . . . don't want anything to happen to you."

"I'm very good at taking care of myself," Alex said. "Now, tell me about the radio. Has the antenna worked out for you?"

"Yeah. Hey, we talked to a guy in Poland tonight. It was *great*! Tomorrow's Sunday, so we're not going to meet, but Monday we're going to try to reach somebody in Japan or Australia. And then . . ."

That began an hour-long discussion about time zones, radio operation, and the world in general. He's a fine young man, Alex thought. Very like Margaret. It's a good thing she'd been here to counter the effects of parents who wanted too much and cared too little.

"Justin, have you considered your future?" he asked.

"You mean college?" The animation drained from the boy's face. "I want to go into engineering. I'd start with mechanical engineering, but I'd like to get into the biomedical field someday."

"MIT?"

"If I can." *If I'm allowed*, his expression said. "Dad wants me to go into business so I can . . . Hey, I don't have to worry about running the company anymore, do I?"

"I'm afraid I can't let you off the hook that easily," Alex said. "I don't have any children, you know."

"Well, hurry up and get some."

Alex laughed.

"I'm serious," Justin said. "Look, I know the company is the family cash cow, but does that mean I've got to hock my life for it?"

"Hmmm. In a way, yes." Alex propped his hip on the edge of the table. "But you don't have to spend all your time doing it. Do I? No, I've got myself a clever lawyer who does everything for me. All he asks of me is that I show up often enough to keep the fear of the Lord in the business types."

"Shit."

"If you take a couple of business courses along with the engineering, I'll see that you go to MIT."

Justin's jaw dropped. "What if my dad says no?"

"Leave your father to me," Alex said. *In more ways than one.*

"Are you serious?"

"Absolutely." Alex held out his hand.

As they shook hands Alex watched the boy's face settle into an expression of stubborn determination. For a moment he caught a glimpse of the man Justin would be one day. Emotion tightened Alex's throat; every few generations a Danilov came along who made him very proud of the dynasty he and Catherine had founded.

Then their hands parted, and Justin became a boy once again. Alex glanced at his watch. "Time for you to get some sleep, young man. It's after three A.M."

"You don't look tired at all," Justin complained.

"I," Alex said, "am a night owl. Come on, let's go."

He waited for Justin to turn out the lights, then walked with him as far as the door to his own room. "Good night," he said.

" 'Night." Justin moved off down the hall, his shadow vastly elongated by the light behind him.

Blood-Hunger enveloped Alex the moment he stepped into his room. Had he been blind and deaf, he would have known Lydia was there.

She lay upon his bed, naked. Starlight picked out the copper tints in her hair and made her skin gleam like mother-of-pearl. She was as lush as a banquet, and all Alex's instincts—revenant and man—screamed at him to partake.

"Hello, Alex," she said. "Your door wasn't locked. I took that as an invitation."

"I didn't expect to find you here."

"Did you think I wouldn't come back after what we shared? It was beautiful. No man has ever made me feel that way before."

"Lydia—"

"You enjoyed it as much as I did. Admit it, Alex."

"Yes," he said. "I enjoyed it." *Too much.* Her breasts beckoned him, the pink-dusky aureoles already taut. And between them, the swiftly fading mark he'd left over her heart. Making love to her had been exquisite, and exquisitely dangerous.

"It was special," she murmured. "Like . . . magic. I felt it in your arms when you held me, heard it in your voice when you called out my name. You trembled."

Yes, he thought. He'd trembled with Blood-Hunger and fear, the need to protect her and the raging drive to consume her.

She held out her arms to him. "Come here."

He wanted a companion in his bed tonight, mind and body and soul. And here Lydia was. Beautiful. Willing. No, eager. His nostrils flared at the scent of woman and desire. Passionate, intelligent, and just spiteful enough to be interesting.

Yes, here she was. But she was the wrong woman.

Tonight, he wanted to be *loved*. And passionate as she was, Lydia didn't know what love was. She only knew desire. Sex and possession, possession and sex.

"I'm sorry," he said. "But no."

"No?" she echoed.

"The first time was a mistake, one for which I apologize. But also one which I do not intend to make again. It won't work, Lydia. *We* won't work."

She sat up, crossing her arms over her chest. "Why not?"

"Because I don't love you."

To his surprise, she laughed. "You *are* naive, aren't you?" Swinging her legs over the side of the bed, she rose to her feet and came toward him, her breasts swaying with the rhythm of her movement. His hands shook with the urge to touch her.

She stopped before him, reaching up to twine her arms around his neck. "No, I think naive is the wrong word. You're a romantic, Alex. A man who believes in the power of true love. I like that. It's very . . . exciting."

Blood-Hunger and arousal swept through him, more powerful than ever before. Of their own volition, his hands spread out across her back, then slid slowly down the graceful line of her spine to cup her buttocks and pull her more closely against him. He ran his open mouth down her neck, feeling the life beating just below the surface of her skin. The darkness within him roared.

"Yes," she whispered. "That's it, that's what I was looking for. Don't think so much, Alex. It makes things much too complicated. Tonight, let's just enjoy each other. Love can come later."

Love has already come. The memory of fathomless amber

eyes touched him, warming him like the sun. Reminding him what had real value. Not this. Never this. He flung off the grasping tendrils of dark-bred desire. Then he reached up, disentangled Lydia's arms from around his neck, and lifted her away from him.

"You can't stop," she said, her eyes, her body still beckoning him. "I want you. I want you more than anything I've ever wanted in my life."

"Until the next toy comes around," he said.

Bewilderment softened her smoky-emerald eyes. "I don't . . . What's the matter? All I wanted was to hold you, and to be held."

"You want to possess. Own."

"I want to make love to you."

"To make love, you must love."

"But I *do* love you," she said.

With the Blood-Hunger under control, he dared touch her again. Gently, he ran his fingertips down her cheek. "No, you don't. You don't even know me."

"But . . . I don't understand," she whispered. "Aren't I beautiful enough for you? Sexy enough?"

"You are the most beautiful and desirable woman I've met in many, many years," he said, knowing she'd never understand why that wasn't enough. "But you're not for me."

She stood, arms hanging limp at her sides, as he found her discarded robe and pulled it around her shoulders.

"Go back to your room, Lydia," he said, leading her to the door. "I can give you only pain, believe me."

"I'll take the pain," she whispered. "If I can have the rest."

He shook his head. "No. Find someone who can love

you as you deserve to be loved. There's a whole world of men from which to choose."

"Not for me." Tears glittered in her eyes, on her cheeks. "Damn you."

"I was damned a long time ago," he said.

12

Thunder rolled overhead as Alex got dressed. It wasn't raining yet, but the air was tense and heavy with the approaching storm. He opened the window and leaned his elbows on the sill. The wind was beginning to kick up. The branches of the mimosa danced like a giant feather duster, and the live oaks creaked and groaned, complaining like a host of arthritic grandmothers.

He closed his eyes, letting the breeze slide over him. It coated his skin with moisture, lifted the fine hairs on the back of his neck with storm awareness.

"It must be a fine thing to be a storm," he said, wishing he could glide off on the wings of the wind, to be deposited at Elizabeth Garry's feet.

"MR. ALEX," the maid called through the door. "Mrs. Danilov said to tell you that the family is eating late and that you're welcome to join them."

"Thank you, Eve," he said. "Tell them to start without me. I'll be down later."

"All right, sir . . ."

"It is *not* all right." Lydia's presence eclipsed the maid's. "Alex, get out here."

He closed the window as Blood-Hunger settled between

his shoulder blades like a sharp-clawed bird of prey. From time to time it buried its beak in him, tearing off little strips of his heart. His only relief lay miles away in Savannah, with Elizabeth.

He sighed. What an idiot he was! In love with a woman he dared not pursue, pursued by a woman he dared not touch. Two women, one for his heart, one for his appetite.

"You'd think after a thousand years I'd know to keep myself from this kind of trouble," he muttered.

Lydia was, as always, stunning. A feast for the senses, even in a spandex abomination that would have been hideous on any other woman. He was a fairly adaptable fellow, but learning to like some of these modern fashions required more flexibility than he seemed to possess.

"Do you like it?" She spun slowly on her toes like a model. The crystal she wore caught the light, cast it back in a claret glow that clashed with the aquamarine of her clothing.

He chose to comment on the woman rather than the attire. "Lovely. Lydia—"

She put her hand over his mouth. "If you're going to talk about last night, don't."

He'd expected either coldness or recriminations; in fact, he would have welcomed them. It would be much, much easier if she didn't want him. But her smile was as warm as ever, her eyes as inviting.

"Do you intend to pretend it didn't happen?" he asked.

"I'm no glutton for punishment," she said. "And I do have my pride. If I thought you really didn't want me, I'd walk away. But you do want me, Alex. I can feel it here." She tapped the center of her chest. "We're a match. Deny it all you want for any reason you like, but we're supposed to *be* together."

"Destiny?" he asked, sarcasm masking his fear that she was right.

"Call it anything you like."

Blood-Hunger was a pulse beat in his mind, pulling up memories of her scent, the way she'd felt beneath his hands. Her blood had been sweet, the taste of her life force hot and vital. He closed his eyes. No. Accepting Lydia's view would be letting the revenant part of him win, letting it choose shadow over substance, pleasure over the clean, sweeping joy of love. And as far as being destined, well, he'd outlived destiny.

"You'd better get downstairs or you'll be late for dinner," he said.

She stared at him, evidently doubting herself for a moment. But she recovered quickly. "Okay," she murmured. "Let's go. We can talk later."

"I've already eaten."

"Then come drink some wine while the rest of us eat." With a smile, she added, "You can spoil Barron's dinner."

"How flattering."

"But true. He's absolutely furious. I've never seen him so pinched looking, and the very mention of your name sends him off into one of those cold staring silences of his. What did you do?"

"Nothing that I know of," he said.

"Liar."

"Among other things."

She took his arm, coming up against him in a rush of softness and perfume. He let her lead him downstairs. Perhaps it was sheer perversity that made him want to confront Barron again.

Why do you bother? You don't need Danilov Industries, and certainly Justin doesn't.

He knew the answer even as the thought appeared: he was a Danilov, bred for strife, weaned on battle. He'd lost his humanity and his soul, but a thousand years hadn't dulled his taste for a good fight. In this too civilized world, the struggle for Danilov Industries was the last remaining battle-field left to him.

The storm broke as he and Lydia reached the dining room. The tall windows framed a darkness ripped by the sudden flare of lightning. Rain started to fall, not in drops, but in an almost solid, wind-driven sheet.

Alex found Barron staring at him, his face composed, but his eyes echoing the roiling darkness outside. Sonya sat half-turned away from her husband, ignoring both him and the cooling food on her plate. A happy couple indeed, Alex thought. Only Justin's face was welcoming, and welcome.

"Hello, Alex," Sonya said, rising from her chair with elaborate casualness to take possession of his free arm. She wore a white gossamer jumpsuit that looked like spun moon-light. "I'm glad you decided to come down. I'll ring for Eve to bring you a plate."

"Just a glass of wine, please," he said. "I ate earlier."

"I'm sure you did." She smiled, glancing from him to Lydia from beneath her lashes. "There's a bottle of wine open on the buffet. Something red and old. I'm afraid it isn't very good."

"Red and old, and not very good? This I have to see." He escorted the two women to the table, then moved to the buffet.

The wine was a La Brocarde from the Rhône region, perhaps twenty years past its prime. Once, this had been one of the best wines in the world. Now, like him, it was a shadow of its former self. He poured it reverently, then held it high to admire the play of light in its depths. Some shadows were better than others.

He returned to the table, intending to take the only safe place, the one on the far side of Justin. But Barron's stare was so challenging that Alex took the hot seat, between the boy and his mother. Sheer perversity, of course. But then he'd never claimed to be a saint.

After meeting Barron's gaze squarely, Alex set his glass on the table, then turned in his chair so he could look at Sonya. There was a special glow to her languid beauty tonight. Perhaps it was because of her husband's obvious jealousy. But perhaps it was his own Blood-Hunger, indiscriminate lover of women that it was.

"You've done your hair differently," he said. "I like it."

She smiled, reaching up to smooth her already smooth chignon. Lightning flashed incandescent highlights in her pale hair. "Why, thank you. I found a new hairdresser today, and he's very good. I think I'm going to keep him."

Lydia laughed aloud. A flush darkened the skin over Barron's cheekbones.

Anger flowed and eddied in the room, currents of ugly emotion beneath the controlled urbanity of modern life. Alex disengaged, preferring to think about his brief time with Elizabeth Garry. That kitchen seemed a haven now. So did the woman. There had been no anger, no games with her. Just those dark amber eyes, honest and vulnerable, and deep enough for a man to lose himself.

Justin's fork clattered on his plate, bringing Alex back to reality with a jolt. He read the anxiety in the boy's eyes, the determination to make peace among his elders. How many times had he played this role? Probably too many.

"So, Alex, how's the fax machine working out?" he asked.

"Fine, mysterious thing that it is. You know, I think there are still cultures on this planet that would worship such a device as a god."

Lydia laughed again. "Who said this one doesn't? When was the last time you saw a business card *without* a fax number on it?"

"Don't be an ass, Lydia," Barron said.

"I think it's an interesting observation," Alex said. "And right on target. As a newcomer to this country, one of the first things I noticed was Americans' fascination with gadgets. Fax machines, Nintendo, VCRs—"

"You didn't have VCRs in France?" Justin asked.

"Some people did. I prefer books. They're quiet, and if you blink or yawn, you don't miss anything."

Barron showed his teeth in an almost smile. "How quickly you were corrupted. A few weeks here, and you've got yourself a VCR, an answering machine, and someone else's home and business."

"True," Alex said. "But then, I've always been an adaptable fellow." He was about to add, "And not one to refuse a good thing when it's offered," but decided that it would be a rash statement in present company.

Lightning speared across the sky overhead. Thunder rolled on its heels. Sonya gasped, clamping both hands on Alex's forearm as the lights flickered. On, off, on again, as though fighting for life. A moment later the room was plunged into darkness.

"Damn," Barron said, moving slowly toward the door, his arms outstretched. "Wait here, everybody. I'll see if I can find a flashlight or candles."

Alex rose to his feet and stepped away from the table— and Sonya's grasp. "Why don't you let me go?" he offered. "I do pretty well in the dark."

Barron kept walking, bumping into the doorjamb on his
way out of the room.

"Alex, where are you?" Lydia asked.

He turned to look at her. She sat with her hands pressed
flat on the table in front of her as though to anchor herself,
her blind gaze searching the darkness. For a moment he
thought he saw a flicker of light in the crystal she wore.
It was brief, just a millisecond long, and was gone in the
space of a blink. A reflection, perhaps.

Wind rattled the windows. Rain beat against the glass as
though wanting to get in.

"Alex?" Lydia called again. "Alex?"

"I'm right here."

"I'm scared."

"Just sit tight. We'll have some light soon."

Even as he spoke two massive bolts of lightning speared
down to strike the tallest of the live oaks outside. For a
moment every branch, every twig and leaf was limned in
eye-searing radiance. Splinters exploded outward from the
trunk. The tree twisted and swayed, groaning like a hurt
beast. Slowly at first, then faster and faster, it fell.

Alex leaped forward as the windows burst inward with a
spray of water and broken glass. He grabbed Justin by his
collar and Sonya by her arm and slung them both toward the
opposite side of the room. Then he hurled himself across the
table on his belly, hitting Lydia in a sort of flying tackle that
flung them both toward the doorway.

The tree smashed down on the table behind him. He
shoved Lydia to one side as a heavy weight hit him in
the back, hurling him to the floor with stunning force. A
moment later he found himself lying facedown beneath a
mass of torn leaves and twisted branches. He took a deep
breath, then another, astonished that he was still in one

piece. Or almost; a grinding pain in his side betrayed a few broken ribs.

"Alex!" Justin cried. "Alex, are you all right?"

"I'm fine," he called. "How about the rest of you?"

"We're all okay. Let me see if I can reach—"

"No, Justin. Don't try to come in here, it's a mess."

He closed his eyes, concentrating on his ribs. Bones drew together with an almost audible grate as his body began to heal itself. The pain grew less with every breath he took. It wasn't long before he was able to push himself up on his elbows, shifting the weight of the branches up enough so that he could look from side to side. To his right, a foot or so from his face, was the main trunk of the tree. He spent a moment pondering whether squashing a revenant with a tree might not be as effective as staking him through the heart. Not an experiment he'd like to try.

"What the hell happened here?" Barron asked from the doorway.

"What does it look like?" Hysteria put a sharp edge in Lydia's voice. "Call the fire department, for God's sake! We've got to get him out of there!"

"The phone's out," Barron said. "I already tried."

"There's a chain saw out in the garden house," Justin said. "I'll get it."

"You're not going out in that storm," Sonya cried. "Justin! Come back!"

"Be back in a minute!" he called, his voice already fading.

Alex wedged his elbow beneath him and levered himself onto his side, then his back. Groping up through the leaves, he found a branch as big around as his thigh. He broke it and pushed it to one side.

"What was that noise?" Sonya yelped.

"I think the tree's shifting," Barron said, no hysteria in *his* voice.

He's enjoying this, Alex thought. He's out there tallying his gains from my dying here tonight.

With a grin, Alex reached out, found another branch, and broke that, too. The tangle of wood and foliage sagged. He held it above him with braced arms, gradually shoving it into a more stable position.

After that, he was able to wriggle far enough out that Justin would be able to rescue him by cutting only a branch or two.

"Alex, are you all right?" Lydia called.

"I'm fine. Somehow I managed to land between two branches instead of beneath them."

"Justin's back. Just relax. We'll have you out of there in a minute."

"I'm relaxed."

Then he heard Barron say, "Here, son, let me have that chain saw."

Alarm shafted through Alex. Revenant he might be, but he had as much regard for his body parts as any living person. "Hold on," he called. "I think I might be able to wriggle out on my own."

"Be careful," Lydia said. "Some of those branches are as sharp as knives."

He squirmed through the tangle, bending the smaller branches, using them to support the larger ones.

"I think I saw something move," Justin said. "Let me have the flashlight."

Alex saw the play of light through the leaves and knew he was nearly out. Feeling rather like the snake in the Garden of Eden, he slithered through a last barrier of treetop-thin branches to freedom.

"Alex!" Lydia cried.

She flung her arms around him, enveloping him in wet spandex and Blood-Hunger. He let her cling for a moment, then gently extricated himself.

The others seemed unhurt, although Justin's face looked as though he'd gotten in a brawl with a mad alley cat. Barron stood with the chain saw hanging from his hand, his face creased with a hatred he'd never have let show in the light.

"Justin, let me have the flashlight, will you?" Alex asked.

"Here," the boy said. "Press that button there."

The light played over the corpse of the tree, the top twenty feet of which lay inside the room.

"It couldn't have fallen in here at that angle," Justin said. "It's almost like it was thrown like a spear."

"Some of your engineering acumen?" Barron asked.

Alex ignored the man's sarcasm; the boy was straight on. "A tornado, you think?"

"Could be. I can't think of anything else that could do it."

"Me, either." Alex directed the beam along the tree, which extended through the outer wall. The rain was still coming down heavily, making the trunk glisten like an enormous snake.

"Look there," Justin said, pointing to a shadowy bulk just visible through the veil of rain. "It's been uprooted. That's what a tornado does."

Alex nodded. He turned the light on the spot where they had all been sitting a few minutes ago. The smashed wreck of what had been the table lay beneath the main trunk.

"Man, look at that!" Justin breathed. "If we'd been sitting there when that thing hit . . . *Pow!* Human pancakes."

"Thanks, Alex," Sonya said.

"For what?" Barron asked.

"Saving our lives." She shuddered. "I've never been so close to dying."

Lydia moved closer to Alex, her Obsession undaunted by the soaking she'd gotten. "I'll find a way to repay you," she whispered. "Somehow."

He had no intention of collecting; the interest on some debts was much too costly.

Suldris stood in the sanctuary of the old church, his arms spread wide as though in imitation of the pale image of the cross on the wall behind him. Rain slashed at his upturned face. Lightning sprang from his fingertips, then reached outward to crawl over the walls and ceiling.

A woman lay on the altar before him. The rain fell on her pale face and pooled in her open eyes. It washed the clotted blood from her throat and hair, sending pink rivulets streaming to the floor.

"Powers of Darkness, hear me," he cried, his voice eclipsing the storm. "Io, Zati, Zata, Abbata! *Coropis su aparantus, daaske erun dageram, coropis su coropis!*"

The air in the sanctuary began to move, picking up leaves and dirt and swirling them into a rotating cloud.

"Io, Zati, Zata, Abbata!" he screamed. *"Coropis su aparantus, daaske erun dageram, coropis su coropis!"*

The whirlwind picked up speed. It screamed around the edges of the room, rattling windows and knocking loose plaster from the walls. The floor of the church bucked and rippled like a live thing. Eyes closed, Suldris stood untouched in the center of it all.

"Go!" he commanded.

The whirlwind vanished. The rain stopped. A single dead

leaf drifted to the floor with a papery whisper.

Suldris let his arms drop to his sides. Exhaustion set in, bone deep, soul deep, and he sank to his knees. Bracing his hands on his thighs, he took several deep, gasping breaths to steady himself.

Opening his eyes was an act of will, knowing as he did what he would see. Slowly, he raised his hands. They had turned to withered claws, his arms fleshless, mere skin over knobbed bone. Puckered scars striated every inch of exposed skin. He reached up, encountering a webwork of ridges instead of a face.

"Danilov," he hissed.

Alex Danilov had done this to him. Or rather, Alexi Danilovich, as he'd called himself then. James Suldris had held the power of life and death over his little corner of Scotland, and not even God had dared interfere. But Alexi had.

Suldris felt his lips writhe back over his teeth as he remembered the night of their final encounter. The torches, the roar of the mob, but most of all, their leader.

The mysterious Russian had come to the village one frigid winter night. There was a sense of overwhelming sadness about the man with a warrior's body and hair the color of the sun. Perhaps because of that, the people trusted him. They told him their tale, showed him the pikes holding the heads of those who dared speak out against Lord Suldris, the gibbets where corpses swung in the wind to be torn by crows and nibbled on by vermin.

Alexi heard their tale. He saw the pikes and gibbets, and passed judgment. He led the peasants against their liege, promising them freedom. All Suldris protections fell before him; no barrier, whether iron, stone, or magic, barred the fair-haired stranger. The Russian had come to Suldris's throne room. Conqueror. He had beaten the unbeatable, taken what could not be taken. The peasants clustered behind him, jackals feeding in the lion's wake.

Suldris faced them with defiance. "Defilers!" He pointed at the villagers, who shrank back. "I will visit a punishment for this that will haunt you for generation upon generation."

But the stranger stepped between him and the peasants. "Your reign of terror must end, James Suldris," he said, his eyes sad and implacable. "This evil is a blight in the eyes of God and man."

"This is my realm, my people," Suldris said. "I will do as I please with them."

"You killed a priest."

"He tried to interfere."

The stranger crossed his arms. "I have seen things in this keep of yours that go beyond abomination."

"You took my son!" cried one of the villagers. "I found his head in your larder!"

"My daughter!" shouted another. "A bairn not half a year old, and you stole her away for your hellish use! And sweet, pretty Rose Forbeis drowned herself in the loch after you defiled her!"

"My wife! My nephew! My husband! My brother!" The shouts rose to a roar that echoed throughout the keep.

Suldris spat on the floor between the Russian's feet. "Yes! I took them all! I'll take as many as I wish, for as long as I wish. I'll take you!" He thrust his thumb at the hulking blacksmith. "I'll take you, or you, or you!" He pointed at three different men. "You're no better than cattle. I'll serve you up on my supper table if that pleases me."

"No," the stranger said. "You won't."

"Is it you who's going to stop me?" Suldris asked.

"Yes."

Suldris raised his hands, chanting. A wind sprang up in the room, extinguishing the torches. The peasants wailed.

"Courage," the stranger said. "I said I would help you."

He held a medallion in his hand, griffin-carved, a cabochon ruby glowing crimson in its center. The glow brightened, grew larger, then leaped from torch to torch. It burned steady and sure, unaffected by the wind.

Suldris spread his arms wide, calling up more power. The wind grew to a gale that tore at the villagers' clothes and hair. Alexi closed his hand into a fist, and the gale died. Snarling, Suldris tried another spell, and another. Each time Alexi countered it.

"So, a sorcerer you are!" Suldris cried.

"You have no name for what I am," the stranger said.

"You can't kill me." Pulling his dirk out of his belt, Suldris slashed at his own arm with it. The skin remained unmarked. "You see? No blade can hurt me, no spear or arrow pierce me."

"So the people told me," Alexi said, his eyes still sad, still implacable. "But that won't save you this time. Recant your foul master, sorcerer. Take up God's path again, and we will spare you."

"I spit on your God! Satan is my brother, my father, my son!"

"Then commend your soul to him," the stranger said.

He laid hands on Suldris then, hands stronger than any man's could possibly be. No matter how the sorcerer struggled, he couldn't break that grip. Alexi dragged him down to the village common, where nine great stones had been set in a circle. A bonfire burned in the center, and above it . . . above it, a great iron caldron. Steam hung above it, born of the water boiling within.

"Nooooo!" Suldris screamed.

"The people have had enough of pain," Alexi said.

The sorcerer howled the most fearsome spells he knew. He fought with his hands, his feet, his teeth. But Alexi merely held him, absorbing everything. Finally exhausted, Suldris tried temptation. "We can share this place, these people. Together, we'll be invincible. Think about it, stranger; we could sit on the throne of England if we wished."

"I want no throne," Alexi said. "The only thing you could tempt me with is peace, and that is something not even God Himself can give me."

Suldris raised his head and stared into the stranger's eyes. There was pain in those cool gray depths, pain and loneliness and knowledge too vast to be contained in human flesh. A shiver ran down the sorcerer's spine. Whether this was demon or angel, he couldn't know. But it was not a man.

"Recant," Alexi said. "It's your only hope."

"May your soul roast in hell," he spat.

"Rest assured, my friend. It already is."

Alexi held Suldris while the villagers wrapped a great sheet of lead around the sorcerer. As the soft metal folded over his face Suldris snapped like a dog, catching the stranger's wrist. A mere scratch, but it was his one last act of defiance. A single drop of blood stung his tongue with its metallic tang. The taste spread throughout his mouth, seeped downward into his throat.

He felt himself being lifted, then dropped. The tiny pocket of air around his nose and mouth grew warm, and driblets of boiling water seeped through the joints in his lead shroud. His skin flinched from the contact, but there was no escape.

After that, he remembered only pain. The lead melted around him, eating its way into his skin, his flesh. He felt his own fat leach out, felt his eyeballs burst from the terrific heat. His mind screamed, since his body could not. Pain . . . Pain.

When it came time for him to die, he was ready. He gave up his soul eagerly, knowing his lord Satan had a place for him in the hierarchy of hell. But when he woke again, it was not in hell, but in the leaden coffin in which he'd been boiled.

He was not alive, not dead. Slowly, his body began to heal itself. Joints that had fallen apart from the boiling grew together again, flesh and skin, bones and organs regenerated. He knew he would never be quite the same; too much had been lost for that. The process of healing took many, many years. Wrapped in a cocoon of metal, he could only endure. And the process hurt. Exquisite, hot-needle pain stabbed through every pore, every shred of flesh in his body. Wrapped as he was in a cocoon of metal, he couldn't even scream.

Another man might have gone mad. But not Suldris. No, he had his hate to sustain him. He would take revenge for this suffering, a life for every moment of pain, a life for every drop of his blood. Blood. He remembered that single drop of blood he'd wrested from the blond stranger, the taste of it, the way it spread through his mouth and seeped into his throat.

Alexi Danilovich was not a man. What, then, was he?

The memory taste of blood was still with Suldris; his body and mind reacted to it, craving it. It was then that he knew what he had become, and what had created him.

He'd have his revenge. If it took forever, he'd have it.

A whimper brought him back to the present with a rush. For a moment he thought he'd made the tiny sound, but then remembered the woman who lay bound and gagged in the next room.

He rose to his feet, groaning. The weather spell had drained him badly. Just now he felt like a bag of bones held together by hope and wires. And Alexi was still alive; Suldris carried the awareness of his enemy's existence in every cell of his body. His brother of the blood. No matter. His time would come.

The woman whimpered again, her terror rising, filling the moldering church like a hymn. Suldris smiled.

"I'm coming, my sweet," he called.

13

Blood-Hunger flew in on the wings of the night. Alex woke to it, agony shafting through him the moment he became aware. He twisted from side to side on the bed as it gnawed at his belly, raked his brain with white-hot claws.

Upstairs, Lydia waited outside his room. His appetite raised its muzzle like a beast of prey on the scent. Live meat.

He groaned, sinking his fingers into the hair at his temples. "Not meat," he said. "She's a woman. A human being. Whatever her faults, her soul is sacred to God. Help me, Lord!"

As always, the Lord ignored him. Creature of darkness that he had become, he had passed out of God's ken. All he had now was Blood-Hunger. Tonight, it was stronger than he. So he fled from it, rushing up the stairs as though it were nipping at his heels, then ghosting out the window on silent owl's wings to avoid the woman who waited outside his bedroom door. Lydia—beautiful, determined Lydia—temptation and disaster in one lovely human form.

There was only one place where his Blood-Hunger couldn't follow: Elizabeth Garry. He had enough presence of mind to slip back into human form and take the Lincoln into

Savannah. Weak, weak to let her shield him, he thought as he drove. He'd always struggled against the Blood-Hunger, but this was like nothing he'd experienced before, a need that raged like a fire burning out of control. The monster within tore at the fabric of what remained of Alex Danilov, and giving it rein would only make it stronger.

He needed help. And although he knew he couldn't be with Elizabeth as he wanted, he had to have a taste of the surcease she offered. He parked a short distance from the Garry house and rolled down his window to let in a wash of humid summer air. The scent of roses was sweet and heady, underscored by the shrill whine of mosquitoes as they hunted the quiet street. Slowly, he bent forward to rest his forehead against the steering wheel.

But it was not the past he sought. Tonight, he was centered on the present and the woman who occupied it. His eyes drifted closed as he sought Elizabeth. She was near, near enough for him to feel the echo of her heartbeat in his own chest. Her serenity beckoned him, offering relief from the pain of Blood-Hunger. To be this close and yet unable to speak to her . . .

"Alex?"

It was her voice. His memory had been playing it over and over to him so often that it took him a moment to realize that she'd actually spoken to him. He straightened abruptly.

She stood outside the car, her hands resting on the base of the open driver's window. For a moment his mind reeled, trying to reconcile the dream and his own need with the reality of the woman.

"Are you ill?" she asked, reaching in to touch his cheek. "Alex?"

He caught her hand. It was smooth and cool against his skin, and the contact washed through him like a crisp autumn breeze. The agony of Blood-Hunger faded, a stale memory like an old toothache.

Why her, out of all the women in the world? Is it some healing gift that touches even such as I?

"I'm . . . all right," he said. "I just got a little dizzy."

"Why don't you come into the house?" she asked. "I was on my way in."

Did he have the strength to refuse? He opened his mouth, honestly not knowing what he was going to say. "I—"

"I promise not to lock you up," she said. "You don't have to run away. Again."

"Will you think me a coward if I do?" he asked, surrendering to another Liz-unconventional conversation.

"Yes."

"Are you always so blunt?"

"Usually. Especially when men who profess to be anxious to avoid my company show up almost at my door."

"I could have been passing through."

"You could have thought up a better lie."

He sighed. "A few centuries ago, they might have burned you at the stake."

"Matilda Rawlins, an ancestor on Father's side, was tried as a witch in 1692. She was acquitted, however. The story has it that some people thought she bespelled her inquisitors."

"That's almost proof positive of guilt," he said. "No self-respecting witch would allow herself to be burned at the stake."

"Are you coming in?" she asked.

"I can't."

Let her go, his common sense told him as she turned away. But his mind had nothing to do with this; it was almost as if he were operating in a world where rational thought did not exist, only feelings. And he felt that if he let her walk away now, he would die. He would *be* revenant, totally, completely, and there would be nothing left for him but to go back to Lydia.

"Walk with me," he said. "The night is very beautiful."

She nodded. He pushed the car door open and got out, only just remembering to close it behind him. For the first time he noticed that she was wearing a yellow sundress that revealed a sprinkling of freckles across her shoulders. Her high heels made her an inch or so taller than he.

"You look lovely tonight," he said.

"I had a date."

Some very human feeling went through him then, chiefly jealousy. Strange that a thousand years of existence hadn't burned that very primitive emotion out of him. "You're home rather early, then, aren't you? It's not quite eleven."

"It wasn't a very successful date."

"I'm sorry."

She smiled. "You don't look sorry."

"So I lied," he said.

"So you did."

He offered his arm; she took it. The trees laid bars of shadow across the sidewalk and street, and her hair turned from dark to gold-dusted and back again as she passed through the changing light. The pulse of her life force was vital and compelling, as powerful in its own way as Lydia's. There were so many things he wished he could say, deep and binding things. But he couldn't, so he walked in silence, savoring her presence as he would a fine wine.

"Are you always this quiet?" she asked.

"Not at all. I have a vast range of meaningless chatter, from the weather to sports to art, and I read the paper to memorize the latest in political jokes."

"Anything to keep the conversation from turning to Alex Danilov?"

"Touché, mademoiselle. You will also note that I find myself void of all normal social skills around you."

She laughed. "I haven't seen you dribble your food."

"You haven't seen me eat."

"Do you prefer to keep this conversation on lighter subjects than our last one?"

"Please."

She let go of his arm abruptly, leaving him bereft. But she merely stooped to pick up a stone about the size and shape of an egg, then came back to again tuck her hand in place in the crook of his arm. He was too deeply mired in his own emotions to assess hers, an unwelcome disadvantage.

"So we'll keep it light," she said, tossing the stone up with her free hand and catching it again. She glanced at him out of the corner or her eye. "Can you juggle?"

"Juggle?" He stopped to stare at her in surprise.

"Yes. I'm trying to learn how to juggle."

"Why?"

She shrugged. "It's as useful a profession as say, textbook writing. Well, can you?"

"I'm afraid that's not a skill I ever acquired, sorry."

"Want to try?"

Again, she startled him. He hadn't played in a very long time. So long, in fact, that he'd almost forgotten how. He looked into her eyes, saw mischief brimming there, and was lost. If he hadn't already loved her, he would have fallen here, this moment. "What do I have to do?" he asked.

"We need two more rocks, preferably about the size and weight of this one."

They cast about for a while, finally coming up with suitable candidates.

"Okay," Liz said. "You go first. Hold two in your left hand, one in your right. Now toss the right one into the air, and at the same time, toss one from your left hand to your right. Catch the airborne one in your left hand, tossing the third stone to your right hand at the same time you toss stone number two into the air. Got it?"

"You're insane."

"Mad as the proverbial hatter. Don't you love it?"

Yes. Oh, God, yes. Instead of answering, he started tossing rocks. It was easier than he thought; trained to use broadsword, mace, spear, quarterstaff, rapier, and almost any blade known to man, his hands took up the motion easily. Unexpected delight went through him.

"This is fun," he said.

Then he made the mistake of looking up at Liz, and completely lost his concentration. The stones fell clattering to the sidewalk.

"Ha!" she cried. "Got cocky there, didn't you? Now where did that thing go . . . ? Ah, there it is."

She stooped to reach into the gutter. "Ouch!"

"What's the matter?" Alex lifted her to her feet. "Are you hurt?"

"Not really. I just got hold of a piece of glass along with the rock. It's not bad."

She held her hand palm outward to show a bright beading of blood at the base of her index finger. The scent of her blood drifted like perfume on the still, humid air, and it was as sweet as the honeysuckle blooming nearby. He shook with the need to taste this essence of Elizabeth, to make her part of him forever. But equally powerful was the need to hold himself apart from her. God, to be only a man!

"Don't worry, Alex. It doesn't hurt," she said.

"Yes," he whispered. "It does."

The world whirled around him as he pressed his thumb against the wound to stem the flow of blood. She stood still, watching him with a gaze that was both confused and speculative.

"What's the matter?" she asked. "You look as if you'd seen a ghost."

Ah, she was too, too perceptive. He felt stripped bare, more vulnerable than he'd ever been before. With a sigh he felt down to his toes, he let go of her hand. "The bleeding has stopped. I'd better take you home; that ought to have some disinfectant and a bandage. God knows what's been in that gutter."

Somehow he managed to ignore the hurt bewilderment in her eyes. He offered his arm. Silently, she took it. He watched her surreptitiously as they walked back the way they had come, trying to impress every nuance of her in his memory. He had the feeling she would dwell there for a very long time.

They reached the Garry house too soon. He gently disengaged his arm and stepped back from her. "Good night, Liz. Thank you for walking with me. Be sure to take care of that cut."

She didn't answer, just stood in the moonlight and watched him. Her gaze held his, and for a moment he felt as though he were floating in a sunset sea, encompassed in deep amber warmth. Then she reached up and touched his cheek.

"Good-bye, Alex," she said.

Then she turned and went in. Alex closed his eyes so he couldn't see the door close.

Alex parked the Lincoln in the garage. To his relief, he saw that Lydia's Corvette was gone. His Blood-Hunger coiled just beneath the surface of his mind, claws bared, but not yet sunk into his being.

Again he thought, Why Lydia? As beautiful and sensuous as she was, so were a thousand others he'd known. But only now, with Lydia, did his Blood-Hunger rise to unmanageable levels. Mere flesh and blood and raw sexuality couldn't do that; her gift with crystals had to be the culprit. Power calling to power.

He walked around to the front of the house, his feet silent even on the gravel walk. The moment he stepped into the foyer, he was greeted with angry voices. Barron and Sonya, in yet another argument. Even the Arbor's solid construction couldn't mute the ugly words or the even uglier emotions that prompted them.

A door banged open at the back of the house, and a moment later Sonya came running into the foyer, Barron a few steps behind her. Alex considered retreat, but then realized he might as well have been invisible for all the notice they paid him.

"I'm not finished talking to you!" Barron hissed.

"You don't talk, you just give orders!"

"If I didn't, you wouldn't be able to get out of bed yourself."

Sonya pivoted slowly on her heel. Her eyes glittered, not with tears, but with hatred. "Oh, really? I seem to have no trouble getting *into* bed without your help."

"So you admit it."

"I have to get it *somewhere*, don't I?"

Barron's face hardened. "Maybe I just don't want to touch something that's been in half the beds in Savannah."

"Maybe you just can't get it up for anything but a dollar bill."

"That's the pot calling the kettle black, isn't it?" Barron

said, low and deadly. "You married me for money, and you're staying with me for the same goddamn money!"

"True."

"You haven't given much value for it."

Fists clenched, she stalked over to him. "At least I'm not a thief," she said. "Worse, you're a hypocrite, kissing up to Margaret, trying to make her think you're the dutiful, loving nephew whose only pleasure was serving her. God, what a joke! And all the while you were waiting for her to die and counting the money you'd get when she did. But she saw through you, didn't she?"

"You goddamn slut!"

She slapped him. He slapped her back with enough force to rock her back on her heels, then raised his hand to strike her again.

Alex stepped between them, catching the other man's upraised arm. "That's enough, Barron."

For a moment Barron's eyes glared naked hate, and he strained against Alex's grip. Then his face closed, locking everything inside.

Glancing over his shoulder at Sonya, Alex said, "This discussion is over. Go upstairs and try to get some sleep."

Her hand shook as she reached up to touch her bottom lip, which was beginning to swell. Then she whirled and ran upstairs. Alex let go of Barron gently, resisting the temptation to hurl the man across the room.

"That was poorly done, Barron."

"Mind your own goddamn business."

"I intend to," Alex said. "And what happens in my house *is* my business."

"As you've reminded me all too often. Your house. Your company. Your way."

"If you don't like it, you're free to leave it all."

Barron smiled, but it was a twisted, ugly thing. "And make things easy for you? Oh, no. Or do you intend to go back on your word and throw us out?"

"A Danilov doesn't go back on his word," Alex said. "Nor does he hit women. You've strayed from the path, Barron. I suggest you look to your heart and see what is left of the family in you."

The other man's face darkened. "How—"

His temper finally roused, Alex grabbed the larger man by the throat—not killing hard, but hard enough to get his attention. "Danilov has been an honorable name because it's been held by honorable men and women. I don't know what your father was like, but fifteen minutes in Margaret's company should have taught you that. I know it's a lot to live up to, but try. Try very hard."

He let Barron go. The other man sank to his knees, rubbing his throat as though to make sure it was still there. "You bastard," he croaked. "I'd sell my soul to the devil to be rid of you!"

Alex turned away. "Careful, Barron. The devil has very good ears, and a rash statement like that can end up burning you."

14

Oblivion loosed its grasp on Alex, leaving him to the night. His Blood-Hunger lay curled within him, present but unroused, the beast quiescent. Lydia must be gone.

"Hello, love," he said to Catherine's portrait.

It remained only a pretty picture, however; what had made it special was gone.

"You always said I cling to the past too much," he said, reaching up to touch the portrait's cheek. "But the future . . . Now that is a truly frightening thing."

He went back to the world of men, carrying his loneliness with him. As if to humor his mood, the house was silent and empty. Eerily so, and for a moment he thought he'd slept a century away like Rip Van Winkle.

"I should be so lucky," he said.

He paused in the doorway of the dining room. The tree had been cleared from the dining room, the shattered wall patched with plywood. The furniture and rug had been taken away. Scars marred the floor, great, gaping slashes of white on the age-darkened oak. Had it been an act of God? No, he decided, turning away from the wrecked room. God would have had better aim.

"If you want me, Lord, all you have to do is ask. I'd

gladly trade the next several millennia for my soul."

The phone rang, nearly startling him out of his skin. He ignored it at first, but it continued to ring. Finally he picked it up. "Hello?"

"May I speak to Alex Danilov, please?"

Elizabeth. Her low, sweet voice flowed over him, through him. Achingly bittersweet. "Hello, Liz."

"Oh. I . . . didn't expect you to answer the phone."

"How are you?"

"Confused, Alex. Considerably." After a moment of silence, she said, "About last night . . . I went over everything we said and did, tried to recreate every word, every scene, trying to figure out what went wrong."

"Liz—"

"Something happened to me. I don't understand it, I don't even know what to call it. And that scares me. I've always been in control. When my ex-husband wooed me and wed me, I was in *control*. But last night I looked in your eyes, and it was like falling into a well. I need to know. . . ." She took a deep breath. "Am I wrong in thinking that you felt something, too?"

Lie. Lie now, and let her go. "No," he said, unable to obey. "You weren't wrong."

"Tell me," she whispered.

"Are the words necessary?"

"Yes."

He took a deep breath, feeling as though he were about to step off a cliff. "I fell in love with you. Instantly, like a raw kid, head over heels and fathoms deep."

"Love," she echoed. "Is that what it is, really?"

"Sometimes. Rarely, but sometimes."

She was silent for a while, and he knew she was assessing his statement. Comparing it with her own experience. "How did you know?" she finally asked.

"I looked into your soul. It . . . fits me, Elizabeth."

"Then what's the problem?"

"You were right when you challenged me," he said. "I was afraid. Am afraid."

"Of me?"

"*For* you. I have nothing to offer you except pain."

"What about your love?" Her voice caught a little on the last word, and he had to struggle to keep from comforting her.

"It won't be worth it, Liz. Not when the price is so high."

Her silence was rife with tears. But when she spoke again, her voice was calm. "You're not being fair. You've made decisions that affect me without giving me the benefit of knowing why. I refuse to accept that. If I'm to pay the price, then *I'm* the one who should decide if it's too high or not."

"You don't understand."

"Then *make* me understand."

"Liz . . ." He closed his eyes. If he obeyed her, he'd be laying his life in her hands. On the other hand, if she didn't value it, then perhaps his life wasn't worth much.

"All right," he said, ignoring the instincts that cried out for self-preservation, "I'll come to you. Leave your window open."

"My window?"

"If you want to understand."

"I hope your explanation makes more sense than this conversation."

"I promise you," he said. "It will be very clear."

He drove to Savannah and parked in one of the narrow side streets that intersected Jones Street. Old live oaks lined the avenue, laying thick shadows across the sidewalk. Alex walked into one of those bars of darkness; a white owl glided out the other side.

Elizabeth's window was a lemon-bright beacon in a darkened house. Alex perched on a branch outside her window to watch her silhouette cross the window, once, twice, again. Then he spread his wings and flew across the intervening space. His claws scraped on the windowsill as he landed.

She whirled, her eyes widening. He sidled along the wood, then hopped onto the back of a nearby chair.

"Shoo," Liz said, picking up a magazine from the nightstand and shaking it at him. "Go on, get back outside. You don't belong here, Mr. Owl."

Alex flapped down to the seat, changing as he did. A moment later he was his usual revenant self, composed, unruffled, and definitely unbirdlike.

"But I've been invited," he said.

Liz dropped the magazine. She stood staring at him, her eyes wide with astonishment. "*Alex?*"

"Do you understand now?"

"I . . . no."

"Let me show you again." He slipped into owl form again, gave her time to register it fully and completely, then resumed human form.

She groped behind her, found the bed, and sat down. "You're not . . . not . . ."

"I am not human." He tried to smile, but felt it twist. "I haven't been for a very, very long time."

"Then . . . what are you?"

"I prefer the term *revenant*. As a writer, you will know the meaning of that term."

"One who returns after a long absence," she whispered. "Or one who returns after death. I have an interest in folklore as well. *Revenant* is sometimes used as a synonym for *vampire*. A mythic being that originated in Slavic countries, if I remember correctly."

"Most persistent, for a myth. Do you remember any other details?"

"A . . . a revenant dislikes garlic—"

"Nonsense."

"Crosses—"

"Untrue."

"And can adopt the forms of animals. I think I read something about wolves being popular."

Alex shifted into the form of a great, silver wolf. Perhaps he wanted to see horror in her, to raise the primitive fear harbored in every human being, and to know finally that she couldn't accept him.

Liz didn't flinch from the beast. There was no horror in her eyes, just the glitter of tears. She came to him, going down on her knees before him. "Did you know," she said, laying her hand on the ruff of fur on his neck, "that your eyes are the same? And they're so sad, Alex. So very sad."

The simple generosity of her gesture awed him. He found himself crouched on all fours on the carpet, a man again. "You're not afraid of me?"

"No." She smiled. "You see, I looked into *your* soul, too. And I saw nothing frightening there."

"I have no soul. I lost it long ago, when I ceased to be a man."

She moved closer, taking his face between her hands and forcing him to look at her. "You're wrong, Alex. How could I feel this way if you were the soulless monster you say you are? Do you think I'm so blind that I couldn't tell the difference?"

All he had to do was reach out and take her in his arms.

He wanted to, so badly that he trembled. Instead he shifted to a sitting position to put some distance between them.

"I can't let you do this," he said.

"Why? Will I have to become a vampire?"

"No. Of all things to fear, that's the least. I've made many compromises because of what I am, but that isn't one of them."

"What compromises?" she asked.

He took a deep breath. "I live only at night; the hours of daylight are oblivion for me. I don't kill, but from time to time I have to . . . take sustenance. That necessity is unpleasant for me, but the biggest burden is the fact that I don't age, and I don't die. You, however, will. One day I'll have to leave you behind."

He watched her take it in, assimilate it, and understand it. "How many women have you loved?" she asked. "How many have you watched grow old?"

"One."

Her eyes widened. "Only one?"

"Only the illusion of love is easy to find, Liz. Real love, the kind that can surmount *my* kind of difficulties, comes around only rarely."

"When?" she whispered.

"I met Catherine in 1808. We built the Arbor, and with it, the family of Danilov. I had nearly forty years with her. When the time came to move on, I felt as though my heart had been torn out."

"Oh, Alex." Liz leaned forward. "Almost forty years? How wonderful!"

Almost of their own volition, his hands went out to grip her shoulders. "Wonderful?"

"To be loved like *that*, even for a day . . ." Her eyes unfocused, as though she were looking back through time.

Her words were so nearly the same as Catherine's that he had to close his eyes against the upwelling of memory. To find two such women, even in a life as long as his, was a miracle. Perhaps the only one he could expect.

She touched him. "Look at me, Alex."

The love in her eyes made him tremble. He spread his fingers out over her shoulders, feeling the warmth of her, the web of bone and tendon and flesh that made up humankind. So fragile a vessel to contain such courage.

"Did you regret loving Catherine?" she asked.

He shook his head.

"Did she?"

"No. Not for a moment."

"Then neither will I." Liz slid her hands around his neck. Her eyes promised things that made him tremble, things that made him reckless.

He pulled her into his arms. She met his kiss eagerly, honestly, holding nothing back. He crested on a tide of emotion, then sank deep, deep, deep.

Time ceased to exist. There was only Elizabeth. Her skin felt like silk against his, her heartbeat rushed through his veins like the sea. He became lost in the feel of her, the taste, the scent. She gave him everything and, in doing so, took possession of him. He was hers now. Beyond life. Beyond death.

Their breath entwined, their bodies, their souls. Loving her was like owning the day again, to walk in the sunlight instead of darkness. She burned like a flame in his arms, his mind, brighter than anything he'd ever known.

"Alex," she whispered against his mouth. "Something like this can't be bad. Could never be bad."

There was nothing of Blood-Hunger in him, no darkness. Tonight, he was only a man. "No," he said. "It can't be bad."

• • •

"John Smith" sat patiently on a bench in Forsyth Square, watching the house across the street. A Jaguar was parked at the curb outside, its sleek hide gleaming like quicksilver beneath the streetlight.

A brown-and-orange tabby cat stalked out from beneath a nearby bush. Smith sat very still, cloaking himself. But the cat sensed him anyway. Hair bristling, eyes glowing golden in the faint starlight, it growled long and low in its throat.

"Cats always know," he said. "No wonder they are favorite among witches' familiars. Come here, little warrior. Come here to Suldris."

The cat continued to growl. Suldris stretched his hand out to the animal. Slowly, its limbs moving in stiff-legged resistance, it moved toward him. When it was close enough, he reached down and picked it up.

"Afraid?" he asked as it spat at him.

He set the cat on his lap, ignoring the fully extended claws. As he resumed his watch of the house across the street, he stroked the animal's flattened ears, smoothing them further against the small skull. All the while, the cat growled.

"Yes," Suldris murmured. "Your kind always knows."

A door opened in the house, spilling a wash of light across the sidewalk outside. Rising, Suldris set the cat on the ground.

He started across the street as a man, a blond woman, and a boy came out of the house. Suldris's interest rose. The woman was unimportant; the boy, however, was another matter. Yes, indeed. The last Danilov.

The sorcerer increased his pace, calling, "Mr. Danilov!"

The man stopped and turned, his eyes becoming wary when he registered a stranger. "Yes?"

"I'd like to talk to you for a moment," Suldris said.

"What about?"

"Alex Danilov. It won't take long."

He watched the man's expression shift from wariness to suspicion to interest. Then Barron glanced over his shoulder at the woman and the boy and said, "Get in the car. I'm going for a walk for a couple of minutes." He turned back to Suldris. "Come on, Mister . . . ?"

"Smith. John Smith."

Suldris led his companion across the street and into the park, where the darkness lay as thick and hot as wool beneath the trees. He indicated the bench he had so recently vacated. "Have a seat, Mr. Danilov."

The man obeyed. His aquiline face was etched with knife-edged shadows, his soul with greed. Suldris smiled; an acquisitive lot, these Danilovs.

"What do you want, Mr. Smith?" Barron asked at last.

"I understand you have a little problem with Alex Danilov. I'd like to help."

Barron crossed his arms and leaned against the back of the bench. "How?"

"There is some evidence, I believe, that is hindering you in your efforts to prevent Alex from taking your company from you."

The man stiffened. "How do you know that?"

"A little birdie told me," Suldris said. Actually, he'd gotten it from Lydia's mind. Appallingly one-track, was Lydia, but an excellent tool that would soon become even better.

"Your 'birdie' has access to some very private information."

Suldris smiled. "What would happen if that evidence happened to disappear from Alex's hands?"

"Ah . . ." Barron drew in a sharp breath. "Is that something you could do?"

"I could."

With a muttered curse, Barron rose to his feet. "And I'm the Tooth Fairy. Good night, Mr. Smith."

"Don't make the mistake of underestimating Alex Danilov. He's a most dangerous man, with resources you can't hope to match. Without my help, you won't have a prayer against him."

"Prayer!" Barron's mouth curled into a sneer. "Last night I told him I'd sell my soul to the devil to be rid of him. Are you the devil, Mr. Smith?"

"Are Danilov Industries and the Arbor worth your soul?"

"Undoubtedly. Are you offering them in trade?"

"No." Suldris smiled. "I'm not dealing in dollars and cents or even in souls. Alex Danilov is my enemy. If helping you hurts him, then I'll help you. It's as simple as that."

Barron snorted. "Right."

"You should learn to trust hate, Mr. Danilov. Love and loyalty are fickle, kindness even more so. Only hate has the power to endure the passing of time or join men in a common cause."

Barron laughed, taking his seat on the bench again. "Most men trust money."

"Only those with too little." Suddenly tired of sparring with the man, Suldris said, "Do you want my help or don't you? If not, we're wasting our time here."

"Yes, I want it."

"A partnership in hate, then?" Suldris held out his hand.

Barron clasped it. "Done."

"A wise man. Getting the documents for you is only the beginning of our association. There are a number of areas in which I can be of service to you, and you to me."

"Whatever I have to do to get rid of that bastard, I'll do."

"Ah, a wise man." Triumph speared through Suldris. Two Danilovs in his net, bound to him by their own words. The trap was nearly complete.

"Alex's lawyer has the documents," Barron said. "Charles McGinnis. He'll probably have copies at his home and office, but I don't have his address—"

"I'll find him."

"I hope you're as good as you think you are," Barron said.

Suldris caught a slight edge of contempt in the man's voice. A true Danilov, this one; full of arrogance and the assumption of preeminence. He studied Barron's sharp, self-confident features, weighing the prospect of killing him here and now. But no, the man might prove useful.

"I'll be in touch," Suldris said, rising.

Barron reached out and gripped his forearm. "No one gets hurt, understand? This is a quick in-and-out job, just get the documents and leave. I don't want the police involved."

Suldris glanced down at the man's hand, then back up into his eyes. Barron let go.

"I'll contact you, Mr. Danilov."

"When?"

"When I'm ready." Suldris turned away.

"Hey, wait a minute!" Barron jumped to his feet. "Where can I reach you? I . . ." He stumbled, cursing as he caught himself. "What the hell is that?"

Suldris glanced down at the small bundle of brown-and-tabby fur. "I believe it's a cat," he said.

"A cat?" Barron prodded it with his foot, then drew back hastily. "Goddamn, it's dead!"

"Yes," Suldris murmured, "it is."

15

"Are you leaving?" Liz asked, blinking up at him sleepily as he pushed the covers aside and sat up.

"It's four A.M., love. Time that you got some sleep."

"When will I see you again?"

He leaned over her, propping his weight on braced arms. "Now that you know what I am, do you want to?"

"What are you saying?"

"I could . . . erase Alex Danilov from your memory. You could go on with your life. A *normal* life."

She shook her head. "Whatever you are, whatever I have to do for us to be together, I accept."

His throat tightened. Acceptance. Hope. A future he could bear. All these she had offered him. To be free of the lies, after all these years . . .

He looked down at her. She was beautiful as only a woman in love could be, her skin flushed, her eyes slumberous, her lips slightly swollen from his kisses. She was as different from Catherine as night from day, yet possessing the same ability to see something to love in him.

His breath went out in a long sigh. "You unman me."

"I don't think so," she murmured.

He glanced down, saw that his body was indeed giving

the lie to his words. "This ought to be impossible," he said. "For man or revenant."

"This whole night should have been impossible," she said. "Look, if you're trying to get out of this, don't tell me it's for my sake. If you want to go, go, but take responsibility for it."

"I'm trying to use my head, which tells me I can give you nothing but grief. For your sake, I should have the strength to stay away."

"Why do you insist on punishing yourself?"

That struck deep. Alex rolled to a sitting position, putting his back to her so that she couldn't see his face. "Perhaps because no one else can. I died, Elizabeth. Not in battle, as I should have, but foolishly."

"How?" she whispered.

"By my own hand. It was an impulsive act by an impulsive young man who had just lost everything he held dear. I regretted it instantly, but it was too late. So I died. And God turned His face from me." He tapped the center of his chest. "There is no soul in here, no salvation waiting at the end of my road. I'm already damned."

He felt the mattress give as she knelt behind him. A moment later her arms came around him, her body against his, and he nearly gasped with reaction.

"I don't believe that," she said, her voice trembling like her arms. "*My* God wouldn't be that cruel."

Breaking free of her embrace, he turned and took her by the shoulders. "Mine is."

"Alex—"

"I'm a vampire, Liz. Night dweller, drinker of blood. A monster."

"You feel like a man to me," she said.

Alex sighed. When he held her, *he* felt like a man, too.

Her words, so seemingly simple, took his world and turned it upside down. She forced him to make human choices, he who could never be human again. She forced him to take the risks of living.

It might be worth it. He might be denied the sun, but perhaps he could find his dawn in her eyes. Slowly, he pulled her against him. Warming himself in her love. Believing.

"Ahhh, Elizabeth, I can't fight you anymore."

"Good."

"Tomorrow, will you come to my home? More than anything else in the world, the Arbor is me. I leave for a time, but it always draws me back."

Smiling, she reached up to trace his lips with her fingertips. "I called Greg Barringer today to get all the gossip about the Danilovs."

"And?"

"Margaret was well liked, respected rather like a force of nature. Barron is not so well liked, but there aren't many who'd dare criticize him to his face. Sonya is rather *too* well liked by some."

"All male, I suppose," Alex said. "Lydia?"

"She's supposed to be gorgeous."

"She is."

"Rumor has it that she's after the new owner of Danilov Industries. Is that so, Alex?"

"Terrifyingly so."

"Did she catch you?"

"Once."

Her breath went out in a rush. "You don't pull any punches, do you?"

"Would you prefer that I lie?"

"No."

With a smile, he reached out to smooth the hair back

from her forehead. "Making love to Lydia was a mistake I can't justify, either to you or to her. I can only make sure it isn't repeated."

"Some women might be jealous."

"Are you?"

"Yes." Her smile was shaky, but genuine. "But your days are safe, and I intend to see that your nights are very busy. Seriously, though; what if your family objects to me? I *know* Lydia is going to hate my guts."

"The Danilovs aren't going to dislike you any more than they dislike one another," he said. "And their opinion isn't going to affect my decision or my actions. But it's different for you. What do you intend to do if your family dislikes me?"

"Alex, my father is an historian. With your knowledge of the past, you can do no wrong. Good Lord, if he knew you'd *lived* those times he studies . . . Believe me, he'll love you. And Mother will accept you because you make me happy. That's all she's ever wanted for me."

She pushed at his chest, and he let her tip him backward onto the bed. He pulled her down with him.

"Now tell me," she murmured. "Exactly how long does it take to get to the Arbor from here?"

"Twenty minutes. As the crow flies."

"Then you don't have to leave for a few minutes yet."

"No," he said. "Not just yet."

Heat lightning lanced across the sky as Lydia turned onto the drive of the old Trinity Church. The air was thick and hot even with the car's air-conditioning going full blast.

She parked the car and got out. Gravel crunched beneath her feet as she walked to the front door. Broken-out windows seemed to watch her, dark, hooded eyes too much like John Smith's for comfort.

Then why are you here? Even as her mind framed the thought it framed the answer: because John Smith was the only one who could give her what she wanted.

The door gaped open a few inches. She reached for it, her fingers wanting to recoil even as she forced them to touch the wood. It felt warm beneath her hand. As though it were alive.

Ridiculous! She pushed the door open and went inside. The sound of her footsteps skittered away on the stone floor to echo in the far reaches of the building.

"God, what a place!" she muttered.

"It has its advantages," John Smith said from behind her.

She whirled, masking her sudden fear. Or hoped she did. "I need to talk to you. About Alex."

"Yes?"

"I've been using the crystal like you showed me. Every night at dusk. But he's not . . . responding. I don't know why; I can *feel* that he wants me. Sometimes the house reeks of it."

His brows went up. "Only a foolish man would refuse such an offering."

"You've got to help me. I'm not tapping the crystal's full potential. You don't know how badly I—" Pride stopped her from finishing the sentence.

"How badly you want him?" Smith supplied. "Ah, but I do. Women always throw themselves at the men who don't want them. I'm sure you're only the latest of many who have wanted Alex Danilov."

She lifted her chin defiantly. "I'm not 'only' anything. He wants me. But he keeps fighting it, and I don't know why or how."

"He fights you precisely because he does want you,"

Smith said. "He can never accept what he is, and until he does, his power will be blunted."

"Power?" she asked. "What are you talking about?"

His eyes grew darker, deeper. They seemed to catch the faint light coming from the open door—caught it, pulled it in, and extinguished it.

"The man you know as Alex Danilov is not a man at all, Lydia. He is old, older than you would believe, and a vessel of great power. Your crystal taps directly into the source of that power."

Confused, Lydia grasped at the only part of the statement she could understand. "What do you mean he's not a man?"

"Haven't you noticed anything strange about him?"

She shook her head.

"I'll give you a hint, then," he said. "Have you ever seen him during the day?"

"Of cour—" Surprise bloomed in her mind. "No."

"And you never will."

"Why not?"

He smiled. "Because he can live only in the night. Haven't you wondered where you got that mark between your breasts?"

Reflexively, she crossed her arms over her chest. "How . . . how did you know about that?"

"That is how he gets his sustenance. Blood, Lydia. Just a small portion of your life to fuel his existence. He gave you pleasure in return, didn't he? Ah, yes, I see that memory in your eyes."

"What are you trying to tell me?" she whispered.

"Come now," he said. "What is it that can only live in darkness, and that needs no sustenance other than human blood?"

What. Not who. She shook her head. But realization hung in her mind like a fat black spider, too ugly to be looked at, too dangerous to be ignored. "I don't know what you're talking about."

"He's a vampire, Lydia," he said. "A very old and powerful one."

"There's no such thing as vampires."

Smith walked around her, forcing her to turn to keep facing him. The air suddenly seemed fetid and close.

"It's time that I told you what I know about him." He put his hands on her shoulders. "Alex Danilov was born in Kiev in 1012, the son of one of Prince Vladimir's knights. A knight himself, he served Vladimir's son."

Lydia didn't know who Vladimir was, but she could add, "You . . . you're telling me Alex is nearly a thousand years old?"

"Yes. A vampire does not age, does not die. Alex isn't your distant cousin; he's your ancestor."

"Ancestor? You mean . . ."

"He founded the American branch of the Danilovs in the early nineteenth century with a woman named Catherine duBrey. His blood runs through your veins—generations removed, but there. It is that tie that made it possible for you to reach him through the crystal."

Lydia barely registered his words. She was thinking of Alex. A vampire. She shouldn't believe it. But too much had happened for her *not* to believe. God, she thought, he's a thousand years old and doesn't look thirty. Eternal youth.

"Ah, Lydia!" Smith said. "Your face gives you away! You want this for yourself."

Yes, she wanted it. A month ago she'd been considering plastic surgery; today, she faced the reality of immortality. So she had to give up daylight hours. God knows she'd done most of her best living at night. A fair trade for living forever. For being beautiful forever.

"Alex will not give you this," Smith said. "Long ago he swore not to make more revenants of his blood. However"—he stroked her cheek lightly with his fingertips—"your crystal is attuned directly to his Blood-Hunger, the source of his power. With my help, you may be able to tap it deeply enough to induce him to bring you over."

Stars whirled in the blackness of his eyes. Lydia struggled to hold on to the thread of conversation. Her mind felt sluggish and numb. "How . . . do you know all this?"

"As I told you, I'm a student of all things arcane. And Alex Danilov definitely falls into that category. The moment I sensed what he was, I began looking into his past. It is well hidden, and only someone with my abilities could have traced him to his origin."

"You didn't want to help me," she said. "You used me to get to *him*."

"True." Cold spread from his fingers to her shoulders and downward, chilling her heart. "Just as you used me. We're two of a kind, Lydia. We take what we want, and damn the methods. But it's Alex himself who forced this. Such tremendous power, and he neither uses it nor wants it. He's a dreamer, an idealist—"

"I . . . called him a romantic," she said.

"Ah, yes. Love. An interesting concept, but useless in application." He smiled. "One thing you must remember about Alex Danilov—he hates what he is. And because he does, he will not give you your immortality, and he won't share his power with me. But if you use your crystal properly, we can both get what we want."

If it were true . . . Lydia's heartbeat throbbed in her ears. *Alex* could give her what she wanted. Once she had him and his immortality, she wouldn't need John Smith at all.

"What do you want me to do?" she asked.

"Bring me something of your nephew's. A lock of hair, some fingernail clippings, an article or two of favorite clothing—"

"Why?"

"To create a spell, my dear. Nothing inimical, just a bit of gentle coercion to nudge Alex in the direction we want him to go. Such a spell requires us to weave a web of those things closest to him. And what is closer than one's blood kin?"

She found herself nodding agreement and stopped the motion abruptly. "No, I can't. Justin's just a kid. He doesn't need to be involved in this."

"Scruples at this late date, Lydia?"

"You never said anything about Justin!"

"You will do it," he said.

"I'll do it." Answering him hadn't been a conscious act; he'd asked, and she'd assented. Panic rose, sour and choking. "No!" she cried. "I never meant to say that! You made me say it!"

"Are you breaking your vow to me?"

"Yes!"

"Did you think your oath of loyalty was only words?" he asked, his obsidian gaze seeming to bore straight into her brain. "Yes, I can see that you did, and that you thought you lied when you spoke them."

"No! I . . . didn't lie."

His smile turned sharp-edged. "Didn't you? It would be easier for both of us if you served me willingly. But serve me you will."

She wanted to protest, but the words wouldn't come. She wanted to run, but her body wouldn't move. He pulled her closer. The air seemed full of voices, chittering like frightened mice.

John Smith leaned close, his breath cold on her cheek, her neck. "I'm a fair master, Lydia. Serve me, and I'll see that you get all you desire. Death will not hold you. Age will not line that lovely skin or make your body sag. The reward for obedience is great. But so, too, is the punishment for disobedience. I think you should have a small taste of that. To remember."

His eyes were full of darkness. She fell into those twin black pits, her mouth open in a scream that had no sound.

16

"Oh, Alex!" Liz said as he made the turn onto the drive leading to the Arbor. "It's beautiful!"

"It was built to catch the moonlight," he said, parking the car just beyond the front walkway. "This is the only real home I've known since I left Kiev. Oh, I've owned many houses in many countries as I moved from life to life. But they were merely buildings, inhabited for a time and left behind without a thought."

She tilted her head back to look up at the graceful columns. "In all these years, only one place you could call home?"

"It was the woman, not the structure."

"I could be jealous of Catherine . . . what did you say her maiden name was?"

"DuBrey. I think you would have liked each other, actually." Had Catherine known he would meet this woman? Had she left him at last to free him to love Elizabeth? Perhaps. "Come," he said. "I want you to see my world, such as it is."

"The present crop of Danilovs included?"

"They're waiting with bated breath to meet you."

"Lydia, too?"

"I haven't seen or spoken to Lydia," he said. "She's out somewhere now, but I'm sure she'll turn up sometime this evening."

"So I'm going to be a surprise for her."

"Yes."

Liz turned to look at him fully. "There's a streak of cruelty in you I hadn't noticed before. Is it the revenant part, or just Alex?"

"How can I know? They're one and the same," he said, accepting the charge. "But both are willing to use a bit of cruelty in the hope of not finding Lydia naked in my bed again. Talking to her was useless."

"Oh." Liz drew in her breath sharply. "You know, I'm suddenly feeling rather cruel myself. It must be a human thing."

"Must be," he agreed, smiling.

He led her up the steps and into the house. She spun in a slow circle in the foyer, and the light from the chandelier picked out the lighter strands in her hair and gilded her ivory dress.

"Such luxury," she murmured. "I'm intimidated already."

"Don't be," he said. "It pales against the gold of your eyes."

"Flatterer."

"Merely a man in love."

Hearing a door open upstairs, he resisted the urge to take her into his arms. A moment later Sonya appeared at the top of the stairs.

"Well, hello," she said, coming down toward them. The hem of her dress belled out around her legs in a cloud of aqua chiffon. "You must be Elizabeth. I'm Sonya, Barron's wife." She turned to Alex. "With the dining room gutted, we've moved family operations—meals included—into the living room. Barron's there now."

"What happened to the dining room?" Liz asked.

"Didn't Alex tell you? Men!" Sonya shook her head. "We had a tree come flying into the dining room during the storm the other night."

"Storm? What storm?" Liz asked.

Alex raised his brows. "It didn't rain in town?"

"No."

"How odd," Sonya said, without any curiosity in her voice at all. "The living room is this way." She moved ahead of them, her dress mimicking her languid movements. "Alex saved our lives that night, by the way. If it weren't for him, we would have been squashed flat. I swear, I've never seen a man move so fast."

"Adrenaline," Alex murmured.

Liz smiled, that same arch, knowing smile Margaret had given him so many, many times over the years. His heart ached with something that might have been regret, or perhaps joy. He smiled back, taking her hand and tucking it into the crook of his arm.

"We're all . . ." Sonya began. Alex looked up to find her staring at him over her shoulder, a very odd look on her face. Then she seemed to give herself a mental shake. "We're all very grateful to Alex for what he did," she said, the brittle tone returning to her voice. "And we're all trying to find an appropriate way to show our gratitude."

"Especially Lydia," Liz said, sotto voce.

"Barron, especially, is very grateful," Sonya continued. "After all, Alex saved his whole world for him—his son and heir, his wife, and his sister—all in one fell swoop." Her smile was too wide for a woman with such bitterness in her eyes. "Here we are."

Alex remembered this space as two smaller rooms;

Catherine's sewing room and a sitting room. The connecting wall had been knocked out sometime in the late nineteenth century, if he remembered correctly, and this room had been born. Modern times had equipped it with a television, stereo, VCR, and attendant conveniences. Alex felt quite alien here.

Barron and Justin occupied opposite ends of the room. The man stood staring out the window, too engrossed in the scene outside; the boy watching TV, too engrossed in a dishwashing-soap commercial. Resentment divided the room into two separate territories.

Another argument, Alex thought, instinctively moving toward the boy.

"Turn the TV off, Justin," Barron said. "We have guests." He came forward, hands extended. "You must be Liz Garry. Alex told us he was bringing you tonight. I'm Barron. This is my son, Justin, and you've already met my wife."

"Yes, I have." Liz leaned around him to wave at Justin. "Hi, Justin. Great shirt."

The boy glanced down at his Grateful Dead T-shirt.

"Thanks. Do you like the Dead?"

"Sure." Liz's smile was pure mischief. Alex had to turn away to keep from laughing.

He led her to a chair in Justin's side of the room, then perched on the arm beside her. A casual, yet supportive we-are-together gesture. He noticed that Sonya, interestingly enough, had chosen a seat in Barron's territory.

"Well, Liz, tell us about yourself. Is your family from Savannah originally?" Barron asked.

"Mom is. She was a Cavanaugh before she became a Garry, but moved away when she was in her teens. It was pure coincidence that my father happened to take a professorship at the university here."

Barron smiled. "So your mother is a Cavanaugh, your father a professor of . . ."

"Medieval history."

"Ah. And what do you do?"

"I write historical textbooks."

"Very interesting. You draw on your father's knowledge, then."

The line of Liz's jaw firmed. "Actually, my specialty is nineteenth-century American history. Dad's expertise lies several hundred years before that."

Barron nodded, apparently unaware of the insult he'd given her. Almost, Alex was amused.

"Barron, stop fishing for information and get the girl a drink," Sonya said. "And while you're at it, get me one, too."

"I'll have a soda, thanks," Liz said.

"Nothing else?" Barron's eyes hardened as he glanced at Sonya. "My wife, for instance, heartily recommends the scotch."

"No, thank you," Liz said, her demeanor as coolly polite as a queen's come to visit the rabble.

Barron turned toward the cart that served as a portable bar. The phone rang, and he changed course to answer it. "Hello? Oh, yes, Mr. McGinnis, he's right here. Just a moment." He held the receiver out to Alex. "It's for you."

There was an odd mixture of speculation and triumph in his eyes. Alex took the phone from him, wondering at that, and said, "Hello, Charles."

"I know you can't talk openly," the lawyer said. "But we've got a problem you need to know about."

"Yes?"

"Remember the evidence I had showing Barron's theft from Danilov Industries? Well, it's gone. A nice, slick job, done I don't know when; I only discovered the theft by accident."

Alex glanced up at Barron, saw that he was watching. "That's very interesting. Has anything been done about it?"

"Not that I know of. I notice you didn't ask *who* arranged this."

"No, I didn't."

"Without that evidence hanging over his head, Barron's going to take steps to contest the will. We need to talk about it, but now I'm not sure *any* phone in that house is secure."

"I agree. Why don't we get together tomorrow night about ten o'clock?"

"Do you mind coming to the house?"

"Not at all." Alex glanced at Liz. Perceptive creature that she was, she was trying to intercept Barron's attention. To no avail. "I have other business in town."

"Okay. Dust off your thinking cap; this is going to get interesting before it's over."

"I agree," Alex said. "See you tomorrow."

Thrust and counterthrust, he thought. He'd underestimated Barron, both his abilities and his lack of scruples. By damn, it *was* a race.

"Is something the matter?" Barron asked.

Alex turned around, smiling in pure, unholy joy. "Not at all. Should there be?"

"Ah . . . no." Barron was obviously taken aback by the smile. "It's just that when a man's lawyer calls him at night, it isn't usually with good news."

"In a life as uneventful as mine, any news is good news."

"Some men might call almost being crushed by a tree an event," Sonya said.

Alex smiled. "That's the past. It's the prospect of an

uneventful future that weighs on a man." He went to Elizabeth and bowed like a courtier. "Would you like a walk in the garden, my lady? It's too beautiful a night to spend it indoors."

She rose and placed her hand on his proffered arm, that old-fashioned gesture that had so moved him the first night they'd met. Just as then, it seemed right in this time and setting.

"Anyone care to join us?" Alex asked.

Sonya shuddered. "No thanks. It must be ninety-five out there."

"I will." Justin unfolded himself from his seat.

"Don't be ridiculous," Sonya protested. "They want to be alone."

"Come on, Justin," Alex said.

As soon as they were out of earshot of the living room, the boy said, "Thanks, Alex," and headed upstairs.

"I thought he wanted to go outside," Liz said.

Alex smiled. "He just wanted out of that room."

"He's not the only one. Alex, that man hates you."

"He's not the first; nor the last, I expect."

"It doesn't bother you?"

He shrugged. "I'll either outmaneuver him or outlive him; either way, he can only affect my life briefly. On another level, I begrudge him even that because I want nothing more than to live here in peace with you."

"You're not a peaceful man," she said.

"No," he replied, closing his eyes briefly. "I am not. But I'd like to try. And as long as this situation exists in this house—"

"Meaning, as long as they live here."

"Yes. And I gave them my word to let them stay. But I'm already tired of sneaking in your window like a thief. I want you openly, Liz. As my wife, before God, and before the world."

"Till death do us part?" she asked.

"Is that acceptance?"

"Yes."

"Once, it was customary for a man to offer his lady a betrothal gift," Alex said, taking a black velvet bag out of his pocket and offering it to her.

She looked at him questioningly for a moment, then opened it. Inside was a medallion, embossed with a griffin with a fierce ruby eye. It clutched a pearl in its claws, possessive as the Danilov clan itself.

"Alex—"

"This is the only thing I brought from Kiev with me, all those years ago," he said. "It was given to me by my father, who got it in turn from his father. It was crafted in Byzantium by a goldsmith named Alsarad, whose talent made him a legend in those times. I want you to have it." He drew a deep breath. "Even Catherine didn't know of this. I . . . wanted you to have something of me no one has had before."

Her fingers trembled as she traced the griffin's contours. "I accept your gift."

He knew it wasn't the medallion she meant. Smiling, he raised her hand to his lips. "We'd better see about buying a house in town. You find what you want, and I'll have Charles McGinnis take care of the rest."

She drew her breath in with a gasp, then laughed. "Alex, you're something else. Lord of the manor, born and bred. No price limits, no qualifications at all. Just find what you like and buy it?"

"I've been rich for a very long time," he said. "Even a bad businessman can't help but turn a profit on funds invested for several hundred years." He opened the French doors and stepped back to let her precede him into the garden.

The night was pure magic. A sultry, druggingly scented breeze tossed the branches of the mimosa, sending shadows darting like dragonflies through the garden. The distant water of the marsh was bejeweled with moonlight, the stillness of the scene broken only by the brief, iridescent flash of a leaping fish.

"You love it, don't you?" Liz asked.

"Yes." He swept his hand in a wide arc. "Wildwood Marsh. It's alive, you know. Lives, breathes, eats, replenishes itself, albeit at rhythms too slow for man to understand. Vast. Older than time. It accepted me, made me part of it. Something of me dwells in its heart. Do you feel it, Liz?"

"Yes." Her voice was a whisper.

The first time he'd come here, he'd looked out over the marsh and knew this was the one spot on this earth that could hold him. Here, he'd build his house and family. Two hundred years, and so many lives later, it looked the same, smelled the same. He felt paper thin, as though he'd been stretched too far between past and present.

"Tell me what it was like," Liz murmured. "When it was new."

She'd touched his mood perfectly, perfectly. He didn't need to close his eyes to remember the past; it was all around him, the world he'd created.

"We were closer to the world then," he said. "In summer, the windows were open to the breeze, and the house was full of the scent of camellias and honeysuckles. The cicadas' song filled the night. Crickets, too, and sometimes the bellow of an alligator would echo over the marsh. Beautiful. Best of all, however, was when Sallee was in a good mood.

Her voice carried all the way from the kitchen, and it was like an angel singing."

"Sallee?"

"The cook. I bought her at auction, freed her, and hired her to work for me. She made the softest, most fragrant biscuits known to man." He glanced at Liz, saw the question in her eyes. "No, I didn't eat them; but the smell . . . Ah, heaven!"

He smiled. "A most excellent bodyguard as well, my Sallee. Six feet tall, broad as that door, and fiercely loyal. One day she caught a man pilfering the silver sauceboat and took out after him with the cleaver. He screamed all the way down the drive."

"You miss it, don't you?" she asked.

"Ah, love, I'm sorry. I've been told many, many times about this habit I have of being maudlin." He skimmed his fingers from her shoulder to her wrist, then took her hand in his. "On a night like this, I admit I miss the happy times I was given. Now, however, I find the present much more interesting."

"Even the new crop of Danilovs?"

"Ah, there you've touched a sore spot." He led her toward the far end of the garden, where human cultivation gave way to the wilder growth of the marsh's border. "Every man hopes that his children will be successful, and their children after them. I gave this family a good start; wealth, love, education, and the drive to do something useful with their lives. To see it all come to this . . ." He shook his head.

"And then there's Justin. You love the boy, Alex."

"Yes," he said. "There's Justin. He's what I meant the Danilovs to be; if it weren't for him, I think I'd walk away from it all. But selfishly, I want to leave something of myself with him."

She stopped, turned to face him. "Alex, most men leave descendants as their mark on the world; if a man has children to carry his name, he will never truly die. Your situation is much different."

"Yes," he agreed. "I try to leave my mark here because I pretend, even to myself, that I'm alive. That I *matter*. And like most conceits, life has a way of puncturing it."

"You're an idiot, you know that?" But her smile was soft and warm, wrapping him up and pulling him close.

"So I've been told many times."

"Stop thinking so much," she said, sliding her hands around his neck.

He pulled her close, hands, mind, and heart moving in perfect synchronization. "Aren't you afraid of what we've begun?" he whispered against her mouth.

"No."

His world faded into a dark amber sea, where there was only Elizabeth. The scent of her skin eclipsed the fragrance of the garden, the beating of her heart overwhelmed the frantic night sounds of the marsh. Holding her, he came to rest even as he was set adrift on the currents of a new future.

A sound intruded. A small sound, but powerful in its anguish. Elizabeth pulled away from him at the same moment he heard it.

Lydia stood a few feet away, her hair lifting in a fiery banner upon the breeze. Her skin seemed to collect the moonlight and cast it back with a milky glow. He'd never seen her look more beautiful. Then he saw her eyes. They were dark with . . . not anger or hurt or any of the emotions he might have expected, but panic.

"Hello, Lydia," he said. He turned toward her, keeping Liz's hand in his. "I want you to meet—"

"Elizabeth Garry," Lydia said.

"Hello, Lydia." Liz stepped forward, her hand extended. "I've heard a lot about you."

Lydia's gaze didn't leave Alex. "Now that really surprises me."

"Alex is nothing if not honest," Liz said.

This time Lydia looked at her. "You're right about that."

"I wanted you to meet Elizabeth," Alex said. "I wanted you to understand."

"Oh, I understand." Lydia pressed her fists against her chest as though she were having trouble breathing. "What's the matter with you, Alex? She's not even *pretty!*"

He slid his arm around Liz's waist, a gesture of deliberate tenderness and possession. "You didn't look close enough," he said softly.

"You're a fool," she spat. "When you could have had—" She broke off abruptly, her lips trembling. For a moment she stood glaring at him, then whirled and stalked toward the house.

"Well," Liz murmured. "*That* went well."

"I'm sorry if you were uncomfortable."

"If she'd been nice, I would have been uncomfortable." Anger sparked in her eyes. "As it is, I just want you to take me home."

"Will your window be open?"

She reached up to lay her hand against his cheek. "My window will always be open."

Lydia stood before her window, watching Alex and Elizabeth Garry. They were silhouetted against the moonlight, their bodies melded as one. Even at this distance, Alex's tenderness toward her was visible in the lines of his body, the way his head tilted as he kissed her.

With a stifled sob, Lydia pressed her hand to her mouth, then jerked the curtains closed. She turned away, catching sight of her reflection in the mirror as she did. Lipstick looked like smeared blood across her lips. She dragged the back of her hand across her mouth. Savagely hurting herself.

"You're the one who doesn't understand, Alex," she sobbed. "He sucked me in. Way, way in, and you're my only way out."

The crystal at her throat burned with a light of its own. Its radiance was dark and heavy, a deeper red than that called pigeon's blood. She put her hand over it, but it shone through flesh and bone as though it had more substance than she.

Maybe it had. John Smith's lesson in obedience had hurt something in her. Call it self-confidence, call it her psyche or her soul, he'd damaged it. Maybe it wouldn't hurt so much if he'd taken it completely; but he'd left her the pieces, and she didn't know how to put it back together.

It had changed her. She was no longer limited to sight and sound, touch and taste and smell. Now she could feel Alex's power. It permeated this house and grounds, stretching even into the marsh. Power. Vast, brooding, tinged with sadness and desperation.

John Smith had his own brand of power, dark and malevolent. Shame stained her cheeks red at the memory of his punishment. He'd ordered her to strip, and she had. He'd ordered her to kneel at his feet, and she had. He'd ordered her to beg for his touch, and she had. His touch . . . Her skin crawled, flesh memory of pain and violation and gut-clenching disgust.

She leaned close to the mirror, stretching her chin upward so she could see the tiny bruise at the base of her neck. Such a small wound to show for what he'd taken from her. He'd offered her immortality. But who wanted to live forever as a slave to *that*?

"Alex," she whispered. "If it were you, I'd beg for it."

And Alex was out there kissing another woman. Lydia would have shared him. But there had been no interest at all in those beautiful pale eyes of his. Alex Danilov, the romantic, was in love.

How had it happened? What was it about Elizabeth Garry that caught and held a man like that? Lydia stared into the mirror, wanting an answer. But her reflection merely stared back at her, as uncomprehending as she. She had everything she'd ever wanted. Youth. Beauty. Sensuality so hot that Alex had trembled when he'd touched her. She'd sold her soul to the devil called John Smith for them. And they weren't enough. *They weren't enough.*

She slipped the crystal up and over her head and cupped it in her hands. Pure power, it sang in her flesh, resonated along her nerves. It was her link with Alex, and also to *him*. One and the other, her experience with both wrapped in this ghost stone. But *he* either couldn't or wouldn't touch Alex. No, he needed her for that.

He'd said the crystal was tied directly to Alex's Blood-Hunger. Lydia shuddered, remembering the creamy greed in Smith's eyes as he'd sucked a piece of her life from her. It was a powerful force, that greed, and in her experience, greed was always stronger than love.

Whatever it took, whatever the price, she had to try. Alex was the only haven from the hell Smith offered.

Humming in counterpoint to the crystal, she sank cross-legged to the floor. The stone seemed to beat with her pulse, drawing her in, enveloping her in a red-tinged whirlwind. Alex's Blood-Hunger. Her way out. She drifted upward on the whirlwind, seeking the lightning.

Alex!

Crystal fire thrummed in her blood. As though in answer, lightning etched the clouds around her. She reached out. It ran along her arms like pure sensuality, delved deep inside her to turn her brain to flame. This she could understand.

Love Elizabeth Garry all you want. This part of you is mine, and I intend to keep it.

Something tugged at her, pulling her away from the lightning with a wrench that sent her spinning into the depths of the vortex. Far below, so far that it was only a pinpoint, was a place so dark it hurt the eyes. It held terror and despair, a malevolent hatred that stank like burned flesh.

It pulled her down.

Alex, help me!

She screamed it with mouth and brain and the shattered remnants of her soul. There was no answer.

The dark place grew larger as she spun downward. Finally, it encompassed all her vision, a vast, yawning abyss waiting to gobble her up. Shrieking, she fell into it. It was cold, cold as John Smith's eyes. The air was full of voices. Cries of pain, of despair, of longing, pitiful and pitiless at the same time. She knew what they were: souls of the damned. Strange, she'd always thought hell was supposed to be hot.

The voices called to her. It was both a plea for help and an invitation to join their ranks.

Never!

Smith . . . her master . . . vampire or demon or whatever he was . . . He wasn't going to keep her.

Closing her eyes, she imagined the lightning, what it looked like, how it felt. The voices faded into the hum of crystal song. She lost all sense of time and direction;

maybe neither existed here. Suddenly the air around her thickened, as though it had turned to gelatin. It cushioned her; her fall slowed, then stopped. . . .

She closed her eyes against a sudden, blinding light. After giving herself a few seconds to adjust, she opened them again. To her astonishment, she found herself standing in Justin's room. It was typically teenager messy, clothes strewn on the floor, CDs and cassettes everywhere, the bedspread awash with magazines. A desk hugged the far wall, piled high with tools and pieces of electronic equipment. Rock stars stared back at her from glossy posters as if wondering what the hell she was doing there. So was she.

She glanced down, shock rocketing through her when she saw that she was holding Justin's hairbrush. Even as she realized it her free hand moved, reaching up to pluck the dark hair from the bristles. Like a puppet on a string, dancing to Smith's orders. Tendons stood out in her arms as she struggled against the movement.

Not Justin, she thought, breathing hard from the effort of not moving her hand. She'd always liked the kid.

But if she didn't . . . He'll punish me, she thought. He'll do *that* again. Or something worse. The fine hairs at the back of her neck lifted in involuntary reaction.

Reaching up, she stripped the hair from the brush and thrust it into her pocket.

One part of her mind seemed to stand back in horror of what she'd done; another part, however, got decisions made and put her feet into motion. She slipped downstairs to the living room.

Barron and Sonya were gone, probably their separate ways. Lydia saw that the small ivory clutch purse she'd noticed before was still lying on the floor beside the armchair. It had to be Elizabeth's; the cheap ivory leather matched the woman's cheap ivory dress.

Inside, Lydia found a thin wallet with nothing but a driver's license and a few dollars in it. But there was also a silver pen inscribed with the initials E.M.G. and a hairbrush in which a few strands of tawny hair were caught. Lydia took the pen and the hair and put them in her pocket.

"Catch as catch can," she said.

A few moments later she headed the Corvette onto the drive, so fast that gravel spewed out from beneath the wheels.

17

Suldris ran his hand down the sweep of Lydia's bright hair. She trembled beneath his touch, and he tasted the sharp rise of her fear.

"I did what you wanted," she said. "Let me go now."

"Let you go?" He raised his eyebrows. "Very well, you may go home."

"That's not what I meant."

"I thought not. You want me to release you from your vow."

Tears glittered in her eyes. "Please. I . . . beg you."

"Ah, Lydia, this isn't the sort of bargain you keep when it's convenient and leave when it is not."

"If Alex—" She broke off, her eyes going wide with panic.

"Alex won't know," he said. "And you are incapable of telling him, no matter how much you want to. Try, if you don't believe me."

He noticed that she was wearing a slim gold chain around her neck. The pendant, however, lay hidden beneath her blouse. He reached out and pulled the necklace free. It wasn't her crystal, as he expected, but a crucifix.

"This isn't your style," he said. "Too plain." Shock came

into her eyes, and he couldn't help but laugh. "I don't fault your reasoning, just your taste. You watch too much television, Lydia. This"—he closed his fingers around the cross— "won't work."

"You admit it," she whispered. "You admit what you are."

"Of course. Unlike Alex, I have no illusions of humanity." He let the crucifix fall. The beams of the cross were twisted now, a parody of what they'd once represented. "And unlike Alex, I have no illusions that this God is any more real than all the other gods mankind has created to keep the dark at bay."

The tears spilled over and ran down her face in twin crystal streams. "What . . . more do you want from me?"

"Obedience," he said. "But that I shall have whether you want to give it or not. I *own* you, body and soul."

She shook her head, still daring defiance.

"There's a woman in the other room," he said. "Bring her to me."

He saw horror mingle with the fear in her eyes as her body obeyed him. Good, he thought. It was time she realized what had happened to her. Smiling, he watched her walk into the other room, moving stiffly and awkwardly as she fought his control over her limbs. She reappeared a moment later, pulling his latest prostitute after her. This one was little more than a girl despite the heavy makeup, and he looked forward to her with much anticipation. Youth was always an added savor.

The whore wrenched free of Lydia's hold. "Leave me alone!" she shrieked, running for the door.

Suldris gestured sharply with his right hand, and the door slammed shut. The sound of it echoed dully in the recesses of the church.

"No!" the girl sobbed. Her absurdly high-heeled shoes scraped on the marble floor as she tried vainly to force the door open.

He walked toward her. She whirled, putting her back against the door, and stared at him with wide, frightened eyes. Then she bolted to one side, her bare legs flashing in the dim light. He followed, slowly, deliberately, pushing her terror to delicious heights. She ran from one side of the chamber to the other, her breath coming in gulping sobs.

"There's nowhere to hide," he said.

She ran to Lydia. "Please, don't let him touch me," she panted. "Help me, help me . . . oh, God, please!"

Lydia's chest rose and fell in a ragged rhythm. She looked up at Suldris, who smiled. With her gaze still locked with his, she peeled the girl's clinging hands away from her shirt and thrust her away.

Suldris had tired of the chase; his Blood-Hunger had been roused to a fever pitch by the prostitute's fear and the exquisite pleasure of the game. As the girl turned to run again he crooked his finger, stopping her. She started to scream, and he stopped that as well.

"Come, my sweet," he said.

Mute, her eyes wild with terror, she took a step toward him, then another, wobbling on her stiletto heels. He opened his arms to welcome her. She was a tiny thing. Even with the heels, her head barely came up to his collarbone. Grasping her by the upper arms, he lifted her so that their eyes were on a level.

And then he sucked her dry, draining her life force like a draft from a cup. It flowed into him, gibbering, to join the myriad others who had fed his power. The husk of what she had been hung limply between his hands, curiously weightless now that the soul had left it. Blood stained his hands, his forearms, and the front of his shirt, and his mouth and chin ran warm with it. He tossed the corpse aside. He'd been right; this one had had particular savor, and his power coursed high on what he'd taken from her.

Dirt grated beneath his shoes as he turned to look at Lydia. She backed away from him, one hand pressed to her mouth, the other stretched out before her as though to keep him away. He followed, backing her against the altar.

She whimpered. Gently, he lifted a lock of her marvelous hair. Blood from his hands stained it, and he lifted it to his mouth to lick the strands clean. Her fear beat through him, sweet, sensual, beckoning.

"You see, Lydia," he murmured, "it's much better to be a slave than the prey, isn't it?"

She nodded.

"Let me hear you say it," he said.

"It's much better to be a slave than . . . than prey," she repeated. Her breath came fast and harsh, as though she'd been running.

"Very good. You may go home now. Remember what you learned this night."

Her eyes widened, as though she was surprised that he didn't kill her, too.

"You're not afraid of me, are you?" he asked softly. Teasing her because he knew her terror.

"You . . . killed her."

"That?" He didn't bother looking at the girl's corpse. "If you want to become one of us, you'll have to get used to such things. A vampire's true power comes not from the blood, but from the life force. Eternal life, Lydia. Eternal youth. Think about it; surely they are worth the price of a few already damned souls."

Greed mingled with the fear in her eyes. He smiled,

knowing that she didn't care about the whore, only that she might share the girl's fate. Truly, Lydia was perfect for the revenant's role. Much more so than Alexi.

"Go home," he said, releasing her hair.

She hurried away. A moment later he heard the roar of her car's engine as she sped down the road.

He turned back to examine the things she'd brought him. A clever girl, Lydia. Or rather, he thought, a jealous one. He lifted the strands of tawny hair up to the light, admiring the play of color. Alex Danilov's lover. This Elizabeth must be special indeed.

He laid the rest of his acquisitions in a row upon the cool stone. The silver pen, the gold-shot hair, the darker hair belonging to the boy, the documents that would free Barron Danilov from his earthly prison but create one of another kind. Lydia he already owned. With them, he'd create a spell. A powerful spell, woven with the essence of Alex's descendants and his love for the mortal woman. Blood ties.

Brother, sister, son—his enemy's direct descendants. The wife-to-be—bearer of the next Danilov line. Everything in this world Alex Danilov held dear. Suldris had to close his eyes against the exultation. Four hundred years. All the pain he'd suffered . . . Now came the time to collect.

"You will suffer as you made me suffer, my old enemy," he said. "I will take it all from you, just as you took my realm, my life, and my power. Not until then will I kill you."

He found the whore's tawdry little purse and upended it. Tubes and pots and small plastic cases—makeup, the tools of her trade—tumbled out onto the floor. Among them was a scattering of coins and a few dollar bills. Suldris stooped and picked up a quarter.

He walked down the road to a green-and-white convenience store. His lip lifted. Had someone dared to build such a thing in *his* realm, he'd have had it burned to the ground. But it did offer what he needed: a telephone.

He dialed Barron Danilov's number. It rang four times, five times, six.

"Hello?" Sleep blurred Barron's voice.

"This is John Smith."

"Yeah?" The blurriness vanished. "You got it, didn't you? Alex got a call from his lawyer tonight, and it was obvious he'd gotten a nasty surprise."

"I told you I could get the evidence."

"That's great. Bring it over now, will you?"

Suldris smiled. "I am not a delivery boy, Barron. Tomorrow night, meet me at the old True Faith Church near Delano. Do you know where that is?"

"Yes, I know where it is. But why—"

"Because I'm busy tonight. If you want the documents, come to the church tomorrow. If not, I'll see if it can be of use to someone else."

There was a moment of silence, then Barron said, "Are you threatening me?"

"Tomorrow, just after sunset," Suldris said.

He hung up on Barron's protest. A most annoying man, he thought, and dishonest in the bargain. There would be little satisfaction in settling with him.

The night's feeding still coursed through him. He felt young and strong, stronger than he'd ever been before.

Strong enough to take Alexi Danilovich at last.

Alex accepted the glass of wine Charles McGinnis held out, then settled back in his chair. The lawyer's study was like the rest of the house; comfortable, cluttered, furnished with antiques that had been used and not just admired.

Charles sank into the opposite chair and balanced his coffee mug on the upholstered arm. "Sorry about the mess. Meg was the organized one. When she died two years ago, I sort of fell into my old bachelor ways."

"Your wife?"

"Yes." The lawyer propped his elbows on the arm of his chair, placing the mug in peril. "She died of cancer."

"I'm sorry," Alex said. "I know what it's like to lose someone you care for."

"Thanks. Then you know you get over it, after a while."

Alex didn't answer; it was obvious that Charles's "*after a while*" hadn't occurred yet. As for himself, losing Catherine had left an empty spot in his heart that nothing could fill. Liz didn't replace her. She was a new love, and would leave a second empty place when she was gone.

Charles was the first to break the silence. "Let's talk about Danilov Industries."

"First tell me about the theft."

"Thefts, if you please. I had two sets of evidence. One was at the office in a locked file cabinet. The other was here at home in my wall safe. There was no sign of forced entry at either place, and the security systems were intact and operational. And both the cabinet and safe were locked the next morning."

Alex blinked in surprise. "They were?"

"Everything pertaining to Danilov or Danilov Industries has been wiped from my computer files, and I mean everything. It's going to take me months to track down all that material again."

"A very thorough job," Alex said, still wondering about that locked file cabinet. "How long has your secretary worked for you?"

"Twelve years. Even if someone bribed her—and I resist that notion—she couldn't have gotten to the safe here. I'm the only one who had access to both."

"Yes," Alex said.

He rose to his feet. Placing his palms on the armrests of the lawyer's chair, he leaned close. The man froze in midblink. Alex delved deep into his mind, searching for falsehood. But Charles was nothing other than what he seemed, a man of talent, integrity, and resourcefulness. A man outraged that his security had been violated.

And now his mind, Alex thought. "I'm sorry, Charles," he murmured, straightening. "But I had to know. Please disregard my intrusion."

He returned to his seat before releasing the man. Charles continued his blink, then straightened abruptly like a boy caught napping in class. "I'm sorry, Alex, did you say something?"

"We were talking about the burglary."

"Oh, yes. I . . . lost track for a moment. It was like a ghost walked in and took those documents. I know there are people good enough to circumvent security systems, but why would anyone lock the file cabinet and safe back up?"

Alex nodded. "I would think Barron would want us to know the evidence was gone. Just to gloat."

"He's not exactly known for his subtlety," Charles said. "You know, I wouldn't have pegged him as having the balls to try something like this."

"He's full of surprises, is Barron," Alex said. "Several nights ago three men waylaid me here in town. Don't look so shocked, Charles. I managed to get away unharmed."

"Why didn't you tell me?" the lawyer yelped.

"Tell you what? That I was attacked, and that I suspected Barron of arranging it because he was surprised to see me when I returned home? Besides, I thought I'd taken care of the problem." Then he laughed, more at his own blindness than at the situation. "My father had a favorite saying, Charles. It goes, only a fool would cut off the viper's tongue and leave the fangs. And that's just what I did."

Charles took a gulp of his coffee, grimaced, and set it aside. "Well, here's the way I see the game developing. First, Barron will contest the will. We counter, of course. Neither you nor Barron will be able to sell your stock until the issue is settled, but that's not a problem for you. The real fight will be over who's going to administer Danilov Industries until it is."

"The object is for us to get our man into the position while Barron maneuvers to get his?"

"Precisely."

"Do you have anyone in mind?"

"Two. Both are honest men, and strong enough to tell Barron, or you, for that matter, to go to hell. He'll have his own candidates, and they'll be outwardly as impartial as ours."

Alex smiled. "Things were easier in earlier times. A couple of hundred years ago, I could challenge Barron to a duel. Pistols at ten paces, and winner take all."

"It does sound like a lot less trouble," Charles agreed. "What do you think he's expecting you to do?"

"Try to steal it back."

"Would you?"

"I am not a thief."

"Chivalry, at the cost of Danilov Industries?"

With a sigh, Alex leaned back against the chair. "Last night I had an interesting discussion with a man. He's an historian, who I think, lives more in medieval times than in these. He believes that mankind lost something important when we came to rely on the courts instead of our strong right arms. He said this has taken our accountability away; a man's honor is now defined more as what he can get away with legally, not as a code of conduct. Perhaps he's right. But some of us haven't left honor behind."

"Honor can be a costly way of life."

"There are worse ways of living," Alex said. "And dying."

Charles leaned forward and held out his hand. "I'm glad you feel that way. Margaret was one of the most honorable people I ever met, and I admired her for it. She said I would like you."

Alex clasped the proffered hand, warmed by the emotion in the man's eyes. "Did she say anything else about me?"

"She wanted me to help you. I agreed to do so for her sake, but she told me I'd come to want to do it for yours. She also said there was something about you I should know in order to protect you properly, but that you would have to be the one to tell me."

Alex looked deeply into the man's eyes, remembering the mind he had delved into a few minutes before. And for the first time he decided to trust someone other than a Danilov. Margaret had chosen this man, although she'd left the final decision up to Alex. Of all the people he had known, he trusted Margaret most. So he told Charles his secret. All of it, from the beginning in Kiev to now.

"You're a . . . I didn't . . . I never . . ." the lawyer stuttered. "This isn't funny, Alex."

Alex rose to his feet and stretched. "No, it isn't." His arms elongated and sprouted feathers, and the rest of his body shifted to accommodate the change. He lunged into the air, his wings beating powerfully, and came to rest upon the arm of his chair. His talons scored the fabric.

"What the hell?" Charles looked like he'd been struck by lightning. "I . . . A bald eagle?"

Alex resumed his natural form. "I thought I'd hit a patriotic note. You would prefer a bat, perhaps? Personally, I hate that form; bats are quite stupid, and eat insects to boot. There are other forms I can take if you'd—"

"That's okay," the lawyer said hurriedly. The color began to come back into his face. "I guess this is why you're not available for business during the day?"

"Yes. And before you ask, I assure you I do not go around killing people like you've seen in the movies." Formally, he added, "I give you my word."

Charles studied him for a long time. Finally, he held out his hand again. "I'll take it." It was a gesture of acceptance, and of friendship.

"Thank you." Warmth settled in Alex's chest as he shook the man's hand. "I'll wire my bank in France and have some funds transferred to your account here. This is bound to be a long, expensive process."

"Years," Charles said. "Hundreds of thousands of dollars."

"It's a good thing I have both to spare, then."

"Is it worth it?"

"As the saying goes, it's the only game in town. And strife keeps a man—or a revenant—from getting bored."

"You could try croquet."

Alex laughed. "Ah, yes, there's the matter of a house. A lady by the name of Elizabeth Garry will be picking something out. I'd like for you to arrange the buy once she finds something. Those funds, too, will be placed in your hands."

"Certainly. Is this lady . . . special?"

"Very," Alex said. "I'm marrying her."

"Congratulations." The lawyer pushed himself up from his chair. "This calls for a drink. Scotch?"

"Wine," Alex said.

They toasted the coming marriage, their friendship, and the prospect of outwitting Barron. They toasted honor and a number of other things as well. Alex left the lawyer sleeping peacefully in his chair, and made his way toward the house on Jones Street.

Elizabeth was waiting.

18

"Open up." Barron's knock was sharp and demanding, and shattered the quiet stillness of Alex's bedroom. "I want to talk to you."

The hot breeze stirred Alex's hair as he turned away from the open window. A good night for a confrontation, he thought as he went to open the door.

Barron strode in. Jamming his fists on his hips, he growled, "Tomorrow I'm starting proceedings to contest the will."

"I thought you might," Alex said.

The man's smile was an insult. "I'm going to have my company back, and I'm going to have this property. Think about it—a high-rise luxury condo right here. Out in the garden . . . let's see, maybe right where the gazebo is, an Olympic-size swimming pool. The arbors will have to go to make room for the tennis courts. It's too bad the environmentalists have made it inconvenient to mess with wetlands, but a man with the right political connections might be able to get around certain regulations. Let's see . . . a few thousand tons of fill dirt, some nice landscaping, and we might be able to put up some more condos."

Alex damped his rising anger; showing it would only please Barron. "Putting the cart before the horse, aren't you?"

"This is my turf, remember? All those judges have known me a very long time."

"Then I can't lose, can I?"

It took Barron a moment to realize the insult, a moment longer to react to it. His face darkened, and his lips drew back in a snarl. "You'd better hope you live long enough to see it."

Alex smiled. "Next time do better than three teenage hoodlums with knives."

"I have," Barron said softly.

He turned on his heel and walked out. Alex sighed. All that money and breeding gone for naught. The man wasn't even a good villain, just a brute. Thank God for Justin, or he'd think the whole Danilov line had ended with a whimper.

A terrible thought. He could accept the end for his name in a war or perhaps a last descendant's glorious plunge from a rope somewhere in the Himalayas. But please, Lord, not with a whimper.

The front door shut with a bang that echoed through the house. Barron had gone.

Now only Lydia remained to be dealt with. His revenant senses placed her downstairs with Sonya. Ah, Lydia. Even that slight contact roused his Blood-Hunger.

He knew she was waiting for him.

There was no help for it; this had to be settled, once and for all. He went downstairs, fighting the urge to walk out the door and go to Elizabeth. There were so many shadows in his life, so many pasts he was bringing to her. This one, at least, could be resolved.

He found Lydia and Sonya in the living room, and as always, he was struck by the difference between the two women. Sonya lay on the sofa like a sleek, lazy cat; Lydia paced the floor, her hair swinging around her shoulders in a bright cascade.

She whirled when he entered the room. "So there you are. Are you alone?"

"If you mean 'do I have Liz with me,' no."

Sonya laughed softly. "Try to get away tonight, Alex."

As she turned more fully toward him he saw a bruise on her cheek. He strode to her, tilting her face into the light. Her gaze skittered away from his.

"My darling brother did that," Lydia said. "He found out about . . . Who was it this time, Sonya?"

"His golfing buddy, Vincent. Actually, I think he was more upset because he's got to find a new partner than because I slept with the guy."

There was an edge to her voice that showed she wasn't quite as flippant as she tried to appear. Alex shook his head. "Why do you do this to yourself?"

Her face closed, pulling in the anger and hurt and shutting him out. Alex turned away. So much bitterness; it was a miracle that Justin had turned out the way he had. But then he'd had Margaret to show him there was something fine in the world, and perhaps that had been enough.

"Come on, Alex." Lydia slipped her arm into his and pulled him toward the doorway.

He let her lead him down the hall to Margaret's study. Or rather, he reminded himself, Barron's study. A number of changes had been made: Margaret's photographs of friends and family were gone, replaced by a rather bad reproduction of Manet's *The Fife Player*; her engagement calendar and address book were gone, and a heavy leather executive chair had taken the place of her armchair. Alex didn't like any of it.

Instead of turning on the overhead light, Lydia switched

on the small desk lamp. Her flame-orange sundress was cut low in the front and even lower in back. As she walked back toward him the light haloed her hair. She seemed a creature of flame, burning as brightly inside as out. His Blood-Hunger surged in response to the sheer sensuality of her. He damped it savagely.

"Lydia—"

"Why did you bring her here?" she asked.

"To show her my home and family and to prove to *you* that there is no hope for us to be together."

"You didn't succeed."

"Why won't you believe what's right in front of your eyes?"

"Because I can't believe it." Again, he caught a hint of desperation in her eyes. "I know what I feel when I'm around you, and I don't think I'm mistaken when I see the response in your eyes. You still want me, Alex."

Right now, this moment, he did. But not the way she thought. Blood-Hunger beat inside him like a multitude of frantic wings, hot, powerful, infinitely dangerous. It rose with every step she took toward him.

She stopped, close enough for him to smell the scent of her. Obsession, woman, and the heady musk of desire. His nostrils flared. The light fell across her face, neck, and shoulders, creating a pool of velvet shadow in the deep crevice between her breasts. Although she didn't touch him, her life force beckoned him powerfully. Such vitality, he thought. Such drive. And all wasted in the empty pursuit of sensation.

"Why couldn't you love me?" she asked. Tears trembled in her eyes. "What don't I have that *she* has?"

"It's something called innocence of spirit."

"I don't understand."

"I know," he said. She would never understand. He sighed, struck with an unexpected, bittersweet ache for what she lacked. Had it been spoiled out of her by a life that was too fast, too easy, or had it never been there at all? She was almost . . . right. Perhaps if he hadn't met Elizabeth, he might have settled for almost. He reached out and touched her cheek with his fingertips. "So beautiful," he murmured. "Tell me, Lydia. What will you do when this fades?"

"I live for today, remember?"

"So you told me. I think I responded that tomorrow always comes."

"Are you going to marry her?"

He nodded.

She glanced away. Although her expression didn't change, tears spilled out of her eyes and ran down her cheeks. A wave of hopelessness came from her, bleak, black despair that staggered him in its intensity.

"Lydia . . ." He reached out.

"Don't touch me," she said, in a toneless voice that was more poignant than a sob. She sank to her knees. Still the tears flowed, sparkling golden in the lamplight.

"Shhh. Don't cry." He knelt before her and put his hands on her shoulders, trying to absorb some of her pain.

She resisted at first, then slowly relaxed against him. He felt the wetness of her tears upon his neck. Her heartbeat seemed to echo in his chest, and he could feel her life pulsing hot and fast beneath his hands. Her need enveloped him, sank into him, ran through his veins as though it were his own.

"Oh, God, hold me," she murmured. "Just this once, hold me."

Man and revenant reacted without thought, sliding his hands down her back to press her more tightly against him.

Her skin was like satin, and hot to the touch. The warmth seeped into his splayed fingers and spread through his body. He felt her arms come around his waist, felt her mouth open against his neck. His pulse hammered in his ears—no, it was hers, but it felt like his.

A whirlpool came into being in him, drawing him down into a well of dark sensation. Lydia kissed his throat, the angle of his jaw, then ran her tongue along his bottom lip. His world narrowed to her lush mouth, the smoky-green eyes that burned with desire as hot as his. She fitted her mouth to his, and he felt as though he'd burst into flame. Sweet, hot . . . Nothing mattered but this moment, this sharp, exquisite pleasure. He slid his hands along her shoulders and downward, finding only bare skin. His work or hers, he didn't know. Or care. He continued his exploration, savoring the lush flare of her hips, the way her skin felt against his palms. Her body seemed to tell him where to touch, and how. He obeyed, reserving *when* for himself. She moaned when he finally cupped the rich weight of her breasts in his hands.

Her head fell back, exposing the smooth line of her throat. Her pulse beat visibly beneath the skin. He kissed her shoulder, the line of her collarbone, the perfumed hollow at the base of her throat, moving ever closer to that beckoning pulsepoint. Blood-Hunger roared in his ears, in his mind.

"Take me," she whispered, sinking her hands into his hair. "Take it all."

He trembled. Life. So achingly sweet . . . Held out to him like a line to a drowning man. He pressed his open mouth over the spot where her pulse throbbed. Her mind was aflame with passion and triumph.

No! Some shred of the man he had been screamed out against this act. It wasn't his life. It was hers. Blood-Hunger sank its claws into his brain, ran shards of jagged pain into his spine.

Elizabeth, forgive me!

Reason washed through him, and with it the memory of what holding Liz had been like. Tenderness, passion, a soul-stretching intimacy—not this mindless coupling. It was that memory that gave him the strength to stop. Gently, he disengaged Lydia's hands from his hair.

"I'm sorry," he said. "I can't do this."

"Alex—"

She reached for him. He got to his feet to avoid her.

"Is it because of *her*?" she asked.

"Yes. But it's me, too."

"I would have given you everything I have to give."

"I know." He had to make a conscious effort to keep from touching her again. "It's too much, Lydia. Too much, and yet not enough."

She sat back on her heels. Naked, beautiful, her body revealing her arousal. Alex had to close his eyes for a moment; the sight would have made a statue sweat.

"You want me," she said. "Or this wouldn't have happened."

"I'm in love with another woman."

"You're in love with her 'innocent spirit.' But you also want this." She touched the triangle of hair between her thighs. "We're good together, Alex. When you touch me, I feel as though I've been set on fire, and I know you do, too. Go ahead and love her, but be honest about what you feel for me."

"This is appetite," he said. "Not feelings."

"So what? My appetite is just as strong as yours." She cupped her breasts, offering them, and the lamplight seemed to linger on them. "And there are worse things for a man and woman to share."

Everything male in him—human or revenant, it didn't matter—responded to the sight. She was Woman, sensuality personified. If he hadn't known she was human, he might have thought she was a succubus come to lure him to his doom.

"Who would it hurt, really?" she asked.

"Elizabeth. Me. You."

"I hurt now, Alex. I'm aching."

Her right hand slid down over her belly. Her knees eased apart in a slow, teasing movement that sent his senses flaring. He turned away sharply, knowing that if he touched her now, he wouldn't be able to stop.

"Put your clothes on, Lydia. Then we can talk."

"Not yet," she murmured. "Look at me."

He didn't dare. A thousand years of experience was no help with this woman. Even his love for Elizabeth failed to protect him. So he did the only prudent thing: retreat.

"This isn't going to go away," she called after him. "It's going to happen again and again because neither of us can help it."

God help him if she was right. Without answering, he headed out to the garden. The night closed around him in a thick, muggy blanket, and the ground seemed to radiate heat. He walked down to the edge of the marsh; although he wanted to run to Elizabeth, he was unwilling to go to her with Lydia's taste in his mouth. He felt drained, sucked dry by his near miss with disaster.

He closed his eyes. Blood-Hunger gnawed at him, taking payment for disobedience, sending small, razor claws raking his spine and gouging at the back of his eyeballs.

Control. Confidence. Honor. All these had been shaken by that brief, powerful interlude in the study. The darkness

within him was growing like a cancer, eating away at the
things that kept him in check. And Lydia, ignorant of the
cost, fanned those black instincts into open flame.

There had to be a reason. Somehow, in all this confusion,
there was an answer.

A door slammed in the house behind him, and a moment
later he heard Lydia calling his name. He stepped deeper
into the shadows before turning. Her face was a blur at this
distance, but he could see enough to know she was scanning
the garden for him. The moonlight leached the color from
her dress, but nothing could quench the fire of the woman
herself.

"Alex," she called again. "I want to talk to you."

He watched her walk toward the gazebo, seeming to flit
in and out of the intervening trees. Blood-Hunger dug deep,
urging him to go to her. His shoulders hunched as a breeze
riffled out of the garden, bringing the scent of flowers and
an overwhelming aura of Obsession and Lydia. The cicadas
thrummed a frantic song overhead. He took a step toward
her, impelled by the roaring darkness within him.

Then the bellow of a bull alligator split the night. The
sound tore Alex out of the Blood-Hunger's grip and swung
him around to face the marsh. Wildwood—cruel and beautiful as only nature could be, but also a haven. The reeds
bowed before him, beckoning, and the graceful, predatory
shape of an owl glided in and out of the moonlight.

Without thought, Alex leaped out over the water. He
didn't fall; strong wings bore him up on the wind as his
body changed. A moment later he followed that swiftly
moving shape into the depths of the marsh.

"Alex?" Lydia called. Her shoes grated on the gazebo's
steps.

The building was empty. A breeze moved lazily through the arched openings, stirring the air without cooling it. She swung around with a hiss of frustration. Alex was close; the ghost crystal beat like a second heart against her chest. She'd almost had him. Back there in the study, she'd felt his loss of control, tasted the stark power of his hunger. If she could just get close to him again . . . She reached up, caressing the crystal with her fingertips.

"Stubborn, aren't you?" she murmured as the stone sang a song of power in her head. "But I'll get there."

Lydia.

Not him, not now! She shrank from that summons, tried to push it from her. But it hung in her mind as though etched with acid.

The doorway of the gazebo no longer framed a moonlit garden. Blackness filled it now, deeper, darker than the night sky, but pale in comparison to *his* eyes. It drew her. She didn't want to go.

But there was no way out. The crystal burned upon her chest, traitor and guide. She sobbed as she was drawn into the darkness, cast adrift in utter blackness.

Between worlds, between realities, she cried out for Alex. But there was no help for her, no choice. She drifted in utter emptiness, terror her only company.

A moment and an eternity later, she stepped out into the sanctuary of the abandoned church.

Tall, black candles filled the votive rack at the far end of the room. The flickering light sent shadows whorling firefly swift around the room. Lydia jerked as a larger shadow came between her and the candles, a gaunt shape that the light seemed not to touch. Although she couldn't see his face, she knew he was looking at her. Into her.

"Welcome, Lydia," he said.

He moved away from her, toward the altar. Lydia breathed a sigh of relief. Then she caught sight of the man who lay supine on the marble slab. Her heartbeat jagged into high gear.

"*Barron?*" she gasped.

"Help . . . me," he panted through bared teeth.

Although he wasn't bound, his arms and legs seemed to hang helplessly. Like a pithed frog, she thought. She watched in growing horror as the tendons in his neck bulged as he struggled to move.

"What have you done to him?" she whispered.

Smith turned around. His eyes were black and mad, twin windows into hell. "I had to immobilize him."

"How . . ." She swallowed the rest of the sentence; she didn't really want to know how.

"You see, Lydia," he continued, "this is the conclusion of a business arrangement your brother and I had. I did him a service, and now I'm taking payment." He took a thick envelope out of his pocket and held it before Barron's eyes. "You see? Here is the evidence I promised. I also destroyed everything relating to the Danilovs or Danilov Industries in the lawyer's files. That should make you happy, eh?"

Barron's face contorted with effort. "Let . . . me go. I'll pay you—"

"Money means nothing to me," Smith said, tossing the packet on the man's chest. "I have everything I need right here."

"Why are you doing this?" Lydia spoke without thinking, then instantly regretted it when he turned toward her.

"Alex Danilov's blood runs in your brother's veins. I will use the man to bind the revenant."

Alex Danilov's blood runs in my veins, too. Lydia backed away. She would have gladly dared the blackness of between-worlds again to leave this place. But that passageway was Smith's, not hers, and the dank wall of the sanctuary stopped her backward progress with a jolt.

Smith went into the next room, reappearing a moment later with a carved wooden box in his hands. He set it on the altar beside Barron. The room stank of danger. Fear crawled along Lydia's spine, lifted the hair at the nape of her neck.

She knew she should run. She knew she should try to do something for her brother. But terror held her frozen, her back pressed against the wall. It was the instinct of the hunted: take anyone but me.

"It is only right that you should know my true name," Smith said. "I was born James Suldris, and I've been looking for Alex Danilov for many, many years. You see, he and I began something, and now it is time to finish it."

Lydia sank to her knees. "You don't want his power," she whispered. "You never did."

"No," he said. "I want to destroy him." Smiling, he looked down at Barron. "You asked me to kill him. I shall. Oh, yes, I shall. Perhaps that will be a comfort to you . . . in your new place of residence."

Lydia watched Suldris's hand move across the top of the box. It was old, so old that the wood was almost black with age. The carved designs seemed familiar and alien at the same time. Staring at them made her feel strangely ill.

"Fascinating, isn't it?" Suldris asked.

Afraid to agree, equally afraid to disagree, she gave an indeterminate shake of her head.

"This comes from a past mankind has chosen to forget," he continued. Flames danced in the obsidian depths of his eyes, but Lydia didn't think they were from the candles behind him. "Once, men thought they had destroyed it, just as they thought they'd destroyed me."

He lifted the lid. Gently, reverently, like a priest handling host and chalice, he took out a knife with a jeweled hilt. The blade was curved, and as dark as Suldris's eyes. "This is no ordinary steel," he said. "It was forged with the blood of innocents in the fires of hell.

"This is my master's blade. No one can own it; I am merely its keeper, bearing it in Satan's work until the time it chooses another," he said. "Power, Lydia. The power of the dark. It can be closed up, imprisoned and forgotten, but it still exists. Ask the children who see monsters in the shadowy corners of their rooms. *They* know the dark."

Lydia pressed her fist against her mouth, only vaguely registering the pain of her teeth digging into the inside of her lip. She knew the dark, too; it was encompassed in this monster's pitiless black eyes.

"What did Alex do to you?" she asked, surprising herself with her audacity.

Suldris bared his teeth in what could have been meant as a smile. But it was a rictus of hate, and took all illusion of humanity from his face.

"Four hundred years ago," he said, "Alexi Danilovich killed me."

Barron lifted his head, a convulsive effort that left his face flushed and sweating. "You're . . . crazy," he gasped.

"Perhaps," Suldris said. "Perhaps."

He pressed Barron's head back down to the altar. Then, in an eerily solicitous gesture, he stroked the hair back from the man's forehead.

"*Vultis melea,*" he murmured. "*Abatus, sua mortus.*"

Barron's teeth shone in the candlelight. "Let . . . me . . . go!"

"Mala un para." Suldris spread his arms wide, the knife held in his right hand.

Behind him, framed by his outspread arms, was the patch of lighter plaster that marked the place where the crucifix had once hung. As he continued to chant the cross-shaped spot began to burn with a strange, colorless fire. It didn't consume, that fire, or illuminate.

Suddenly, impossibly, the cross began to move. Lydia sank to her knees. With a groan that vibrated the bones in her skull, the cross rotated. Faster and faster, until it was a blur of light.

As suddenly as it had begun, it stopped. Upside down— the mark of Satan.

"Sathan, Baal, Astarot, Belphegor," Suldris howled. *"Su humanis paragor, es mala, es mala."*

Colorless flames licked along the edge of the blade. He grasped Barron's hair and pulled his head back. And then he brought the knife down in a slashing arc.

Blood spurted. Gouts of it splashed across the walls and even the ceiling. Lydia recoiled, gagging. The smoke from the candles swirled toward the altar, driven by a breeze she couldn't feel. Shadows lurked in the depths of the smoke, half-seen, half-real, terrible to see.

Suldris's voice rose to a shout. *"Ruha se coropis, se aron Belial. Ilan, Ilas, Sathan rua eschalyas. Bel sahe, bel sahe!"*

The smoke grew thicker, darker. The shadows in it coalesced into a single large one. It was humped and twisted, its head a crested horror. Twin points of red marked its eyes.

It looked at her.

Lydia couldn't bear that gaze, couldn't look away. The thing kept watching her as it bent to fasten its mouth over the gaping slash in Barron's throat.

A thin wail rose, whether hers or Barron's, she didn't know. She watched her brother die, his eyes fading as though a light had turned off in them. His body crumbled, falling in on itself until there was nothing left but scattered piles of gray dust. Her terror for herself was too great for her to feel anything for him.

Suldris let his arms fall to his sides. Reverently, he bowed to the thing that crouched beside the altar. It inclined its head in a regal gesture, then disappeared with a clap of air that sent gray dust sifting through the room. The stink of its evil hung in the air, rank and powerful.

Slowly, Suldris turned toward her. She heard the scrape of his shoes on the floor, the rasp of her own breathing.

"Come here, Lydia," he said.

She scuttled along the wall to the corner. *Not like this. Oh, God, not like this!*

"Please," she whispered. "Please, leave me alone."

He walked across the room to her. Bending, he lifted her to her feet. Terror had taken the strength from her legs, and she hung like a doll between his hands.

"This is your destiny, Lydia, just as it was your brother's. And the boy's. I have summoned him. You and he will be the tools with which I fashion the spell that will destroy Alex Danilov."

"Don't," she sobbed. "I did everything you wanted, I helped you . . . . Please, let me go."

As gently as a lover, he carried her to the altar and laid her down. The marble was cold. She could feel wetness against her back as Barron's blood soaked into her dress.

"You shouldn't be afraid," Suldris said. "It is an honor to serve the Lord of the Dark."

She tried to speak, but only managed to whimper. Suldris placed the point of the knife at the base of her throat. She shook her head, denying what was about to happen to her.

But instead of slitting her throat, he cut her dress and underpants away, leaving her naked. She made an abortive attempt to cover her breasts, but a shake of his head stopped her.

"What . . . what are you going to do?" she whispered.

He didn't answer. Dipping his finger in Barron's blood, he painted a design in the center of her chest just over her heart. Her skin twitched as he painted another on her belly. Then he spread her legs wide so he could do the same to each inner thigh.

Arousal spread through her. It didn't lessen her terror; instead, it heightened it because she couldn't control her body. Still, it licked hotly along her veins, made her hips shift rhythmically. Suldris grasped her ankles and pulled her forward so that her lower legs hung over the edge of the altar. A moment later he entered her. It was not an act of passion, but possession, his mind thrusting as deep as his body.

She closed her eyes, not wanting to look at him as he did this to her. Pain/pleasure, pleasure/pain. The degradation of being stripped bare, body and soul. But anything was better than what he'd done to Barron.

"Lydia."

Whimpering, she looked up at him. His eyes were twin pits of blackness in which pinpoints of hellfire swam.

"In a way it's a shame you're related to Alex Danilov," he said. "Otherwise, I might be tempted to keep you. As it is, the blood that runs through your veins is far more important than your other qualities."

He grasped her thighs in a grip that made her gasp in pain, then leaned down and fastened his mouth on the big vein in her neck. Impaled, body and soul, she arched her back in exquisite agony. Time blurred as he drank from her.

Finally, he raised his head. She stared up at him, dully registering that her blood stained his lips and her life raged in his eyes.

"Say 'I belong to the Lord Satan,' " he commanded.

"I belong to the Lord Satan," she said, knowing what this would cost her, but too weak to fight him.

"My soul is his. I will serve him in this world and the next."

"My soul is his. I will serve him in this world and the next."

The designs Suldris had painted on her body burst into flame, the same colorless fire that had burned upon the wall. It didn't hurt, didn't consume, and yet she felt it eating into her flesh.

He leaned over her. "Take me, Dark Lord," he said. "I am your handmaiden."

No! A small, sane part of her mind screamed. *Don't say it!* But her mouth opened, and the words came out without her bidding.

"Take me, Dark Lord. I am your handmaiden."

Suldris raised the knife over her. The blade winkled darkly, seeming to drink the light. It was then that she knew it for what it was: a window into the dark abyss of evil. Poised to take her into the blackness. A hulking shadow lurked behind Suldris, and she could feel its lust. Bestial. Unconquerable. It was then that she realized that Barron had had an easier fate.

With a strength she didn't know she'd had, she fought to raise her hand. Fought and won. She just managed to clamp her hand over the ghost crystal before the darkness claimed her.

19

The Arbor's white columns almost seemed to glow in the moonlight as Alex drifted across the lawn on silent wings. He came to rest on a branch outside his window. Blood-Hunger was an ache deep inside him, present, but only an echo of what it had been. Lydia was gone, then.

Respite. Now was his chance to use his mind instead of his instincts.

He launched himself off the branch and glided into a patch of shadow to change himself back to human form. "And now, my lovely crystal gazer," he murmured, "let's find out why you have this effect on me."

The downstairs windows were dark, as were those on the family's side of the house. Here in the west wing, however, almost every light was on, and the heavy thump of rock music vibrated the windowpanes. Alex smiled; without Justin, the house would be a very dull place indeed.

He slipped upstairs to Lydia's room. As before, he found the chamber full of crystal song. It should have been a sweet sound, but there was a twist to it, a dissonance that was too faint to identify but that set his nerves on edge. He closed his eyes, listening with his mind instead of his ears.

The strongest voice came from a large, flat-sided quartz crystal that occupied the top shelf of a bookcase near the bed. Alex picked the stone up and balanced it in his palm. Its song grew stronger, running along his nerves like static electricity. His Blood-Hunger stirred. *Recognizing this touch.*

The implications were staggering. Untutored, without the help of any of the old grimoires, Lydia had harnessed the power of the stones. And her motive? Love. Since she lacked the ability to love, however, it was the Blood-Hunger she touched, not his heart.

"Lydia, Lydia, what have you done?" he whispered.

It was a dangerous binding, to him and to her. And the longer it existed, the more dangerous it would become.

He sent his awareness into the stone, hoping to follow the path she had taken. The crystal was a world in itself, an ordered place of latticework angles and refracted light. Lydia's touch was a memory here, a teasing wraith that taunted and cajoled but never fully showed itself.

He followed it deeper and deeper into the stone. Music surrounded him, grew louder and stronger as he went. The dissonance put an edge to the song, a resonance that made his teeth ache. Shards of rainbows flowed over the angled fretwork, seeming to beckon him onward. Finally, he reached the crystal's heart.

And found it empty.

His breath went out in a gasp. Lydia had taken a ghost crystal from this place. Made real what was not-quite-real.

Magic. True magic, power of a kind he hadn't seen since mankind had turned to machines. He entered that empty place, wandered in a wasteland of agony. The regularity of structure had been shattered, supports bent or broken, facets burst, angles twisted into madness. The rainbows broke apart and fled. This was the source of the dissonance, where the harmonic structure of the crystal's song became as twisted as its heart.

Pain, pain . . . around him, in him. A scream too vast to be contained, a scream that encompassed all the world. The crystal's need resonated in his bones, ran like acid through his veins.

Return what was taken. Make me whole.

Alex couldn't. If he'd had the ghost crystal in his hands, he wouldn't have known how to obey. He fled the pain he couldn't ease, fled the need he couldn't fill. The crystal's voice chased him through the echoing structure, bouncing from angle to angle and facet to facet. Whorled colors, the crystal's pulse, skimmed ahead of him.

Suddenly he burst free, back to his own body. He sank to his knees, gasping for breath. Echoes of pain belled in his mind. How could Lydia, with her gift, have borne the stone's agony? How could she have slept in the same room with it and not been aware of what she had done?

The ghost crystal must have been equally injured during that brutal separation. And it was that sick, twisted stone that fueled her burgeoning power. It was that sick, twisted stone that held the strings to his Blood-Hunger.

He shuddered as the crystal hummed in his hands. Its pain was no longer buried deep inside; his touch had released it, and it thrummed at him in a key that was more felt than heard. Unless the ghost crystal was returned to its rightful place, the mother stone would remain in agony.

He looked down at it. From here, there was no sign of the yawning emptiness in its depths. *Like me.* Seemingly unflawed on the outside, the inside flawed. It had no heart; he had no soul.

"At least it wasn't your own doing," he murmured, stroking the stone's flat side.

It would be a kindness to end its suffering now. He got to his feet and raised the crystal overhead, fully intending to smash it against the fireplace. The crystal song rose to a wail.

"I'm sorry," he said. "I'd help you if I could, but my powers are not those of a healer. Your mistress—"

He shook his head. Lydia couldn't help, either. He may have lacked the capacity to heal, but she lacked the capacity to care. It might not hurt so much if he could be angry at her. Lydia was so completely, unselfconsciously selfish, however, that anger seemed inappropriate. Sadness, perhaps. Regret for a wonderful talent wasted on someone for whom compassion was only a word.

The crystal cried.

Alex tensed his arms, ready to throw. Then, with a sigh that seemed to start at his toes, he lowered the stone. He couldn't do this; it felt too much like killing.

Gently, he set the crystal back on its shelf.

"I'm sorry," he said again. He left the room, closing the door to shut out that anguished voice. But the echoes of it followed him. Demanding. Pleading. *Help me, help me!*

"Looking for someone?"

Sonya's voice brought him around with a jerk. She leaned against the wall a few yards away, arms crossed, mouth twisted in a less than nice smile. And she was wearing very little beneath her expensive lace peignoir, something she took pains to let him know. He sighed; if he hadn't been preoccupied with the crystal, he might have avoided this meeting.

"I happened to be looking for Lydia," he said. It was the only possible answer, considering where he was. "Have you seen her?"

"She took off an hour ago. I didn't get the impression she was very happy with you."

That makes two of us. "She'll get over it."

"I expect she will."

"Well, good night," he said, turning away. "I'm going to change, then head up to Savannah."

"To Elizabeth Garry?"

"Yes."

She pushed away from the wall. "I'll walk you to your room. I'm going that way anyway. It's after eleven, time for Justin to pry his nose away from that radio and get to bed."

Alex inclined his head, accepting her company with a graciousness he didn't feel inside. The crystal's wail followed him. It was more real to him than the touch of Sonya's hand when she tucked it into the crook of his arm.

"I've been hoping the novelty of this ham radio would wear off," she said. "I swear, he's up at all hours calling people around the world."

"I wouldn't worry about it," he said. Pain echoed in his mind, the agony of that empty place in the crystal's heart. "There are worse hobbies for a teenager to have."

"I suppose so. Barron called his lawyer today."

Alex blinked, surprised by her sudden shift. "Oh?"

"He's going to contest Margaret's will. Apparently he's found a way around the evidence you've got."

"Apparently. Look, Sonya—"

"I can get it back for you. For a price."

He raised his brows.

"A million cash," she said. "I want out."

"You want out in style."

"That's right."

"What made you change your mind?"

She glanced away, then back. "I saw how you looked at Liz Garry. And how she looked at you. Ever since you brought her here, I've been thinking about it. I've been married, I've had lovers, but I've never been *loved*. I want that before I get too old to appreciate it."

He stared at her, truly astonished. "I thought you liked being a Danilov. You'd give it up for love?"

"As you say, there are worse things. I just don't want to be poor when I do it."

"What about Justin?"

She smiled, but it was much too brittle for humor. "Do you think he'd like the Riviera?"

Alex shook his head, more in disbelief than to answer her question. He wasn't sure Sonya could find love or recognize it if she did. But, whispered the cynical corner of his mind, a million dollars could buy her a reasonable facsimile.

As they walked down the hall toward the west wing, the crystal's voice faded to a vague, nagging ache at the back of his skull. Not forgotten, but bearable. The portraits lining the walls almost seemed to be watching him as he passed; if he'd been a man of too much imagination, he might have seen sympathy in their eyes. Danilovs. Some good, some not so good, all possessing their own brand of eccentricities.

This generation was no different. Barron, Lydia, Sonya—Justin, too, in his turn . . . They would pass, just like all the others, and their portraits would hang somewhere in this house.

And I will still be here.

His door was a beacon, promising solitude. He needed a few minutes alone, and a shower to wash off the taint of all that had passed tonight. Elizabeth was waiting. She was his future, and he didn't want to bring her the sourness of his present.

Reaching his room at last, he disengaged Sonya's hand from his arm. "Good night," he said.

She darted around him, putting her back against his door. "I could love you, you know."

"No, you couldn't," he replied with a gentleness he didn't feel. "My appeal to you is the prospect of hurting Barron. And for some strange reason, yourself."

She lifted one shoulder in a shrug. "Why did you pick Lydia?"

"I didn't," he said. "I picked Elizabeth."

He expected her to counter, but she didn't. Her eyes showed more thoughtfulness than disappointment. He realized with a shock that his refusal had pleased her. Strange. Then again, not so strange; perhaps she just wanted to test his love for Elizabeth. He felt a stirring of kinship with her.

"I hope you find what you're looking for," he said.

"I do, too. No, wait," she said when he turned away. "I'm not finished. Just a quick warning, and then I'll let you go. Lydia's very determined, you know. She'll make your life a living hell until you give her what she wants."

"No one can give Lydia what she wants," he said.

She drew in her breath sharply. "You know, you might be right about that. But convincing her may be another story."

"I'm not going to convince her. I'm going to move out as soon as Liz finds something she likes in town."

"If you were smart, you'd kick the lot of us out."

"I gave my word that you could stay."

"Barron would kick *you* out in a heartbeat."

"Some of us live by different rules than Barron," he said. "You might try it."

"You're a fool, Alex Danilov."

"Frequently," he agreed. "But at least I have the satisfaction of knowing it's my own brand of foolishness."

"Foolishness is foolishness, no matter whose brand."

He laughed in genuine amusement. "You're right about that. Good night, Sonya."

"Let me know what you decide," she said. "About the money."

"All right."

Once in his room, he went straight to the phone and dialed Liz's number. It rang twice before she answered.

"Hello, love," he said.

"Hello, yourself. I was getting worried, Alex."

"I'm sorry. I've had a rather . . . incredible evening."

She laughed. "A Danilov evening, no doubt."

"Perceptive, as always."

"Will you come at all?"

"The hounds of hell wouldn't keep me away. But I want a shower and a change of clothes first, so I'll be a while. Why don't we go out for a change? I know a place that doesn't close until the sun comes up."

"Don't tell me. Vampires?"

"Jazz musicians." He wanted to be with her so badly he could almost taste it. "Say yes, Elizabeth."

"Yes."

"I'll be there in an hour."

He headed for the shower. Time seemed to hang suspended while the hot water pounded his shoulders and back. It had been a night of many surprises: Lydia with her astonishing show of magical talent, Sonya with her equally astonishing epiphany. And the impetus for both? Love. Such a gentle emotion, love, but powerful enough to prompt one woman to tap another world, another to leave the one she'd sold herself to inhabit.

He turned, letting the water needle his front. Was love the answer to all human ills? Of course not. Like life itself, it was sometimes beautiful, sometimes cruel, intensely pleasurable, and intensely painful. Full of bumps and hollows, unexpected curves and tricky turns. But what a ride!

Lydia was incapable of love. As for Sonya . . . It might be worth a million dollars to see if it made her happy.

Suldris walked up the steps of the house on Jones Street. The door swung open as he approached, then closed behind him after he passed. The house was dark and close, filled with the presence of sleeping human beings.

Such peaceful little lives. So frail, so brief, to be Alex Danilov's doom.

His preparations were complete. The bait was prepared, the trap set. Only one spell was yet to be made. And when this night was done, Alex Danilov would have nothing. No family, no past, and no future. The sorcerer's nostrils flared at the hot scent of fresh blood.

"I'm going to take it all," he murmured. "Everything you love, everything you value. Just as you did to me."

He slipped upstairs. Silently, stealthily, although an army couldn't have stopped him tonight. He'd drunk many lives in the past few weeks. His mind rang with the echoes of their passage Power. Wrought from death and the devil himself.

He entered the nearest bedroom, where a middle-aged couple slept. The woman's mother and father, no doubt. Mere grist for Suldris's mill; their lives would bind the woman that much tighter. He took them quickly, so quickly that their dying hardly rumpled the bedclothes.

Heat flushed his cheeks, his brain as he tasted their deaths. Ah, Satan, it was a good night. A very good night. He turned toward the door. It was time to meet Alex Danilov's beloved—the best trap of them all. Her life force was sweet and strong, and only a few dozen feet away. He followed that beckoning scent down the hall to the bedroom at the far end.

She lay on top of her covers, fully dressed. But the room was dark, and her chest rose and fell with the deep, regular breathing of sleep. Her lover was late.

Suldris smiled; Alex was going to be later still. He moved to the right so as to get a better look at her face. In repose, it was strong and serene, the sort of face that aged well. He didn't find her beautiful. She was just . . . a woman. What, then, made her precious to Alex Danilov?

Just then she sat up, startling him with the suddenness of her movement. Although the room was too dark for her to see him, she stared straight at him as though she'd pinpointed him by other means. Interesting.

"Alex?"

"No," Suldris said. "An acquaintance of his."

She reached for the bedside lamp. He let her; part of the pleasure of this was her knowing what was happening to her. Light flared in the room.

"Who are you?" she asked.

He swept her a bow. "My name is James Suldris. I knew Alex Danilov . . . a very long time ago."

"What are you doing in my room? How did you get in here?" For all her challenging words, her eyes were dark with fear.

"I go wherever I please. Tonight it pleased me to meet Alex's lover. I know you're expecting him—"

"No, I'm not."

He smiled. A most perceptive woman, this Elizabeth Garry. She'd observed him, judged his danger, and acted to protect Alex. How touching.

"Of course you are, Elizabeth," he said. "Why else would you call his name the moment you awoke?"

He looked deeply into her eyes, saw the awareness in them. The sweet thrill of shock went through him. She knew

what he was. Had known from the moment he walked into
the room. She *believed*.

"Alex told you what he is," he said.

"Of course," she said, still afraid, but also defiant. "He's
a Frenchman of Russian extraction, a businessman, a—"

"Revenant," he said, compelling her.

Her mind was a stubborn one, resisting his invasion with
a strength that surprised him. But that strength was only
human; he overwhelmed it, bent it back upon itself. Later,
he'd release her so she could *feel* what was happening to
her. But now he wanted the truth.

"Now, Elizabeth, tell me," he murmured. "You know
Alex is revenant."

"Yes."

"Do you love him?"

"Yes."

"Has he prepared you to come over?" He reached out and
tilted her face upward. "Has he put the seeds of immortality
in you?"

"No. He won't."

"Tell me why," he said, although he knew the answer.

"Because he thinks of himself as damned, and refuses to
damn anyone else."

"How nice to know he retains his idiocy to the end."
He let his hand drift down to her neck, to feel the pulse
beating there. "A revenant is a being of great power, and
Alex perhaps the most powerful of all. Tell me, Elizabeth.
Why are women always attracted to such creatures? Is it
the power or the strangeness that appeals to you, that you
can love a monster?"

She blinked, and for a moment it looked like a light had
gone on in her dark amber eyes. "He feels like a man to
me," she said.

Suldris let out his breath sharply. Now he understood Alex's fascination with this woman. It took innocence of spirit to believe the unbelievable, generosity to accept the fantastic. Innocence, generosity—rare commodities in any age. To be loved for what one was, man, revenant, good, bad . . . A gift of inestimable value, precious because it could not be bought or coerced. It could only be given.

Suldris smiled. He would take that innocence from her. Not to keep it. To destroy it.

No. To make *Alex* destroy it.

20

The screams began at midnight.

Alex was on his way downstairs when he heard the first one. A woman's voice, high-pitched and frightened. Whirling, he ran back upstairs.

"Sonya!" he shouted.

She screamed again. It pumped him to even greater speed, and he had to catch the doorjamb to make the turn into the hallway.

"Sonya! Justin!"

The door to the radio room opened, spilling an elongated spear of light into the corridor. Sonya's shrieks subsided to muffled crying. Alex skidded to a halt as Justin appeared in the doorway.

Something about the boy's stance struck Alex as odd; it was stoop-shouldered and oddly limp, like a marionette whose strings have been cut.

"Justin?" he asked. "Is everything okay?"

The boy's head came up, but there was no recognition in his eyes. He started forward. Alarm beat dark wings in Alex's chest. There was no trace of consciousness in the boy's mind. Something else controlled him, moving arms, legs, and head in a terrible parody of movement.

The stink of magic rolled down the hall ahead of him, and Alex took a step backward in astonishment. A Summoning! In this time, in this place! Dear God in heaven, had the whole world gone mad?

Sonya, her eyes wild with terror, staggered out of the room the boy had just left. Blood streamed from her nose, making a scarlet webwork over her mouth and chin.

"Stop him!" she cried.

Justin kept walking, a strange, loose-limbed stride that wasn't his own. Alex thrust his arm out as the boy went past. Justin stopped, his chest pressed against the restraint. His eyes never changed.

Sonya ran forward. "Justin, wait for me. Please, let me help you."

"Don't touch him," Alex said.

She ignored him, grasping the boy by the arm. He shoved her away with a ferocity that sent her sprawling. Then he sprang forward, dodging past Alex like a broken-field runner.

Alex sprinted after him, catching up with him at the head of the stairs. The boy turned on him, biting, scratching, kicking, gouging, fighting like a mad cat. For all his revenant strength, Alex had trouble holding him.

Despite the savagery of the battle, Justin never cried out, and his expression remained as blank and blind as a doll's. The rasp of his breathing was loud in the eerie silence.

They teetered at the edge of the stairs. Alex wrapped his arms around Justin and let himself fall backward, skidding painfully across the oak floor. The impact jarred the boy out of his grasp.

Justin scrambled away on all fours. Alex lunged forward, catching him by the ankle, and drew him back. The boy twisted his body at an impossible angle and swung at him, catching him on the cheekbone with Summoning-driven power.

Alex's head snapped back from the force of the blow, but he managed to keep his grip. Hurling himself up and over, he bore Justin back to the floor.

"Stop it, stop it!" Sonya shrieked. "Justin, what are you doing?"

Alex caught the boy's flailing hands and pinned them to the floor. Justin snapped at him like a rabid dog. Levering his forearm beneath Justin's chin, he forced the boy's head back to expose his throat. Then he carefully pressed the carotid artery to cut off the blood supply to the brain.

"Are you crazy?" Sonya screamed. Her nails scored Alex's skin as she fought to drag his hands from her son's throat. "Alex, stop! Don't hurt him!"

Alex ignored her, even when she pounded at his face with her fists. A moment later Justin's head lolled to the side. Alex laid bonds of magic across his mind to keep him unconscious.

"You killed him!" Sonya cried.

"He's not hurt. I only knocked him out," Alex said, grabbing her wrists to keep her from hitting him again. "Did you want him getting out . . . like that?"

She took a deep, shuddering breath, and some of the wildness drained from her eyes. "Okay," she panted. "Okay."

She sank to her knees beside the boy and pulled him into her lap. The unexpected maternal gesture made Alex's throat tighten. Maybe, he thought, there was hope for her after all.

"It's going to be all right, baby," she crooned. "Don't worry about anything, you're going to be all right." Tears ran down her cheeks, making pale streaks in the blood. "I was listening to him talk to some guy in Iceland when all

of a sudden he jumped up, knocking the radio right off the
table, and started for the door. When I tried to stop him,
he hit me."

"Let me see that." Alex took her chin in his hand and
gently forced her to look up.

As bad as her face looked, most of the blood seemed to
have come from her nose. Her upper lip was slightly swollen, and there was a small cut at the corner of her mouth, but
otherwise she seemed unhurt. He took out his handkerchief
and wiped the worst of the mess from her face.

"Are you hurt anywhere else?" he asked. "Did he knock
you unconscious or—"

"No." The tears continued to flow. "I'm sorry I hit you.
But . . . He's my son." She said that as though it explained
everything.

Perhaps it did.

"He was like a wild animal," she said, then shook her
head. "No, he was like a zombie at first. *You* saw what I
meant. His eyes . . ."

Alex nodded.

"Then I put my hand on his shoulder, and he turned on
me. I never even saw his fist coming until it was too late.
Oh, God, Alex! What's wrong with him?"

"I don't know," he lied, knowing the truth would not
have been believed.

The stench of the Summoning hung over the boy, so
strong that it seemed impossible that she couldn't sense
it. He scrubbed the back of his hand over his face, then
levered himself to his feet. He felt filthy, tainted by the
mere contact with that dark spell.

"Could he have taken drugs?" Sonya asked. "I've heard
horror stories about crack and angel dust, how they get a
person so wound up that they can get shot several times

and still keep coming at you—"

"Stop, Sonya," Alex said. "You're frightening yourself to no good purpose." He bent and gathered the boy into his arms.

"What are you doing?"

"I'm going to secure him until I can find a way to deal with this."

"You mean tie him up? Absolutely not. He needs to go to the hospital." There was an edge of hysteria in her voice. "I'm going to call Dr. Cavendish and have him meet us—"

Alex caught her gaze and held it, delved into her mind and held that, too. He didn't have time to argue. Justin didn't have time. *We don't need a doctor. Go back to bed, Sonya. You're very tired.*

"I . . . I'm very tired now." She rose to her feet. "I think I'll go to bed."

"Don't worry, Sonya. Take a hot shower, then get a good night's sleep. Forget about what happened tonight; everything will be fine in the morning."

"Everything will be fine in the morning," she parroted.

She turned away, a bit jerkily because of his control. Alex waited until she disappeared around the corner, then carried Justin into his room. Not to tie him up, as Sonya thought; no ropes could hold someone who was in the thrall of a Summoning. Only magic could counter magic.

The world *had* gone mad, the boundaries between it and the world of magic blurring in a way he hadn't seen for centuries. Lydia tapping into his Blood-Hunger, pulling the ghost crystal into reality, this Summoning . . .

Was this Lydia's work? No. True, she had talent. But it was raw and untutored, a thoughtless outpouring like her sensuality. No one with any experience would have left that ragged wound in the crystal's heart. And a Summoning required not only experience, but great discipline.

He laid Justin on the bed, leaning over him to brush the tumbled hair back from his forehead. This boy was the last of Catherine's line, the last of her blood.

"It can't end here, Catherine," Alex murmured. "I have such hope for this one."

Hope! He chuckled at his own absurdity. "Who was it that said, 'He who lives upon hope will die fasting'? Ah, yes, Benjamin Franklin. I wonder if he was right."

Bracing his hands on the footboard, he closed his eyes and tried to break the Summoning. But it had been woven so tightly into the boy's being that it was hard to tell where Justin ended and magic began. An intricate binding, created with great subtlety and power.

Frustration tightened his throat. He could beat death himself, he could pull this house down like a modern-day Sampson, but he couldn't destroy that spell without destroying something of Justin, too. The memory of that shrieking, empty place in the crystal's heart was too fresh for him to take that risk with the boy's mind.

All his revenant power, useless. It would be like using a sledgehammer to carve porcelain, and equally destructive. Justin moaned, fighting the bonds of unconsciousness.

So young, Alex thought. So vulnerable. How had he become ensnared in this?

"It's my fault, Justin," he said. "This is dark magic, wielded for a purpose. A sorcerer capable of constructing such a spell had bigger game in mind than a fifteen-year-old boy."

There. He'd said the word he'd been avoiding: sorcerer. A practitioner of the Arts, perhaps another revenant. Alex had made many enemies among his "own" kind. A hate rightfully deserved; he had destroyed many of them through the years.

"So," he murmured, "you bait the trap with this innocent boy, hoping to draw me out. All right, you've succeeded."

Brave words, but he had no other choice; the spell would remain until Justin obeyed it. And, Alex thought, find the point of Summoning, and perhaps he'd find whoever or whatever had created it.

There would be a reckoning.

He released the binding spells that kept the boy unconscious. Justin's eyes snapped open. He sat up, swung his legs over the side of the bed, and headed for the door with that same almost alien gait.

"Yes, go," Alex said. "But not alone."

He followed the boy through the house and out into the garden. Wisps of mist coiled close to the ground. Justin's feet left a trail of dark splotches on the grass as he walked toward the garage. He opened the door, disappearing into the darkness within.

Alex shifted into owl form and flew in after him, perching on one of the rafters to watch the boy lift a bicycle down from the rack and mount it. The bike wobbled a bit as the boy—or the Summoning, rather—struggled to adjust to this new balance.

Alex launched into flight, following Justin down the drive and out into the street beyond.

The boy turned onto the road that led to Delano. As Alex flew he wondered what sort of changes had occurred in the little town that had begun as a handful of cabins for the freedmen who worked at the Arbor. Catherine had named the town, and had used her considerable influence to protect the inhabitants. A small bit of light in the dark years of slavery.

Instead of going into town, however, Justin turned off into a dark, cypress-lined lane. A few yards farther on, and the road widened into a seamed and rutted parking lot. Ahead, Alex saw the remains of a small church. Holes gaped blackly in the roof, and slabs of fallen stucco lay like exposed bones in the moonlight. It took him a moment to place its name. Ah, yes, the True Faith Church. Begun by old Rosswell Huygens in the late 1920s, it apparently hadn't long survived its founder.

Justin let the bicycle fall and walked up the steps. Alex went with him, drifting on wings and caution. The air inside the building was thick with decay. Things scuttled away from Justin's feet, small things accustomed to solitude and darkness.

The boy headed toward the sanctuary. Once, it had been a place of worship. But there was nothing of God here now; black malevolence lurked in that room, unseen, unheard, yet all too real.

Justin moved forward, blinded by the Summoning. A lamb going to the slaughter. Alex shifted into man form and moved up beside him.

Dark blotches stained the white marble of the altar, and the sickly reek of death hung heavy in the room. Justin stopped beside the altar, suddenly, completely, a robot who had been given an order.

Still, nothing happened. The silence was complete. Dust motes drifted in the faint moonlight that slanted through the windows. Alex trailed his fingers across the surface of the altar, and brought them away red. Blood. Still liquid, but his revenant senses told him it was hours old. Heartsblood, shed in magic. It wouldn't dry until the spell was complete.

One of the blotches looked too regular to be a puddle, and Alex reached to pick it up. His hand closed on a wadded mass of paper, already disintegrating because of the blood that had soaked it. Alex retrieved a hand span of writing, enough for him to tell that these papers had contained the evidence against Barron.

Who died here?

Justin picked something up from the altar. Fear beat a tattoo in Alex's brain when he saw that the boy held a chain from which a small wine-dark crystal hung. A light burned in its depths, faint but definitely there.

The ghost crystal. But it should be clear, not red.

Justin stood motionless, the chain suspended in his hand. The crystal spun slowly. It had no voice. Something terrible had happened to Lydia in this room; the stone held the memory of it in its depths, a scream no less potent because it wasn't heard.

"Lydia, Lydia," Alex whispered. "What have you done?"

Something dark whipped toward Justin. Alex flung the boy aside and met the attack himself. But the thing had no shape, no real substance; it was as though a piece of the night had come to life. His hands passed right through it.

Justin lay where he'd fallen. No longer manipulated by the Summoning, his arms and legs splayed bonelessly, like those of a broken doll that has been discarded on the ash pile. Completely vulnerable.

Alex stood over him, turning in a slow circle to keep the coiling darkness in sight. It flitted along the edges of the ceiling like a wasp looking for a place to nest. Finally it settled in the far corner. It grew darker and deeper, and if Alex stared at it long enough, he could almost see sparks floating in the blackness.

Feeling a tightness on his skin, Alex glanced down at his hand. The blood had dried.

A breeze drifted out of the darkness. It plucked at Alex's hair, sent dust balls and dried leaves scuttling across the floor. This was no normal wind; hot, moist, tainted with a carrion smell.

Alex moved so that he stood between Justin and the darkness. There was no running from a spell such as this; he either won or died. Something moved in that black pit. Amorphous, darker than the darkness itself. Its scent was evil itself, a gritty putrescence that came from the deepest pit of hell.

"Beast, thy name is Abomination," Alex said, spreading his arms wide. "Show yourself!"

A pair of long, oddly jointed hands emerged from the darkness. Chitin gleamed blue black in the moonlight, and each finger ended in a curved, deadly claw. Killing hands. They scrabbled for purchase, leaving deep furrows in the wall.

The claws caught and held. And then *it* came.

Red eyes, scales, a crested monstrosity of a head . . . A thing that hadn't visited this world since mankind put magic aside. Hellspawn. It climbed down the wall like a spider, its long, spurred legs giving it purchase on the plaster. Reaching the floor, it straightened, raising its head to stare straight at Alex.

"You are . . . not a man," it said. Tusks flashed white in its mouth.

"No. But I dwell among men. It is you who has no place here."

"Give me the boy."

"He's not for you, spawn of Satan."

"I was sent to take him." It bared its tusks at him.

"Come, then," Alex said. "Try."

The creature slid along the wall, forcing him to shift

position to stay between it and the boy. Then it leaped into the air, coming at him in a vicious arc. He caught it by the shoulder and arm and heaved with all his strength.

Howling, the Hellspawn smashed down on the altar. The impact shattered the thick slab of marble, sending white chips of stone spinning through the room. One struck Alex on the cheek, slicing it cleanly. Blood dripped down his face.

The creature's nostrils flared. With incredible speed, it attacked him again. Again he flipped it up and over his head, this time hurling it against the wall. The building groaned like an injured beast.

"Go back to your master," Alex said.

It snarled at him. Alex picked up a chunk of marble and flung it at his opponent. The Hellspawn dodged, and the stone smacked into the wall behind it with a force that brought plaster raining down from the ceiling.

The creature began to circle again. Alex spun with it, knowing he was at a disadvantage. With Justin to protect, his options were limited. His opponent, however, could move at will, attack at will. And it was too intelligent to spring at him again. Instead, it continued to feint and circle, obviously seeking a way to close with him.

He needed a weapon. A sword, a spell, something to give him an edge. But the room was empty, and a spell that would contain a being such as this would take far more time than he had.

The creature sprang, but not at him. Like a grasshopper, it leaped up toward the ceiling, hit, clung, then launched itself toward the far wall. Landing, it again clung for a moment before springing toward another perch. Its velocity increased with every jump.

Alex picked Justin up with one hand and backed toward

the altar. He laid the boy down between two hunks of stone, gaining a small measure of protection for him. Then he spotted a gleam of metal in the remains of the lower part of the altar.

Plaster grated as the creature launched itself straight at him. Alex flung himself flat. He kicked upward as it passed over, catching it in the chest. Its clean trajectory became a head-over-heels tumble, and it landed hard enough to shake the building.

Alex rose to his knees, then drove his fist straight into the altar. Stone burst outward in all directions. He wrenched that piece of metal free, coming away with a three-foot rod of solid steel.

It was spotted with rust, but it would do.

Something grabbed him from behind. Something fast and strong, strong enough to hold a revenant. Another Hellspawn! He'd been so occupied with the first that he hadn't seen the second come.

It's hand clamped over his face, claws digging into the skin beneath his jaw. The metal bar clattered to the floor as Alex reached up to keep his face from being torn off. He pried at the armored fingers, bending one back until it snapped. The creature howled. It dragged him backward, away from Justin.

The first Hellspawn pounced on the boy. Flinging him across its shoulder, it raced toward the spot of darkness from which it had come.

"No!" Alex shouted.

With a convulsive effort, he heaved himself toward the metal bar. His fingers raked it, missed. Another heave. Catching the bar up in both hands, he drove it backward like a spear. He felt it pass through chitin, flesh, then chitin again. The Hellspawn shrieked, a steam-whistle cry of death.

Dark liquid spattered the floor, hissing like acid when it hit the stone.

The first creature was just disappearing into the darkness. Justin's limp hand dangled for a moment, then slowly disappeared into the void.

Shoving free of the dying beast behind him, Alex leaped for the corner. He reached up, groping, and by a miracle connected with Justin's leg. Then he reached farther to the arm holding the boy. Bracing his feet against the wall, he heaved backward with all his strength. A wail ululated out of the darkness. Justin dropped back into the room, still clutched in the Hellspawn's severed arm.

Alex caught the boy. "Thank God," he muttered, lowering him gently to the floor. "Justin!"

Something clamped around his neck and jerked him upward. Before he had a chance to react, he was pulled into the darkness.

21

Blackness closed around Alex as he struggled to pull the Hellspawn's hand from his neck. One by one, he pried those chitinous fingers up and broke them. The creature screamed and gibbered, finally wrenching away to fall into the darkness.

"Back to your master, beast," Alex said.

Alex hung motionless, watching as the Hellspawn grew smaller and smaller, dwindling to a spot, a point, a speck, and finally disappearing. It might have taken a moment or a hundred years. This was the Abyss—betwixt and between, neither heaven nor hell. Time and space had no meaning here.

He closed his eyes, opened them again. There was no difference. Blackness all around, without feature, without texture. It just . . . was. He would have given much to have a single star. To wish on, perhaps.

There was no way home. Soulless, immortal, he had no place in either heaven or hell—or in the world of men, for that matter. He'd expected to be punished one day; perhaps, as Liz had said, he'd *wanted* to be punished.

"But not now!" he shouted into the darkness. "I'm needed back there!"

The Abyss swallowed his words, negated them. There wasn't even an echo to prove he'd spoken at all.

If he hadn't been able to see his body, he might have thought he didn't exist. A figment of his own imagination. He tried to laugh, but couldn't.

The darkness seemed to tighten around him, wrapping closer and closer, covering his mouth and nose, smothering him. He fought for control.

The Abyss is endless. You can't fall, you can't smother.

If he could just hear something, anything. He sang to himself for a while, but that didn't work. He needed something other than Alex. He needed to go home.

"I have to go back," he cried. "Don't you understand? My family is in danger!"

Something snapped in him then. He began to scream, flailing his arms and legs like a frantic swimmer. He cursed God, he cursed Satan, he cursed his own stupidity.

The Abyss ignored it all.

He raved for a long time. Perhaps forever. Finally driven into a state of panting exhaustion, he stopped screaming and curled into a fetal position. He squeezed his eyes shut, preferring the abyss of his own mind to the darkness without.

He ignored the first light touch on his cheek. Imagination—or perhaps his own hand, starved for sensation, had strayed without his knowledge. But a second touch came, gentle, yet truly there, and he opened his eyes.

"Catherine," he murmured.

She floated beside him in the darkness. Young, as young as she'd been that first time he'd met her, and achingly lovely. Her eyes were as blue as he remembered.

"Catherine," he said again, reaching out to stroke a lock of shining, dark hair. It slid like silk through his fingers.

"It's been so long, so very long."

He drew her in, cradling her against his chest. The scent of lavender surrounded him. Memories washed over him like the tide; her laughter, the touch of her hands, the look on her face when he showed her the home he'd built for her, their first child, brought into the world with his own hands.

"Is this heaven, then, that you're with me?" he asked.

She raised her head and looked full into his eyes. "You left me," she said. "Just walked away and left me."

Shock hit him like a fist in the guts. "You told me to go."

"You wanted to go. I grew old, and you moved on."

"It wasn't that way. Catherine—"

"You took the easy path. You always do."

He opened his arms, letting her drift away from him. Her face was the same, but her eyes were implacable.

"I gave you my youth."

The voice came from behind him. Startled, he swung around to see another Catherine. She wore the gown he'd had sent all the way from Paris because it exactly matched her eyes.

"I built my world around you."

To his left, a third Catherine.

"I gave you my nights."

"I protected your days."

A fourth Catherine and a fifth. The same blue gown, the same accusing voice.

"I bore you nine children."

"I forgave you your past."

"I gave you my future."

More Catherines. He turned around and around, and always there were more. Telling him what she had given him, telling him what she'd given up.

He had only one answer for them all. "I know."

They floated in a circle around him, staring. Were they real? Real enough. She *had* made those sacrifices. And he'd let her, blinded by his own need to be loved. He had tried to cherish her enough, but perhaps there was no such thing as enough.

And he'd been ready to do the same to Elizabeth.

"I gave you my love," one of the women said.

A gentle voice. He scanned the host of faces, searching for eyes to match it. He found her, a mature Catherine, half-hidden in the crowd.

"Catherine?" he whispered.

She came forward. Her hair was silver-shot, bound into a knot at the back of her head. Lines had begun to form around her mouth and eyes. This was the woman who had borne nine children to carry his name. The woman who shared her joys and sorrows with him, whose face was the first thing he saw upon waking, the last before oblivion claimed him.

"You don't hate me," he said, looking into her eyes.

"No. Never."

He reached out, traced the creases that bracketed her mouth. "Why have you chosen to come to me as *this* Catherine?"

"They"—she pointed to the others—"are the young girl who fell in love with you. I am the woman who kept loving you through the years, and who never regretted for a moment that girl's decision. I wanted you to see that woman."

"I left you to die alone."

"Not alone," she said. "I had children and grandchildren, and I had a lifetime of joy to take with me. Your name was on my lips when I died."

"Why did you stay at the Arbor?" he whispered. "All

these years . . . Was it just to comfort me?"

"No. To comfort me. Heaven itself was not enough to take me from you."

He held out his hands. She placed hers in them, palm to palm. The moment she did, the other Catherines vanished.

"Hello, love," he said. "It's been a long time."

"Not so long," she replied.

"What were those others? Echoes of my own discontent?"

She smiled. "Does it matter?"

"Yes."

"There is no answer but the one that is right for you."

"I don't understand," he said.

"I know. And still lost, I see." She lifted her head, questing. "Come, Alex. It's time for you to go. Elizabeth needs you."

His face must have shown his astonishment, for she laughed and said, "Did you think I'd mind that you found happiness again? I had forty years with you. I knew love such as few women even dream of, and that joy will be with me through eternity."

"But—"

"But. You and I had our time, Alex. Now I dwell here, and you belong elsewhere."

He stared at her in astonishment. "Here? You're not supposed to be here! Have you been trapped, like me?"

"Shhh." She put her hand over his mouth. "You've always worried too much over things you couldn't change. In this, I know more than you. Trust me."

Smiling, she brushed her fingers over his lips, then took his hands in hers again. She drifted backward, taking him with her. At first the motion was imperceptible. Then he began to feel the sensation of speed; more and more until he was buffeted by it. Wind tore her hair from its fastenings, sent it whipping around her head in a shining halo.

Then he realized that the wind came from behind him, and he was moving toward its point of origin. He glanced over his shoulder. An oval of light hung like a sun in the blackness, and he knew the door had been opened again.

"Hurry," Catherine said. "It won't be open long."

"Come with me."

She shook her head. "I'm dead, Alex. In any world."

"I can't leave you here! To face this torment alone—"

"The pain you felt came from yourself, as always. I have never chosen pain. Although I float in nothingness, this"— she touched her heart—"is full. And I have my memories to keep me warm. It's enough of heaven for me."

He tightened his grip on her hands. "I can't accept that. This time I'll hold you. I'll bring you through."

"Impossible," she said. "Even for you."

He held her with all his strength, but she slipped through his fingers somehow. Her dress had become transparent, and with a shock he realized her flesh had also. Only her eyes were the same. And her love.

"Catherine!"

"Remember me." She thinned, like fog on a summer morning. "Give my regards to Elizabeth. Love her as well as you loved me."

The wind bore her away from him. Lavender surrounded him, a last caress.

"Noooo!" he shouted, even as he was sucked backward toward the doorway.

The wind tumbled him end over end, and finally spewed him into the room from which he had come. Stunned, he lay facedown on the clammy stone of the floor. Just within his field of view, he saw the steel rod he'd pulled from the altar. It was bent, its surface pitted as though with acid, but there was no sign of the Hellspawn.

Has it been a day, a year, or a century?

Someone groaned. A boy's voice, nearby . . . Justin! Alex sat up and scanned the room. Justin lay in the far corner, his eyes closed, arms and legs curled tight in obvious agony.

Alex scrambled to his feet and ran to the boy. "Justin, can you speak? Tell me where it hurts!"

"My head," he moaned. "Ohhh, man, it hurts!"

"It's the Summoning. A spell like that leaves one hell of a headache behind."

Justin's eyes opened. "Huh?"

"Never mind." Alex's legs suddenly felt rubbery. He'd only been gone a few minutes, then. It had felt like eternity. He hadn't expected this gift of time, but it was very welcome.

The boy struggled to a sitting position. His mouth dropped open as he looked around the sanctuary. "Where am I? How did I get here? Alex, what happened?"

"The impossible."

"I don't get it."

"Neither do I, exactly." Alex searched Justin's mind, heaving a sigh of relief when he found no lingering traces of the Summoning. "Go back to sleep. The headache will be gone in the morning." *And so will your memories of this.* He sent the boy back into unconsciousness, catching him by the shoulders to keep him from falling backward.

Light sparked in something on the floor nearby. Lydia's crystal. Alex leaned over and picked it up. After a moment he slipped the chain over his head. The stone was warm against his chest, and sharp as a rebuke.

"I'm sorry," he said. "I failed you. I don't know how, but I did."

What enemy had set this trap for him? A very powerful one, to open a door beyond. But such a spell carried a very high price; dark magic always did. Had Lydia paid it?

That triggered an even less welcome thought: had Catherine's soul paid the price of getting him out?

Two burdens for him to carry, two debts that must be paid.

"Who did this?" he whispered, reaching up to touch the crystal with his fingertips.

But the stone remained silent. Perhaps Lydia could have awakened it, but he lacked that gift.

A tenseness prickled the air, a feeling of hushed anticipation that made the hairs rise up on the back of his neck. Dark magic and hatred. The stink of it thickened, filling his mouth and nose, coating his skin like rancid oil.

Another trap.

Dust sifted down from the ceiling. Alex glanced up, saw moonlight gleaming through a crack in the roof. Even as he watched, it grew perceptively wider. He snatched Justin up from the floor and ran for the door. The church groaned like a hurt beast, then, with a shriek of splitting wood, started to come down around him.

A fist-sized hunk of plaster slammed into his shoulder; looking up, he saw a whole section of the ceiling break away. He flung himself forward, hurdling a pile of fallen timbers. The floor heaved beneath his feet.

His breath came in quick pants as he pelted toward the front door. It started to swing closed. His vision narrowed to that steadily narrowing opening; once that portal shut, he and Justin would be trapped.

If he could just . . . Now! He leaped for the opening. The door scraped his back as he went through, but he made it.

His balance skewed by Justin's weight, he sprawled heavily on the ground.

Safe. They were safe. Alex laid the boy aside, then turned to watch the church's demise. It seemed to take a long time. The roof crumbled into the interior section by section, and the walls groaned as they fell in with almost surreal slowness. Dust hung in the suddenly quiet air.

"Gave it one more try, did you?" he muttered.

Sighing, he got to his feet, then bent to lift Justin to his shoulder. "And now, my young friend, it's time to put you in a place where our enemy can't find you. I have some hunting to do tonight, and I don't want to risk you again."

He brought Justin into Wildwood, wading along a long-remembered path until he reached a small, mounded island crowned with trees. He laid the boy down on the grass. Then, turning, he looked out over the marsh.

This was the heart of Wildwood. Untouched by man, as unspoiled as the day he'd found it. A necklace of tiny islands dotted the sea of marsh grass like emeralds on a woman's breast. A breeze played across the grass. Great billows ran in its wake, catching the moonlight like sparks on a cat's fur.

The marsh knew him. Unlike Man, it had never forgotten the old ways, the old powers. Alex spread his arms wide. "Ancient One, I call upon you. Help me. As I have protected you, so do I ask you to protect this boy."

Movement played across the surface of the grass. But this time there was no breeze. The stalks bent, whispering to one another. Alex felt the marsh stir around him. Life, too vast and enduring to be counted in human terms, or even in revenant. Foxfire burned among the trees, ran in lightning-bug spurts along the top of the grass.

Something big roiled the water, plowing the grass aside as it moved toward him. A moment later it broached the surface in front of him. A huge, knobbed head, slitted eyes that glowed from within, a double ridged back slimming to a long, powerful tail that moved sinuously through the water.

The great-great-great-grandfather of all alligators.

It opened its mouth, six-inch teeth gleaming white in the moonlight. Then the great reptile bellowed. A paean to its power, its age, its vast experience and savagery. Alex stared down the ribbed gullet, awed by the sight. This was no beast; this was Wildwood itself.

Alex bowed. "Greetings, Ancient One. You honor me."

The alligator's mouth closed with a snap that seemed to echo throughout the marsh. Then, with ponderous grace, it climbed out of the water and settled down beside the boy. Its eyes glowed yellow. No power on this earth could touch Justin now.

"Thank you," Alex said.

He shifted into owl form, circled the island once, twice, then soared off on the nearest breeze. Someone had brought dark magic into this time and place, striking at Alex through those he loved. Elizabeth was in danger.

First, Alex wanted to make sure she was safe. Afterward . . . afterward he would find his enemy. It was time they met.

Which was the hunter and which the prey, only the night could know.

22

No mortal owl could have flown as fast as Alex did that night. Straight toward Elizabeth; if his unknown enemy intended to strike at him through those he loved, then she was surely in danger.

Moonlight turned the Savannah River into a ribbon of molten silver. The city spread out below him, a dusting of golden lights among the trees. So beautiful, so outwardly peaceful. But beauty could hide many dangers, and peace was the most fleeting state of all.

He sent his revenant senses ranging down, down, through the quiet squares and along the streets. He could find nothing out of the ordinary, no aura of dark magic anywhere.

Sleeping minds, content and safe. And among them, Liz Garry's. Hers stood out like a beacon amid the multitude, eclipsing the lesser lights. She was dreaming about him. It was no schoolgirl's dream, this, but pure desire, a woman's need for the man she loved. Everything male in him, human and revenant, responded to that call.

He angled down into the city in a long glide. Elizabeth's call grew stronger, drew him even faster. He hurtled through the headlight beam of an oncoming truck, and brakes squealed as the driver reacted.

I'm coming, Liz!

The house on Jones Street was dark and silent. He could sense no enemy lurking in those quiet rooms, no stranger, nothing of the dark. Only Liz. Sleeping. Safe. Alex let his breath out in a sigh of relief.

Her window was open, the curtain belling outward in the breeze. Welcoming him. Alex flew into it an owl, came down to the floor a man.

Liz lay on top of the covers, naked. Long, lean curves and secret, shadowed places, skin that looked like porcelain in the dimness. The griffin medallion hung on a gold chain around her neck, the ruby catching the moonlight and sending it back in a scarlet glitter.

She shifted position slowly, sensuously, arousal evident in every movement. Alex's nostrils flared. Tenderness and desire, love and possession and the simple human need to touch and be touched—all entwined in a great crashing tide that drew him toward her.

He leaned over her, brushed his lips across her forehead. "Hello, love."

Her eyes opened. "Alex," she murmured. For a moment she just gazed up at him, then a frown creased her forehead. "What's the matter? You look so . . . frantic."

"I've had a hell of a night," he said. "Everything's all right here?"

"Of course. What could possibly happen?"

"You've had no strangers come to the house, no phone calls, nothing out of the ordinary?"

"No, nothing. What's the matter, Alex?"

He sat down heavily on the side of the bed. "Someone kidnapped Justin tonight."

"*What?* My God! Is he—"

"He's all right. I managed to get him back before they took him . . . too far."

She knelt behind him. "And you think you were the reason for the kidnapping, or you wouldn't have come here looking like you'd seen a ghost."

"Yes. I don't know who's behind this, but he has already struck at me through someone I love. Get dressed; I'm going to take you to a place where you'll be safe."

"In your arms is safe enough for me," she said.

"Liz—"

"Shhh." She moved, sliding around him so that she was sitting in his lap. Of their own volition, his arms went around her. The griffin medallion dug into his chest, but the pressure was insignificant compared with the feel of the woman he held.

"I was dreaming about you," she whispered. "No, don't say anything. I just want to hold you for a minute. That's all . . . just a minute."

Winding her arms around his neck, she pulled him down for a kiss. Alex sank deep, deep, deep. The world receded. There was only Liz, her taste, her scent, the feel of her skin beneath his hands.

She moaned softly, and he drank the sound from her lips. Her heat sank into him, running through his veins to pool deep in his body. He'd never felt like this before. This was new, powerful, sweeping away a thousand years of caution, a thousand years of experience.

"I love you," she whispered against his mouth.

He lifted her, shifting her onto the bed. As he came down to her she enclosed him, wrapping him in arms and legs and the musky perfume of her flesh. Her heartbeat felt like his own. She pulled at his clothing, tearing buttons off in her haste. He helped her, needing to feel skin against skin as much as she.

"I want you," she said, pulling him down, pulling him in.

It was like falling down a well. And all pleasure, a sharing such as only those truly in love can experience. He went, a willing sacrifice. A small, sane corner of his mind beat frantically for attention, but was submerged in a wild, roaring tide of sensation. He tore his mouth from hers, cupping her face between his hands so he could look into her eyes. There was nothing serene about her now; she was like a flame in his arms, vital, consuming, as reckless as he. He wanted to do everything at once, wanted it to last forever.

Wanted to be with her forever.

He had the power.

One drop of his blood. One drop, and she would be his true partner, the bride he could cherish throughout eternity. He kissed her mouth, her cheek, the smooth curve of her throat where the blood pulsed close to the surface.

"I can't stop myself any longer," he said.

"Don't try. Don't stop. Please, Alex, don't stop."

"Are you sure?"

"More sure than anything in my life."

He closed his eyes, unbearably stirred by her acceptance. "There's no turning back. This is forever, Liz."

"Yes," she moaned. "Yes, yes, yes!"

The taste of her blood was sweeter than any he'd ever known, rich and promising. He could *see* the threshold she had to cross, and it didn't seem monstrous now. No. It was welcoming. No more loneliness, no more wandering the earth, a lonely expatriate, waiting for the time when he could go home again. Like a bridegroom carrying his new wife into the house he'd built for her, so he would carry Elizabeth into immortality. Proudly. Offering everything he had, everything he was or would be.

He felt her mouth against his own throat. As he brought

their minds together, merging them for the final leap, he felt . . . he felt . . .

Darkness.

It matched the raging darkness within him, called to it. The mindless sensuality of Blood-Hunger. His. Hers. *Hers!*

"No!" he shouted, tearing free of her. He leaped off the bed, stood staring at her in trembling horror.

She sat up. Her body was still flushed from his loving, her eyes unshadowed by anything but concern for him. And love, as clear and straightforward as he remembered. He could feel the heat of her from here.

"Alex, what's wrong?" She looked honestly bewildered. *She doesn't know!* "How do you feel, Elizabeth?"

"I . . . Why, I feel fine. Why shouldn't I?"

There was no lie in her eyes, or in her face. But when he delved into her mind again, he again found the darkness. It was deeply buried, planted with such care and subtlety that he hadn't sensed it. A trap. Like the one at the church, set for him, and baited with the one thing he couldn't resist. He'd been sucked in by his loneliness and his love for her, by all the regrets of his past and his fear of the future.

He reached up, frantically feeling his own neck for a wound. Finding the skin unbroken, he let his breath out in a long sigh. Thank God! It had been so close, so very close. He'd almost dragged her into the hell that was his existence, almost cursed her soul and stole her salvation. Eagerly, blindly. God! Even thinking he was doing it for her! Whoever had set that trap hated him savagely.

And knew him well.

Liz climbed off the bed and came to kneel before him. "Alex, you're scaring me," she said. "Talk to me."

"Are you sure no one came to the house tonight?" he asked. "No stranger?"

"I'm sure," she said.

Again, nothing but truth in her eyes. He shook his head, wishing he could accept it, wishing he hadn't seen what lurked in her mind. She reached out, laid her palm flat on his chest.

His Blood-Hunger roared.

She came against him then, fitting herself to him like another skin. His arms accepted her. She was his match, body, mind, and soul. Perfect. Intelligent, compassionate, sensual, and yet still possessing that innocence of spirit that had captured his heart.

Take her! Take her now, and you will never be alone again!

"Take me," she said, echoing the voice within him.

He bent his head and kissed her as gently as the revenant within him would allow. Yes, they fit. A match made in heaven. And if he did what she wanted, what he wanted, it would be forged anew in hell.

She surged against him, lifting her hips in an invitation he fought to ignore. This wasn't Elizabeth, begging so wantonly for damnation. It was the spell.

He couldn't do it. Not like this. Not. Like. This.

Somehow, somewhere, he found the strength to break the kiss. He lifted his head, his thumb making restless circles over her lower lip while he stared deeply into her eyes.

"Take me," she whimpered.

"I cannot," he said. "For your immortal soul, I cannot."

He caught her gaze, held it. Carefully, he went into her mind, treading the pathway the other had taken to set the spell in place. It was a black thing, that spell, a shadowy creeping horror that grew like a cancer in the brightness of her mind. Outrage bloomed in him. For this foulness to touch her . . . He took a deep breath, fighting for calmness.

There was no gentle way to remove such a thing. So he did it quickly, stabbing into the center of that darkness. Killing it. She cried out at the wild, sudden flash of pain, then slumped against him. He caught her in his arms.

"I'm sorry, love. It had to be done."

"What . . . what happened?"

"Someone placed a spell in your mind."

She reached up and touched her forehead with fingers that trembled. "A spell to do what?" Her voice was barely audible.

"To make me kill you," he said. "And make you revenant."

"Oh, God."

Not wanting to see horror come into her eyes, he laid her down gently and got to his feet. "It almost worked. I was a breath away from doing it." He raked his hands through his hair. "It preyed on my love for you, twisting it, turning it into a weapon I'd cut my heart out rather than use."

"Alex—"

"I'm a monster, Liz. Whoever did this knew that, and used it against me."

"Help me up," she said.

He turned. She had struggled to her feet, listing precariously to one side as she tried to find her balance. He put his arm around her waist, supporting her weight as she leaned against him.

"Take it easy," he said. "You're going to be dizzy for a few minutes, but it will pass."

"I don't care about that," she said through clenched teeth. "Could this spell have been set from a distance?"

"No. He had to be in this room. He . . . had to touch you."

She drew in her breath sharply. "Alex, my parents are home tonight."

"They were? I didn't . . ." *She was the only living thing in this house.* "Are you sure?"

"Very. They said they were going to bed early."

"I'll go check on them. You lie down for a few minutes and let the dizziness pass—"

"I'm going with you."

"No."

"Then I'll go alone." She pulled away, staggered, then struck at him when he put his arm around her again. "It's all over your face!" she cried. "You think they're dead!"

"I—" The lie stuck in his throat.

"They're my parents. It's my right."

He put his arm around her shoulders, supporting her as she walked toward the door. It *was* her right.

Every step she took grew surer as she began to recover. Her face was set, her jaw thrust forward as she hurried down the hall to her parents' room. Courage. Simple, human . . . irrational in the face of what she was dealing with. Once again, Alex was awed by it.

She turned the knob, hissing in frustration when the door didn't give.

"It's locked," she said. "Open it, Alex."

He would have given everything he possessed to spare her this. But he only nodded, reaching around her to grasp the knob. Wood shrieked as he forced the door open.

He moved into the doorway, blocking it. Phillip and Marianne Garry lay in bed, the covers pulled up around their shoulders. Such a peaceful scene.

Or would have been if their faces weren't chalk white, their eyes open and staring as though something horrible had filled their last moments.

"Let me by." Liz pushed at his back.

Bowing to the inevitable, he stepped aside. She flipped the light switch, bathing the room with the harsh, unforgiving glow of reality.

"Ohhh, God!" she moaned.

He touched her cheek, felt the wetness of tears. She reached up and took his hand in both of hers. Seeking support, seeking strength. He gave her all he could.

"Let's go," he murmured.

She shook her head. Dropping his hand, she moved toward the bed.

Heartsblood! Alex took a step toward her. "Liz, no! Don't!" he cried, knowing she wouldn't listen.

She pulled the covers down, then stood frozen, gripping the blankets with white-knuckled hands as she stared down at what was left of her parents. Their chests gaped open, a mass of shattered bone and torn meat. Meat. Slaughtered. Like cattle for the market, not knowing why they had to die.

"No," she whispered. "Oh, God, no!"

Her face was as white as those of the poor, pitiful things that had once been her parents. Alex gripped her shoulders hard, rocked by the intensity of her pain.

"You knew," she said. "You knew."

"I knew."

Her head fell back against him, and he could feel her pulse racing hot and fast. Alex closed his eyes, unprepared for the sheer, visceral power of her grief.

"What kind of monster could do this?" she cried. "They were gentle people . . . . Oh, God! Why, why, why?"

Because of me, Alex thought. He welcomed the coiling heat of anger that tightened his chest. He looked down at the pitiful remains, fixing the picture in his memory.

Two more lives to be tallied to his account. So be it. He accepted them.

He pulled the covers from Liz's hands and covered the corpses. Gently, as though gentleness mattered to them. Their mutilated bodies covered, they regained their humanity again.

Elizabeth moaned.

"Let's go," he said, putting his arm around her shoulders.

"No. Not yet. I . . . want to say good-bye."

He let her go. She leaned down, kissed her mother's cheek and then her father's. The gesture was filled with such tenderness that Alex turned away hastily, unable to bear it.

"I love you," she said.

He flinched as though the words had been a lash. It wasn't until he felt her hand on his shoulder that he realized she had spoken to him.

"You should hate me," he said.

"Hold me, Alex. Please, just hold me."

Whirling, he opened his arms, and she came into them, burying her face against his shoulder. "It hurts," she sobbed. "Oh, it hurts!"

His throat was too tight for speech, so he swung her up into his arms and carried her back to her room. She cried for a long time. He was glad she could, even more glad that she wanted his comfort.

When the worst of the storm was over, he stroked the wet hair back from her forehead and said, "Pack your things. You're coming with me. I won't risk you again."

"You'll find him, won't you? You'll find him and punish him?"

"Revenge?" he asked softly.

"You saw what he did to them. They suffered, Alex. I

could have handled anything but that." She tilted her head back to look at him, her eyes shadowed with hate. "I want him to pay for that."

He understood her rage, accepted it. Shared it. Barron, Lydia, Justin, Liz, Phillip, and Marianne—this unknown enemy had struck at them all. And why? Because he was afraid to strike at his real target.

Enough was enough. *Coward! Sneaking around with your spells and your evil. You want me, you'll get me. I'm going to take every one of those lives out of your hide!*

Taking her face between his hands, he made her a vow. "You have my word. As God is my witness, he'll pay for what he's done tonight."

23

Suldris walked through the quiet darkness of Lafayette Square. Waiting. A few hundred yards away, the twin towers of the Cathedral of John the Baptist speared into the sky. There was a reddish tinge to the moon tonight. A killing moon.

He hadn't expected the trap at the church to work; in fact, he would have been disappointed if it had. He didn't want things to be nearly so easy for Alexi. Now the real bait had been taken. The sorcerer smiled, pleased that something as simple as love had been the key to the Russian's downfall. Such blindness, such utter foolishness from a being so old and powerful . . . In a way, it was a shame.

"You really should have known better, my old enemy," he murmured.

He turned toward a nearby bench, where one of the city's vagrants slept. The fellow was young, despite the dirt, passably handsome despite his thinness. Fifteen, sixteen at the most. The taint of AIDS was in his blood. No matter. Blood was blood, and not even AIDS could kill the undead.

Suldris walked toward the boy, his shadow flitting in and out of existence with every passing cloud. "Hello," he said.

The vagrant awoke with a start. Suldris stood looking down at him, savoring the dawning of alarm in his eyes.

"Who the hell are you?" the boy asked.

"My name is John Smith. I'm new in town."

"Lookin' for company, huh?"

"Isn't everyone?" Excitement began to grow in Suldris. The hunt, always the hunt. He needed this boy, desired his willingness. At least for now. "Are you available?"

"Could be."

Ah, thought Suldris. He's a careful one. "I'm lonely, and I'm willing to pay for your time. Interested?"

"Five bucks for a blowjob, twenty for a fuck. Anything else is extra."

Suldris took a sheaf of bills out of his pocket, saw the boy's watery blue eyes widen with greed. Smiling, he pulled out two twenties and held them out.

The boy snatched them and stuffed them into the back pocket of his filthy jeans. Then he fell to his knees, fumbling with the zipper on Suldris's pants. The sorcerer pushed him away gently. "Not here. Come to my place."

"That's going to cost more."

Suldris dangled the wad of bills between thumb and forefinger. "Will this buy the rest of the night? I'd like a little conversation along with . . . the rest."

"Maybe." The boy took the money from him and counted it. "Four hundred and eighty dollars, man. For that, you can have the rest of my life."

"Done," Suldris said, draping his arm around the boy's shoulders. "Come with me . . . What's your name?"

"Christian."

Surprise brought a chuckle to Suldris's lips. "Is that your given name?"

"Nah. It was Fred before I hit the streets. They call me Christian because I like to sleep in churches in the cold weather. Always manage to find a way in. Sometimes I sneak in, sometimes I con the pastor into thinkin' he's gonna convert me."

"Ah, I see." Suldris took the boy's chin and turned his face toward the cathedral. "Now, Christian, look at that. Beautiful, isn't it? But so useless. Mankind has many follies, but that is the worst of all. God. Pah! He takes their faith and their money, but does nothing for them in return. They live out their squalid little lives in blind contentment, trusting Him to give them their reward afterward. Faith. Bowing and scraping to a God that doesn't hear, and wouldn't do anything for them if He did.

"The great myth of salvation," he continued. "It keeps them bound, tames their rebellion. And Alexi—after all these years, he's still burdened by it. I suppose I should be glad of it, for it is his greatest weakness."

He looked at the boy, whose eyes were beginning to glaze over with boredom. Little Christian, he thought. You ought to pay more attention to the last hours of your life.

He led the boy to an old, run-down building tucked away in a nearby alley. Most of the paint had peeled away from the frame boards, and the windows were covered with dark, weather-beaten plywood.

"Hey," Christian said. "This isn't—"

Suldris placed his hand on the back of the boy's neck. "I just bought the place. I'm staying in a couple of rooms at the back until I get the rest of it fixed up."

Christian went in, a little reluctantly, a little defiantly. And why not? Suldris thought, following him. He's got nothing to lose, not even his life. The inside of the building was pitch-dark, redolent of dry rot and mouse droppings.

"Don't you have any lights in here?" the boy asked.

"In the back."

Suldris grasped Christian's hand and led the way to the rear of the building. This room had once been a storeroom. Now it was littered with the corpses of wooden packing boxes. Spiderwebs hung from the ceiling, heavy with the small, shrouded corpses of insects.

Still holding Christian's hand, Suldris lit a candle that had been stuck in its own wax on top of a nearby packing box. The boy recoiled as the light revealed Lydia's motionless body.

Her eyes were open and empty, her skin inhumanly pale. But her beauty remained; but for the coppery gleam of her bright hair, she might have been a lovely statue.

Christian gasped. "Shit! What the fuck is going on here?"

He started to back toward the door, but stopped when Suldris grasped his shoulder.

"This is Lydia," the sorcerer said. "Don't be afraid."

But he was. The smell of his fear was delicious.

"What's wrong with her?" he whispered.

"Nothing. She's perfectly normal . . . for what she is."

Suldris let a moment of silence pass, then said, "Aren't you going to ask, Christian?"

"Ask what?"

"The next question—what is she?"

"I . . . I . . ." The boy's terror beat high in the room. Suldris smiled. Human beings were all the same; even the already doomed want to live. He drew the boy closer to Lydia. "Lovely, isn't she?"

The sorcerer lifted a handful of her hair, then let it sift through his fingers. It caught the candlelight, casting it back in a riot of auburn sparks. She stared straight ahead, not reacting.

"This is my servant, Lydia," Suldris said. He took the boy's hand and held it against her cheek.

"She's cold!" Christian cried. "Christ, she's dead!"

"Essentially, yes. But this is no death such as your kind knows; decay cannot touch her, or disease, or age. Eternal youth, just as I promised her."

The boy recoiled. "Big deal."

"She is my servant," Suldris continued. "Perfect obedience. I made her, Christian, with magic and her own soul. Now I need to animate her, and for that I need *your* soul."

Christian tried to wrench free. Suldris, expecting such a move, tightened his grip on the boy's hand and forced him to his knees.

"No," Christian screamed. "No!"

"You're dying anyway," Suldris said, almost gently. "I'm just hastening the process a bit. At least this way you can be of some use to the world." He caught the boy by the chin and forced his face upward. "Look at me."

Christian shook his head frantically. "No!"

"Look at me."

"No! N—" The boy's mouth went slack.

"Very good, Christian."

With the dark blade, Suldris made a neat incision in the boy's wrist. He dipped a feather into the pooling blood and drew a circle around himself, Lydia, and Christian, then another, larger one around it. Between the two circles, at north, south, east, and west, he drew four pentacles. On Lydia's forehead, a fifth.

Careful not to break any of the lines, he stepped out of the circles and began to chant. The knife vibrated in his hand as a dark mist sifted into the area bounded by the circles. It grew ever thicker and darker, until the figures of Lydia and the boy were completely obscured. There was a hint of movement deep within the smoke, and soft, malevolent whispers.

Suldris smiled; his gift had been accepted. The whispering stopped. He clapped his hands sharply, and the mist shrank, folding in and over on itself until it was a tiny point. Then it disappeared.

The boy, the crate, even the puddle of blood were gone. Lydia alone remained. She stood in the center of the circle, the pentacle on her forehead still gleaming wet in the candlelight.

Suldris held out his hand. "Come, Lydia."

She stepped forward, flawless, graceful, lovely enough to make a man's heart turn over. Only her eyes were empty.

Suldris's triumph was sweet and hot, hot as the hatred that burned in his chest. The end of the hunt was in sight.

He wiped the blood from Lydia's forehead. In a way, it was a shame he couldn't share this ecstasy with her. But she was much more useful like this, lich instead of lover. Unquestioning. Obedient. She carried Alex's heritage within her, and with it, the seeds of his destruction.

Tonight, Alex Danilov would die. Again.

"Come, Lydia," he said. "We have work to do."

Alex followed Liz down the hall. She rushed past the door to her parents' room, the suitcase she carried banging against her shins as she walked.

"There are some papers in the living room I need to take," she said, glancing at him over her shoulder.

"Lead on."

She went down the stairs and down the hallway at the same headlong pace. Alex followed, wishing she *could* outrun her grief. God knows, he'd done plenty of running himself. Speed, distance, action—none worked. Only time did, and that was one thing that couldn't be rushed.

He found her standing in the center of the room, staring around her as though she'd never seen it before.

"I'm never going to see this house again, am I?" she asked.

"No."

"What are you going to do, burn it?"

He nodded.

"Because the police are going to get just a little excited about two bodies from which the—"

"Stop it, Liz."

"—the hearts have been forcibly removed." A note of hysteria crept into her voice. "It's a hell of an ugly world you come from, Alex!"

Because he wanted to hold her so much, he didn't. "I know."

She walked slowly to the bookcases at the far end of the room. Picking something up from the shelf, she balanced it on her palm and turned back to Alex. He saw that she was holding a glass paperweight. Inside it was a scene of a London street in winter, tiny, perfect in every detail. She shook it, causing a snowstorm to swirl among the buildings.

"Dad bought this for my eighth birthday," she said. "I used to keep it on my nightstand. The lamplight made the snow turn gold, and staring into it was like looking into a fairy palace. . . ." She set it aside hastily.

"Take it," he said. "It's part of you."

"Part of me," she repeated. Her eyes were haunted. "My father's books, his research, my mother's collection of porcelain cats . . . Is this it? Is this all that's left?"

"If you believe that, then whoever killed them has beaten you."

She drew in her breath sharply, then nodded. Tears glittered in her eyes. "Let's get out of here," she said. "I can't stay in this house any longer. Not with them upstairs . . . like that."

He reached out. She placed her hand in his, a gesture of trust that made his throat tighten with emotion.

"Wait," she said. "I almost forgot something." Slipping the paperweight into the pocket, she straightened her shoulders and turned back to Alex. "Okay, I'm ready now."

Then she crumpled. Completely, bonelessly, like a doll tossed carelessly on the ground.

"Liz!" he cried. "What's wrong?"

He fell to his knees beside her. Pain washed over him, searing-hot agony like needles being driven into bone. Her pain. He slipped his arm beneath her shoulders and lifted her against him.

"I . . . hurt," she moaned. "Oh, God. Alex, make it stop!"

Entering her mind was like breasting a solid wall of agony. It was then that the full horror burst on him. The first spell had been a trap. By breaking it, he had unleashed a worse one. Subtle, insidious, incredibly swift, it raced through her body. He tried to catch it, but it had no form, nothing that could be held. It was Elizabeth herself, bone and blood and flesh given a lethal half twist.

This was what her parents had died to create. Alex closed his eyes, fighting for control. He'd done this to her. Unknowingly, perhaps, but he'd done it. And somewhere out there, his enemy was gloating.

"No," he whispered, holding her close. "No!"

Like a string of dominoes, her defenses were toppling, bits and pieces of Elizabeth crumbling. He fought for her. But the spell was too fast, too strong, too tightly wound into her being. He propped one thing up, only to have five more fall around him.

She was dying.

24

Liz moaned sharply. Her back arched as the pain grew worse. Much worse. Alex held her, fighting to keep her with him even as he felt her slipping ever farther away.

"Don't let go," he said. "Don't let go."

Astonishingly, she smiled at him. Unable to bear it, he pressed his forehead against her hot cheek.

"Look at me," she whispered.

Obeying her was the hardest thing he'd ever had to do. Her eyes held pain, fathoms of it, but also trust. A gift without price. And also a burden, because he'd failed her.

She reached up, touching his cheek with her fingertips. "I . . . thought we'd have more time."

"We will. I'm not going to let this happen to you. Just hang on. If I can just trace—"

"You've run out of time, Alexi." The voice came from behind him, and was as dry and hard as flint.

Alex swiveled to face the man who had spoken. No, not man. Revenant, reeking of blood and spent human lives. The tall figure was cloaked in a darkness even Alex's vision couldn't pierce.

"Free her," he said.

The dark revenant laughed. "Don't you want to know who I am?"

281

"Free her!"

"She has, oh, fifteen minutes of life remaining to her. At the end of that time, she will belong to me. Body and soul, Alexi. Forever. The only way to save her from that fate is to kill her yourself."

"No!"

"Oh, yes."

Cradling Liz in his arms, Alex got to his feet. He laid her down on the sofa and turned to meet his enemy. "Only a coward strikes at innocents."

"Ah, but it's always the innocents who suffer, in love or in war. You should know this by now." He stepped forward.

Alex saw his face for the first time. A face from the past, sharp-planed and cruel, filed in memory with flames and screams and the foul reek of death. And the eyes . . . Alex shuddered. The Hellspawns' eyes had been kinder.

"Suldris," he said. "I remember burying you."

"What was left of me. But I drank your blood, Alexi. A single drop, taken quite by accident. It was enough to bring me back to pain. Centuries of it. And now I'm . . . just like you."

"There's no need to be insulting," Alex said. "Even as a man, you were monstrous. Now I'm surprised even Satan can stand you."

Suldris bared his teeth. Then he stretched out one hand and slowly closed it into a fist. Liz shrieked, a cry of such agony that Alex nearly screamed with her.

"Stop it!" he shouted, shifting his weight onto the balls of his feet. "Stop it, or I'll tear you apart!"

Suldris inclined his head. With a gasp, Elizabeth relaxed against the cushions.

"It's gone," she said. "The pain's gone."

Alex backed to the sofa and took her hand in his. The pain was indeed gone. But looking into the black pits of Suldris's eyes, he knew this respite was only another form of torment. Freeing her would be an act of mercy, and James Suldris had never been merciful.

She sat up. "Alex? What's the matter?"

"He knows me too well," Suldris said. "Look at his face, Elizabeth. You will see the answer there."

"It's . . . going to come back, isn't it?" she whispered.

"Oh, yes," Suldris said. "I merely wanted to give Alexi time to appreciate what is happening to him. And to meet someone." He glanced over his shoulder into the hallway. "Come in, my dear."

Alex jerked in surprise when Lydia came into the room. She was as beautiful as always, glowing like a flame against Suldris's darkness. Then he looked into her eyes. Empty. He looked into her mind. Empty. And her soul? Empty as well.

The ghost crystal beat like a heart against his chest, but it couldn't ease the chill gripping him. "Oh, Lydia," he murmured. "I'm so sorry."

Liz rose to her feet and grasped his arm with both hands. "I don't understand. What's—"

"Lydia is my servant," Suldris said. "And a very good one. Complete obedience as only a revenant can command. She feels no more ambition, no troublesome yearnings, no vanity. Lydia, my sweet, show the nice lady what I mean."

Lydia dragged her fingernails down her own cheek, flaying the skin in four parallel stripes. Dark blood welled in the cuts, then overflowed and trickled sluggishly down her chin. It was all the more chilling because she didn't flinch, didn't change her expression at all.

Hearing Elizabeth gasp sharply, Alex drew her close against his side. "Don't worry, love. She can't feel anything," he said. "Suldris made her into what is called a lich, or zombie. Dead, but animate. A soulless automaton. She'd cut her arm off if he told her to."

"That's what you will be, Elizabeth," Suldris said. "Once the spell reaches its climax, all the pain will end. And you will be mine."

"No!" she cried. "God, no!"

"God has nothing to do with this," Alex said.

Suldris smiled. "How true. Think, Alexi. Isn't this delicious? Lydia, your lover, and Elizabeth, your love. A matched pair. You had them for a while, but I'll have them forever. And what about your precious salvation then, hmm? Their souls will wander, tormented, belonging neither in heaven nor in hell."

"Why?" Liz asked. "Why are you doing this?"

Suldris glanced at her, red sparks swimming in the obsidian depths of his eyes. "He took my life, my power, everything I'd spent a lifetime building. Now it's my turn. I'm going to strip him of everything he values, and then I'm going to rid the world of him at last."

"You never built," Alex snapped. "You sold your soul to the devil, and he gave you what you asked for."

Suldris inclined his head, then turned his gaze back to Liz. "Nevertheless, I had an empire. A small one, but my rule was supreme. My people obeyed me—"

"They hated you," Alex said.

"True. But that didn't matter as long as they obeyed me. If I asked a man to deliver up his property, he did it. If I asked for his wife or his son, he did that, too."

"No wonder Alex killed you," Liz said.

"It was none of his business." Suldris raised his hand and pointed at Alex. "What right had you to judge, vampire? You have walked this earth for nearly a thousand years—how many men have died by your hand?"

"Enough to know when to kill," Alex said. "And when not to."

"Ah, then you should feel right at home with your decision tonight," the dark revenant said, dropping his arm to his side.

"You can kill her, you can make her revenant, or you can give her to me. Choose, Alexi."

Alex felt Liz tremble, and knew the pain had returned. He shifted her back down to the sofa. Black spots jagged across his vision when he saw that she'd bitten her lower lip to keep from crying out. But it was helpless rage. Helpless. He sat down beside her, unable to do anything but hold her hand as the dying began again.

"I'm not very"—she paused, drawing her breath in sharply—"religious. But right now . . . I think I'd . . . like to pray. Help me, Alex."

He stroked a lock of hair back from her forehead. "Our Father, Who art in heaven, hallowed be Thy—"

"Pray all you want." Suldris laughed, a bitter, raucous sound. "He won't save you from me, Elizabeth."

"Bastard!" Alex surged up from the sofa.

"Yes, come," the dark revenant said. "You're weak, Alexi. You've let your scruples blunt your power. I, however, have not. I've drunk many lives. Many. I'm stronger than you. And while we fight Elizabeth will die. Then she'll be mine anyway."

Rage won; Alex started forward.

"No." Liz's voice was a whisper, but it brought him back to her instantly. "Promise me something," she said.

He ducked his head, terrified of what she might ask.

"Don't let him . . . have me."

"Liz, you can't—"

She covered his mouth with her hand, silencing him. Her fingers shook, but her eyes were very sure. "Yes, I can. Make me like you, or let me die, but don't let me become . . . that."

"How can I promise that?" he whispered against her hand. "Oh, God, Liz!"

"Promise."

He opened his mouth to answer her, even then unsure of what he was going to say. At that moment her gaze shifted to a point behind him. Her eyes widened.

Danger!

Alex tucked his chin against his chest as Lydia's hands came around from behind him. Her fingernails groped along his face, searching for his eyes. He grabbed her wrists and shoved her away, giving himself time to get to his feet.

She charged him again. Expressionless, silent, implacable as a machine. And completely without fear, of him or for herself. Alex whirled like a bullfighter, helped her past with a push.

She sprawled awkwardly, thumping against a table with enough force to knock the breath out of her. But Lydia had no breath. No weaknesses, either; a zombie felt no pain, had no sense of self-preservation. She had nothing to lose. A creature of darkness, created by evil, bound by the touch of Satan.

And yet she still looked like Lydia. Beautiful, flawed, tragic Lydia.

He'd almost loved her. And that *almost* had brought her to this; if he'd been able to either love her or find true indifference, she wouldn't have gone to Suldris.

She came at him again, her fingers curved into talons. He knew he should destroy her now. But he couldn't. Instead, he grabbed her by the shoulders, using her own momentum to swing her around and hurl her back to her master.

The dark revenant touched her shoulders, and she froze, kneeling at his feet.

"Coward," Alex hissed. "To make her do your fighting for you."

"I have no qualms about fighting you," Suldris said. "I'm merely amusing myself by forcing you to do it. You'll have to damage her, you know. The only way to stop a zombie is to dismember it. And we both know how much you hate hurting innocent people."

"You make it sound like a fault."

"It is, when you allow it to destroy you."

Alex heard a muffled groan behind him. Time was running out. He took a step backward, then another.

Lydia scrambled to her feet. She matched his retreat step for step, and he knew she'd be on him the moment he tried to reach Elizabeth.

"You see, Alexi? You should have destroyed Lydia when you had the chance," Suldris said. "Now you're paying the price. As I told you, this regrettable hesitation toward taking life will be your undoing. Or rather, your ladylove's, since you've lost your chance to help her."

Without turning his back on them, Alex said, "Elizabeth, can you throw the medallion to me?"

"Ah . . . I'll try."

"No," Suldris said. Again, he closed his hand into a fist.

Elizabeth's breath grew raspy. Alex flinched; for a moment he thought she'd fainted. Then she began to speak.

"I don't . . . take . . . orders from you. . . ." Her voice faltered, then grew stronger. "I don't belong to you, you damned . . . pig!"

Her courage brought tears to Alex's eyes. Without looking at her, he knew she was pulling the necklace up and over her head, balancing it in her hand, throwing it. He whirled. The medallion spun around and around as it arched toward him, the cabochon catching the light in a glory of crimson sparks.

It slapped into his hand, still warm from Liz's body heat. He grinned at her. She smiled back, a glorious smile full of love and defiance.

"Get him," she panted. "Get him for me."

Then that inner light went out as though someone had blown out a lamp. She turned on her side, curling in and around the pain. Light glistened off the beads of sweat on her forehead.

Lydia hit him broadside. He went down with her on top of him, kicking, punching, gouging for his eyes. He hit her, an open-handed slap that rocked her head back. It had no effect at all. She grappled with him, her strength incredible.

Suldris began to laugh. Bestial laughter, full of triumph. The sound of it sent a red tide of battle rage through Alex. It was the same wild fury that had carried him through the steaming battlefields of Iroslav's Russia, his sword chopping men like firewood, his body soaked with their blood and his own.

He surged to his feet, the zombie clinging to him, teeth and nails and unnatural strength. He peeled her away, raised her high overhead, then hurled her at the dark revenant. Without glancing away from Alex, Suldris smashed her aside with his forearm. She crashed into a bookcase, bringing it down on top of her.

Alex scooped the medallion up off the floor. Holding it in the palm of his hand, he invoked its power. The ruby began to glow.

Wood splintered as Lydia wrenched her way clear of the bookcase and stood up. Her right leg was broken; bone flashed palely amid shredded flesh. Even that didn't stop her. She moved toward him, dragging the useless leg. Her shoe scraped along the carpet, an awful sound.

Alex stared into the jewel, concentrating. Lydia staggered forward. Suddenly she hit an invisible barrier, lurched back, then moved forward again. And again was stopped.

"You used that little trick in our last meeting," Suldris said. "This time I'm prepared. Come here, Lydia."

She obeyed. Suldris grasped her arm and raised it to his mouth, bit down savagely. Blood welled, dark as his black, black eyes. Then he held her arm high, letting the blood flow down over his hand.

"You see this, Alexi?" he purred. "This is Danilov blood. Hers and Barron's and, in essence, yours. It gives me the lever I need to break you."

Alex folded his arms over his chest. "Indeed?"

"Indeed."

Suldris cupped his hand, gathering Lydia's blood. He began to chant softly. Colorless flames sprang into being on the surface of the dark liquid, sending a coil of sickly smoke up toward the ceiling.

"Now, Lydia," he said. "Continue."

Alex didn't watch her; he watched Suldris.

Lydia lurched forward, hands outstretched, fingers curved into claws. Her eyes empty, empty. Alex cupped the medallion in his hand, letting it work for him while he concentrated on helping Liz breathe. In, out. In, out. He was losing her anyway, inch by inch.

A second more, a minute, anything, Lord.

The scrape of Lydia's dragging foot seemed to echo in the room. Alex stared past her at the dark revenant, saw the cruel mouth curve into a gloating smile. The beautiful lich staggered onward, pitiful and deadly.

And bounced off the invisible barrier again.

Suldris's smile sagged. "Wha . . . ?"

"The blood in her veins isn't mine," Alex said. "My name is the only thing I gave my dynasty; Catherine's children were fathered by another."

"Impossible!"

"Revenants cannot produce children. Another small drawback of our unnatural condition. If you'd done anything with humans except kill them, you'd know that. And now, if you'll excuse me, I have something more important to tend to."

He turned back to Elizabeth, and was shocked at the transformation pain had wrought in her. It was as though her skin had thinned, becoming almost transparent; he could see the fine veining at her temples and her closed eyelids.

"You can't save her!" Suldris shouted. "Keep me away all you like; death will claim her for me."

Alex raised her hand to his lips. Even the reflection of her agony was intense. It wrapped around him, ate into his being like hot acid. He accepted it, absorbed it as he searched its depths for a way to free her.

Her eyes fluttered open. "I'm dying," she whispered. "You tried, Alex. Now . . . let me go."

"I can't."

"Whatever . . . you decide is fine. Just don't let him . . . have me."

He closed his eyes. She was slipping away fast, and there was no way to hold her.

"If you love me," she said, "you won't let him have me."

If I love you!

She sat up with a convulsive effort and wrapped her arms around his neck. Waves of her pain jagged through him. "He said you're weak . . . because you haven't taken any lives."

"Not you," he said, trying to look away from her eyes and failing. "Not you."

"Don't you think that . . . together . . . we're stronger than that asshole?"

He drew in his breath sharply. "Liz—"

"Do it," she hissed. "Now!"

A roaring darkness hovered at the edges of her mind. Suldris's spell, come to take her. Alex glanced at Lydia, looked deeply into her beautiful, vacant eyes, and then tightened his arms around Liz.

"Now," he said.

25

Alex closed his eyes and kissed her, gently, tenderly, as though he were going to keep her forever. And then he carried her over the threshold. She clung to him, trusting him. Light surrounded them. It was pure joy, the sound of children laughing, of streams splashing through placid meadows, of soft summer dreaming. He'd never been so close to his God, so near the salvation he'd lost so many years ago.

Liz smiled at him. There was no more pain in her, no more fear. The light beckoned her. Not him. Never him.

He drew in his breath sharply. This was the moment. He could make her revenant now, and then he *could* keep her forever. The light swelled around him, exquisitely beautiful, exquisitely bittersweet because he could never be a part of it. He reached out and touched her face. He'd hardly had any time with her.

Take her now, and you will never be alone again. Almost, he obeyed. But then he looked into her eyes, saw the trust in them. "Whatever you decide will be fine," she'd said.

If he held her, he would deny her the light. So he opened his arms and let her go.

Their hands touched. Her fingertips lingered against his for a moment. Then a bead of light sparked into being between their fingers, grew larger and brighter as the distance increased. She drifted away from him, her hair a bright nimbus around her head.

"I'll love you forever," she called.

Her voice faded. She disappeared into the light. Gone. And yet something of her stayed with him. Her courage, her strength, the essence of her vitality became part of him. It was a union of spirit he hadn't expected. This was not the revenant's claiming of his victim's life, but Elizabeth's gift to him.

He was not alone.

So, he thought. There are miracles even for such as I.

Alex opened his eyes. Liz lay against his arm, eyes closed, face serene. She was still warm. Gently, he laid her down on the sofa.

"So, you found the courage to do it," Suldris said. "You may have saved her soul, but I will still possess her body. She will serve me, just as Lydia does, and when I'm finished with her, I'll throw her away like the garbage she is."

The sorcerer began to chant. Beside him, the bric-a-brac on the coffee table rattled. Glass screeched across wood as ashtrays, figurines, books, and pencils leaped into the air, followed a moment later by the table itself. Then they all hurtled forward, smashing into the invisible barrier.

"It won't hold for long," Suldris said. "Pah! I overestimated you. You're no threat, just an old, tired vampire without the courage to face life. You've drained yourself all these years, because you were too *moral* to drain others. Think of the power you could have had!"

"And what would that power have gained me?"

"You could have ruled the world!"

"I didn't want the world." *I only wanted Elizabeth, and respite.*

"But I do." Suldris's lip lifted in a snarl. "And after you're gone, I'll take it."

He pointed to the bookcase, to a nearby wing chair, to the fireplace tools. More, and more, until the air seemed full of things. Then the sorcerer flung them all at the barrier. It shuddered under the impact, began to falter.

"You can't hold it," Suldris said.

Alex hadn't tried; the barrier spell had been given to him many, many years ago by someone he'd helped. He'd used it twice, both times against James Suldris. Now its power was fading. He laid the medallion on Elizabeth's chest. "Protect her," he whispered. His fingers lingered on the ruby for a moment, and he felt a pulse of warmth, like a benediction.

Then he leaped straight at Suldris.

In the split second before impact, he saw profound surprise on the dark revenant's face. He'd guessed right; Suldris hadn't expected a physical battle.

They crashed to the floor, Alex on top. Kneeling on his enemy's chest, he felt along the floor for a piece of the shattered bookcase.

"Fool!" Suldris hissed.

Lydia grabbed Alex's throat from behind. Shifting one hand to his hair, she bent his head back. Alex saw Suldris's clawed hand slashing toward his throat. With a shout, he flung himself backward.

Lydia's breath hissed in his ear. Foul, like day-old meat. She clung to his back, tearing at his neck with her teeth. He dragged her around in front of him just as Suldris's swooping dark form blocked the light.

The sorcerer's arm rose and fell, something dark glittering in his hand. Lydia jerked, her eyes widening in pain. Pain! Impossible, Alex thought. A zombie feels no pain.

He caught her in his arms as she collapsed, blood spurting from her mouth.

Cursing, Suldris tore her away from Alex and tossed her aside. He raised his arm for another strike, and it was then that Alex saw the black knife in his hand.

Ah, that blade! Forged in Satan's furnace, tempered with blood and the suffering of human souls. Capable of killing even a revenant. Alex dodged as Suldris whipped the knife in a deadly arc. It missed his throat by a hairsbreadth, catching his upraised hand instead. It sliced across his palm like fire. Alex closed his fist against the upwelling blood.

"I'm going to suck you dry," Suldris panted. "I'm going to take your power and use it as it was meant to be used."

"For evil?"

"We *are* evil. Predators. Does the wolf love the rabbit it runs down? Does the hawk feel sympathy for the mouse it hunts on the ground below?"

"Even as a man, you were a blight upon the earth," Alex said. "It's time for mankind to be rid of you."

"And who's going to do it?" Suldris jeered. "You?"

"This *is* between you and me, isn't it?"

The sorcerer laughed. His face blurred, almost as though it were melting. Gone were the hawkish, cruelly handsome features. In their place was a mask of striated scar tissue.

"So, that's what you really look like," Alex said. "You match your heart, Suldris."

"You did this to me. You know nothing of pain. I had centuries of it. Terrible, screaming pain while my body regenerated itself. And through it all, I could only see your face."

"So. And now it's time to finish what I started."

Suldris bared his teeth. "You can try."

Moisture glistened on the black knife—Lydia's heartsblood. What remained of her lay crumpled on the floor.

Discarded. Used. Something bloomed in Alex's heart. Not rage. Anger was for those who hadn't lost as much as he had this night. No, it wasn't rage he felt, but outrage.

He moved in and under the knife, grabbing Suldris's wrist and forcing his arm upward. Then he clamped his other hand on the sorcerer's neck. A moment later he felt Suldris's long, bony fingers lock onto his own throat. Caught in a deadly embrace, they staggered from one end of the room to the other.

"You can't beat me," Suldris hissed. "I've drunk enough lives to destroy two of you!"

"I don't have to beat you," Alex panted, tightening his grip on the sorcerer's wrist. "It's nearly dawn. All I have to do is hold on until then."

"And destroy yourself?"

"If I can take you with me."

Suldris arched his back, slinging Alex hard into a window. It shattered, and he felt a thousand points of pain as bits of broken glass stabbed into his back. He wrenched sideways, bringing the dark revenant with him. They crashed through the wall into the dining room.

They fell to the floor in a shower of plaster and shattered two-by-fours. Releasing the sorcerer's throat, Alex grasped one of those jagged shards of wood. "Tonight, it ends," he said, plunging the makeshift stake toward his enemy's chest.

Suldris moved with a suddenness that took Alex by surprise. Instead of hitting the sorcerer's heart, the wood entered his body just beneath his collarbone, passing through to the other side in a spray of blood and scraps of flesh. He howled, a terrible cry of rage and pain, and tore out of Alex's grasp.

As Suldris staggered backward Alex went after him. The sorcerer kept him at bay with the knife, great, sweeping, savage cuts. Alex leaped into the air, shifting into owl form between one instant and the next. He slashed at Suldris's eyes with his claws, beat at his head with powerful wings. His talons scored bloody stripes down the dark revenant's face.

Blinded, confused, Suldris stumbled. The knife fell from his hand. As it skittered across the floor Alex shifted back into human guise and dove after it.

His hand closed on the hilt, and it almost seemed to squirm in his grasp. He recoiled, repulsed by the serpentine feel of it. Pure evil, that blade.

Hearing a soft, stealthy sound behind him, he knew the time for scruples had passed. He snatched the knife up and whirled to face the dark figure swooping down upon him. The sorcerer stopped almost in midstep, staring with slitted eyes at the blade.

"That knife won't serve you," he said. "It knows its master."

Alex smiled, dropping into a knife fighter's crouch. "Yes, it does. But you aren't the one, James Suldris. And one feast is as good as another to this servant of Satan."

He leaped upward out of the crouch, slashing his arm in a long arc as though it was a sword he held, not a knife. The blade passed through the sorcerer's neck as though through smoke. For a moment Alex thought he'd missed. Then Suldris's mouth opened. Wide, wider, his tongue writhing as though it had a life of its own. Blood welled, a ruby necklace around his throat, then poured down over his shoulders.

The knife shifted in Alex's hand, an almost imperceptible motion. He knew what it wanted. "You see, I *do* accept the role of predator," he said. "It's just that I prefer to hunt wolves to rabbits and hawks to mice."

He plunged the knife into the center of the dark revenant's chest. Black smoke roiled out around it. Suldris's eyes widened in terror and agony, and the awful realization of the fate that waited for him. In terrible slow motion, his head fell backward, hitting the floor with a meaty clunk. A moment later his body followed.

The final dissolution came quickly for the sorcerer. Skin, muscle, and flesh shriveled and fell away, bones crumbled into dust. The knife clattered to the floor. It seemed to wink at Alex like a fathomless black eye.

"I hope you enjoy serving your master now, James Suldris," Alex murmured. "You cheated him out of four hundred years. He'll have to work hard to catch up."

He turned away. A breeze entered through the broken window, hot, humid, heavy with the fecund scent of the marsh. It stirred his hair, plucked inquisitively at his clothing. The pain in his slashed hand eased. He inclined his head, accepting the gift.

The breeze moved on. It stirred the dust that had been James Suldris, lifted it into the air, and scattered it.

A few motes drifted for a moment in the moonlight, and then disappeared.

26

Alex knelt beside Lydia and brushed the bright, tumbled hair back from her forehead. He hoped he had freed her. Reaching up, he touched the crystal. It was still silent. Perhaps it would always be, now that she was gone. He took it off and tucked it into her outstretched hand, gently closing her fingers around it.

"Fare thee well," he murmured, rising.

Elizabeth lay where he'd left her, the medallion clasped in her folded hands. She looked as though she were sleeping. He tried a kiss, hoping, like Prince Charming, to wake her. Her lips were pliant, but cold.

He pressed his forehead against hers for a moment. Then his nostrils flared, stung by the ozone reek of singed wiring. It pulled him into the dining room, where he found the black knife burning with an eye-searing flame.

The blade glowed yellow, then red, then white. Fire burst out from it, licking along the wood flooring with unnatural speed. Even as Alex watched, the rug burst into flame. The fire gained strength with every passing moment. It leaped to the curtains, devoured them, then roared upward to the ceiling.

There wasn't much time. Alex ran back into the living room, lifted Liz into his arms, and carried her out. If he

299

were a logical man, he'd leave her. But he wasn't. And he couldn't.

The house was well aflame by the time he reached the street. Sirens wailed behind him, but he knew no power on this earth could put out that fire until there was no more for it to consume. There would be no evidence of what had happened in that house, nothing but a few charred bones to show that human beings had died there. It was providential, really, just what he'd planned to do himself.

Somehow, he wasn't thankful.

The eastern sky had lightened; dawn wasn't far away. Alex shifted Liz in his arms, then began to walk. He didn't know where he was going, didn't much care. He just walked.

An owl hooted, loud in the predawn stillness. He looked up, startled, and found himself at the entrance to Colonial Cemetery. The twisted branches of the live oaks hung dark and ghostly in the mist, their shrouding of Spanish moss blurring their outlines.

Alex had avoided this spot all the years since Catherine's death. In a way, it had been his way of keeping her with him; a death not seen was a death not accepted. Now the cemetery drew him powerfully.

Passing through those quiet graves was like passing backward through the centuries. He walked through the ranks of headstones, feeling the weight of all that time, all those lives.

A large vault loomed out of the mist. Although he'd never visited here, he knew what it contained. This was Catherine's last resting place. An angel was carved into the marble above the door, her wings spread out protectively over the lintel.

"So, Catherine," he murmured. "This was the one house I couldn't build for you."

He grasped the handle. Once it had been bright brass. Now it was black with tarnish. He pushed hard; metal shrieked as the lock gave way. Air whiffed out, stale and musty, as he carried Elizabeth inside. It was cool here after the heat outside. And so empty. He didn't know what he'd expected—some lingering presence, perhaps.

An inscribed bronze plate had been set into the wall. It said, simply: CATHERINE DANILOV, 1788–1872. Mummified flowers occupied an urn below it. Once, they might have been lavender. Time had turned them into an amorphous brown mass that crumbled the moment the moist outside air touched it.

"Hello, love," he said. "Here I am, at long last."

He laid Elizabeth on the floor. Her hair spread out around her, the sun-colored strands bright against the gray floor. He wished . . . He wished too many things. Impossible things. But the memory of that glorious light was still strong, and he was glad he'd given her to it. Glad that he'd made the decision for her, not for himself.

Taking the medallion from between her hands, he slipped the chain over her head. The cabochon winkled gently in the faint light.

He couldn't say good-bye. Instead, he combed her hair with his fingers, memorizing how it felt as it slipped through his hands. Then he straightened and turned toward the door.

The eastern sky had lightened to mauve. In a moment the sun would peek over the edge of the world. It was going to be a beautiful dawn. He wanted to see it. Just once, he wanted to see the sun. He was ready to pay the price.

Stay.

He wasn't sure if it was the wind or his own mind.

Stay.

The breeze danced into the vault, bringing with it the scent of flowers. And something else. Something he'd searched for so long and hard that he almost didn't recognize now that he'd found it.

Peace.

All these years, he'd hated himself. Considered himself an abomination, an outrage in the eyes of man and God. A drinker of blood, preying on his own kind. Soulless. Evil.

But tonight, he'd looked into the face of evil, and it was not him.

So, what am I, then? he asked himself.

Alex Danilov. Not a man, certainly. Soulless, perhaps. But not evil.

He sighed as the sunlight spilled out over the city and came rushing toward him in a golden flood. For nearly a thousand years, he'd been denied this. He watched it, drinking in the sight.

"Oh, God, so beautiful," he murmured.

The light reached the cemetery, sparkling on the dew-wet bricks of the wall and gilding every branch, every leaf, every curling wisp of moss. A slanting beam speared toward the vault.

He slammed the door. Closed once again in darkness, he assessed the damage. He would survive. His skin tingled from a burn, seared nerve endings sending frenzied messages of pain. But pain was something he was accustomed to bearing, and he had the memory of that glorious dawning as payment.

He lay on the floor beside Elizabeth. The fragrance of her skin hadn't faded, and it tugged powerfully at his heart. Would it fade in time, turn to corruption? Surely. He closed his eyes against a sudden stab of pain; this was not the bed he'd expected to share with her.

But deep inside, he found joy. She had given him a part of her spirit, back there in the light. And as long as he kept it, he would not be alone.

"Good night, love," he whispered. "Say a prayer for me."

Could he bear another thousand years? Perhaps not. But he could bear today, and for now that was enough. Besides, he had much work to do. Catherine's soul dwelled in the Abyss—for his sake. Justin had lost a father—for his sake. Alex Danilov was needed.

Life beckoned. Sweet, painful, full of strife, full of surprises, every day an adventure if it was allowed to be. Not always to be enjoyed, but always to be *lived*. If he didn't understand that by now, then he didn't deserve the two women who had loved him.

As the dark, clutching fingers of oblivion claimed him, he almost smiled.

The man curled up in the lee of a large stone crypt, scorning his friends who had refused to accompany him here. So what if it was a graveyard? A place to sleep was a place to sleep, and this was better than sharing space with the queers and crazies. And then only until the cops showed up to run them all off.

"Yeah, Jackson," he muttered. "This is the life."

The stars winked down at him, as uncaring as his world. He leaned back against the stone wall of the crypt and closed his eyes, shutting them out. Shutting it all out.

A sudden squeal of metal on metal brought him upright, every hair standing on end. The noise came from the front of this crypt, and sounded like . . . like a door opening.

He shook his head, denying the sound, denying his own perceptions. Realizing that his breath was coming in harsh pants, he quelled it.

A moment later he saw a man walk away from the crypt, a man whose hair gleamed bronze in the starlight. He moved as though his body hurt. But silently. Jackson strained to hear the slightest footstep, the slightest sound of twigs breaking, but failed.

Jackson waited until the man had disappeared into the shadows of the street beyond the cemetery entrance, then waited several more minutes to be sure. Then he walked around to the front of the crypt.

A stone angel cast a winged shadow over the door. He forced himself to reach into that fringed darkness and grasp the handle. Hinges groaned in protest as the door swung open. Inside was a greater darkness and the scent of long-spent flowers.

Instinct urged him to leave, but the lure of good, clean shelter drew him inside. His vision slowly began to adjust to the darkness.

And then he saw it . . . her. Lying on the floor, her hands clasped over her breast. Her face too white, her body too still. Something gold flashed between her fingers. A lot of gold.

"Goddamn," he whispered. "Goddamn."

He knew he should run. But something drew him forward; greed, curiosity, morbid fascination—whichever, it pulled him toward her.

Heart pounding, he leaned over her. She seemed to be holding a medallion of some kind. Maybe a necklace; he could see the links of a heavy chain between her fingers.

Leave it.

He rejected the thought. That necklace was going to buy him food and shelter for a long, long time. Still, it took a lot of willpower for him to reach out and touch those pale, cold hands, to pry them away from the necklace. Then, as though in sudden capitulation, her arms fell to her sides, leaving the medallion to glitter upon her breast.

"Yeah!" He closed his fingers around the necklace.

Her eyes opened, freezing him in place. Cold horror clamped its hands around his neck as he met that blind, blank gaze.

"Alex?" she said. It was almost a sigh. "Alex."

Jackson's hand opened nervelessly, dropping the necklace back onto her chest. Her eyes closed.

The rasp of his breath echoed in the dark, close chamber, but he couldn't stop it any more than he could stop the trip-hammer pounding of his pulse. He scuttled backward on hands and knees, not daring to rise, not daring to turn his back on her.

He tumbled over the threshold, feeling the free night air like a blessing. Metal rang harshly as he slammed the door closed.

As he pelted toward the entrance he thought he heard her calling again in that sweet, soft voice.

Alex. Alex!

Epilogue

Alex stood ankle-deep in water at the edge of the marsh, Justin beside him. Wildwood was full of sound this early September night, crickets chirping madly, frogs croaking, mosquitoes whining shrilly as they hunted. All rushed and frantic as though they sensed the ending of summer.

"Watch this one," the boy said, skimming a flat rock across the surface of the water. Concentric circles spread out from each point of contact. "Two, three, four . . . five, hah! Beat that."

Alex crouched, squinting, then launched his own stone. "Five for me. Looks like we're tied. What was the bet again?"

"That database program, as if you didn't remember."

"We're going to . . . Shh." Alex put his hand on Justin's shoulder, turning him toward the shoreline to the left, where twin phosphorescent sparks hovered in the brush.

Justin nodded. He stood as silently as Alex, waiting. After a few moments a raccoon waddled out from the bushes, two half-grown kits trailing behind her. The trio stopped at the edge of the water to drink.

Alex watched the boy, not the animal. Although Justin didn't remember what had happened to him that terrible

306

night, he had changed. A stillness had taken root, a deep, abiding sense of the world around him. Wildwood had protected him for a few short hours, but it would never quite let him go.

A branch cracked sharply, sending the raccoons scurrying into the underbrush. Alex sighed, his revenant senses placing the newcomer. A familiar presence, and not completely welcome.

"Hey, it's Lieutenant Rhudwyn," Justin said. "I wonder what he wants this time."

The policeman stopped at the edge of the land, the toes of his polished shoes a scant inch from the water. "Mr. Danilov?"

Alex turned to face him. "Hello, Lieutenant."

Rhudwyn was wiry and slim, with a creased, clever face. His hair receded over his temples, making his widow's peak even more pronounced. Lieutenant Martin Rhudwyn had been assigned to investigate the disappearance of Barron and Lydia Danilov, and had done it intelligently and persistently. A bulldog in a terrier's body.

"Sorry to bother you so late," he said, "but you're a hard man to get hold of during the day."

"I don't mind the hour," Alex said. "Come inside and we'll get a cup of coffee."

"No, thanks. I'm pushed for time just now." Rhudwyn glanced at Justin. "Maybe we should talk alone."

"If this is about his family, he has a right to hear it," Alex said. The boy nodded.

"Whatever you want," Rhudwyn said. "I'm not even sure this is significant. I just wanted to check with you on the off chance it might be. All this time, you'd think there'd be some sign of Barron or Lydia, especially with the kind of media coverage we've gotten. A kidnapper would have asked for ransom. Hey, even if they'd absconded with the family fortune, they'd have surfaced *somewhere*. And from what I've heard, Lydia isn't the kind to live quietly and anonymously."

"And . . . ?" Alex prompted.

"I've been asking questions around Danilov Industries, and rumor has it Barron was skimming company money. Know anything about that?"

Alex shook his head. "Did you find any evidence?"

"No."

"Then I don't see where it's significant."

"What about the million dollars that suddenly appeared in Sonya Danilov's bank account?"

"That came from my personal funds," Alex said. "Let's call it a down payment on the rest of her life."

"She'll verify that?"

"All you have to do is ask. She's right up there in the house."

"Why do you keep coming around, anyway?" Justin demanded.

"Son, I've got a case here that smells bad, and isn't going to get better with age. Two prominent citizens disappear without a trace and apparently without reason, and I've got the chief breathing down my neck to find out why."

Alex spread his hands. "No one wants answers more than we do, Lieutenant Rhudwyn."

"Yeah. You know, Mr. Danilov, you're lucky you were on a plane to Paris the night they disappeared."

Alex inclined his head, accepting the implication. Fortunately, computers made it easy to create a trail where none existed; thirty years ago, he'd have been hard-pressed to account for his movements.

"Oh," Rhudwyn said, his face too bland, "I've also got

some interesting news about the Garry fire."

"I didn't know you were investigating that as well," Alex said.

"I'm not. I'm just keeping up with everything related to the Danilov family, and the fire qualifies. You'll be interested in knowing that dental records have identified the bodies of Phillip and Marianne Garry."

Alex didn't have to fake his astonishment. "And no one else?"

"Right."

Not Lydia!

"So you see, Mr. Danilov, now I've got three missing persons instead of two," the detective said. "You wouldn't know what happened to Elizabeth Garry, would you?"

"No."

"Weren't you engaged to her?"

"Yes."

"Kind of strange for her to run away, wasn't it?"

"She wouldn't run away, Lieutenant."

"Then where is she?"

"I don't know," Alex said. "I've been mourning her."

That, too, was very real. Grief, as deep and painful as a man could feel. He saw Rhudwyn register it, but not necessarily accept it.

Finally, the detective nodded. "Well, I've taken up enough of your time. If you hear anything, give me a call, eh?"

"Of course," Alex said.

Rhudwyn turned away. "Be seeing you."

It was a promise. Alex knew the man wasn't going to give up until he found some answers, and the normal world held no answers for what had happened that night.

"Lieutenant!" he called.

Rhudwyn stopped and glanced over his shoulder. "Yeah?"

"Welsh, aren't you?"

"My grandpa was. Talked about the homeland like it was some kind of mystical place." Rhudwyn lifted one shoulder in a shrug. "Impractical. All I inherited from him was his name."

Alex smiled. "Welsh blood tends to breed true."

The policeman stared at him for a moment, then walked away. Alex watched him until he disappeared around the corner of the house.

"He thinks you know something," Justin said.

Alex skipped another rock across the surface of the water, his hands moving with automatic precision while his mind worked on another level. Rhudwyn's instincts were right; something very strange was going on. Lydia's body should have been found. Perhaps something about Suldris's binding spell had caused it to disintegrate, or perhaps the dark blade had taken her with it when it had returned to its master. All in all, very strange.

"Do you think my father is dead?" Justin asked. It was the question he'd been avoiding the past weeks, the one Alex had sensed growing more imperative with every passing day.

"Yes."

"Do you *know*?"

A blunt question. It deserved a blunt answer. "I didn't see his body. But he's dead all the same. You feel it, too, don't you?"

Justin looked away, then nodded.

The roar of a bull alligator echoed over the water. Deep, fierce, stirring the primeval instincts buried within. Silence fell over the marsh. Awe, fear, respect, perhaps all three. Alex glanced at Justin, saw a momentary glimmer of moonlight in his eyes.

Yes, he thought, the boy has changed.

"Are you going to stay?" Justin asked.

Alex looked out over the marsh. An owl hooted softly and was answered by its mate. "This is my home," he said.

Some of the tension went out of Justin's shoulders. He hefted a stone and sent it skipping over the surface. "Six," he said, satisfaction deepening his voice.

Alex took his turn. "Five. Looks like you get the program after all."

"Yeah."

Smiling, Alex cocked his head to one side. "I think I've been hustled."

"Yeah."

Laughter brimmed in Justin's eyes, bringing echoes of joy to Alex's heart. And deep inside, something of Elizabeth responded. Sometimes, he thought, life is good. Throwing his head back, he sucked in a deep breath of marsh air.

This spring, he'd plant some lavender. Just for the memories.

Death is the veil which those who live call life:
They sleep, and it is lifted.

—Percy Bysshe Shelley
Prometheus Unbound